Further From the Middle

by

Ronald Ray Schmeck

Further From
the Middle

Library of Congress Control Number: 2007903582

International Standard Book Number: 978-1-60126-047-5

Printed by
Masthof Press
219 Mill Road
Morgantown, PA 19543-9516

Prelude

This is my second book about the Pennsylvania Dutch. Let me be clear right off. I'm not some cultural anthropologist or historian. I'm Dutch. I wanted to reminisce now that I'm retired. But I didn't want to offend one of my *Pennsylvaanisch-Deitsch* buddies by reminiscing something embarrassing, you know. So, I fictionalized, as they say. *Geschichtenerzählen*. That's storytelling. I put together pieces of family, friends, personal events, values I remember, and I tried to illustrate *dutchifiedness* with made-up stories, or *geschichte*. I know none of the people in the stories will get their feelings hurt, because like I said in the Prelude to *The Other Side of the Middle*, I turned things around so much my own mother wouldn't know who is who. I even turned the map around. Anyway, I have nothing but warm and tender memories about them and those long-ago days. Life was good then, I'll tell you. This is fiction and yet, still and all, these characters seem real to me and my wife. We talk about them as though they're real. What's real anyway?

My main character, Arsenic Schlank, is a hardheaded Dutchman who combines traits of my Pop and some uncles on both sides of the family. His wife Peach and friend Maggie are combinations of my Mum and various aunts. At least two of the characters are combinations of myself and one other person. In one case, I describe a real person directly but changed his or her gender. The dialect I put in their mouths, and italicize in the text, is the dialect I remember from childhood. Is it THE one and only Pennsylvania Dutch dialect? No. In my opinion, there is no such thing as one and only one. Heck, the dialect they use in Lancaster's a little different from the one they use in Reading, and they're just down the road from each other.

What I try to present in my novels, using syllables common to English speakers, is a dialect similar to what I heard from friends and relatives when I was a child. I rarely have a character speak at length in dialect, because I never learned to do that myself. Adults of the Lutheran and Reformed church, the first ones that went out in the English world to look for jobs and get involved in politics, they tended to avoid speaking much *Pennsylvaanisch-Deitsch* around kids, because they didn't want to burden them with the discrimination that many of them had experienced after the wars with Germany. Better to be more anonymous, they figured. You never know if a person in authority bears a grudge against Germans. No use showing all your cards to everybody until you know them better.

Like I said, I'm one of the people I'm talking about. I wanted to tell stories that retain the flavor of what I remember personally. I'm entertained by my memories everyday. Maybe my readers will be too. If you sound out the italicized dialect words in my books, you'll find them to be entertaining and sometimes funny. Also, some of the phraseologies might make you chuckle. We kids played with speech a lot. For example, there was an old man who'd yell at us if we took a shortcut across his fields. We called him "Old Yeller," after a dog we'd seen in the movies. Is that dialect? I don't know. It's funny. On a more serious side, I remember an old drinking mug inscribed, "I tell the truth and only drink what's clear." My Mum had that on our kitchen windowsill and pointed to it at certain times for emphasis. You have to admit, it's a cute way of saying a meaning. It just occurred to me that when my Pop lost something, he would say he "found it missing," like "I was going to fix the door hinge but I found my screw driver missing." Once again, I think it sounds cute, and it makes you think, "wait a minute, what did he just say?"

I'm not going to bother to set you up for this second story by connecting it to the first one. If you read the first one, the connection will be obvious, and anyway, the second one stands nicely on its own. Whether you happen to read *The Other Side of the Middle* before or after *Further From the Middle*, please do read them both. Together, they form a nice overview of the Dutch culture that I remember. A culture both reserved and warm, earthy and clever, forceful and gentle.

Arsenic and his family and friends were just getting used to being past midlife, or the other side of the middle, when I finished the first book, but you got the feeling that nothing stays the same, one little crisis after another. And now here we are in this second book, with Arsenic even older, or further from the middle, and more crises coming down the pike and yet good times follow bad as sure as the sun comes back out after a thunderstorm. I hope you feel like I do when you finish *Further From the Middle*. Everyday I thank God for having given me a chance at life. It might not be your perfect designer life, but it sure is fun anyway.

- Ronald Ray Schmeck

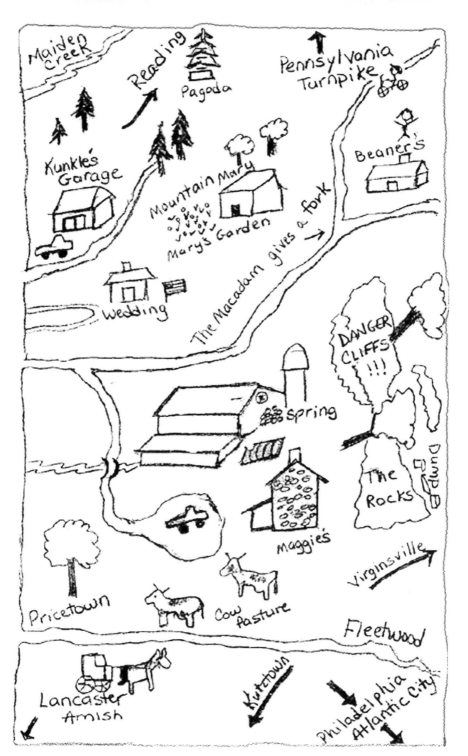

CHAPTER 1

The rattlesnake bit Arsenic on the calf of his right leg as he stepped over a branch lying across the trail. Then, it slipped away feeling certain, as rattlesnakes do, that Arsenic had struck first. Arsenic, on the other hand, felt insulted. He was on a man-made trail, not cutting through the brush.

Oh well. The snake was being a snake. Arsenic was carrying a heavy walking stick but made no move to strike back. The damage was done. Besides, he didn't own the trail.

The day had started early with the smell of bacon and eggs rousing Ricky from his bed. Arsenic was naturally an early riser, but since his wife's death, he'd taken to rising long before sunrise and sitting and thinking. His son, Randy, had commented, "Pop, don't you think you need more sleep?" And Arsenic replied, "*Ach, venn I'm dead, I'll be aschleep all da time!*"

Right after breakfast, he and Ricky had begun their hike down into the ravine next to their mountain cabin. It was shortly after daybreak.

A track switchbacked down the east side of the cut. Rising sunlight bounced off the west wall but dwindled fast as they climbed deeper into the notch. Gurgling, sloshing sounds echoed from a stream churning along the floor of the hollow toward the Susquehanna River. Birds getting morning drinks along the creek echoed warbles, twitters, and squawks. The dark green canyon was misty, and light from the early robins-egg sky bred a vague teal blue haze with mysterious dark shapes behind it.

Several times Ricky took shortcuts across zigzags of trail. Arsenic followed but found himself slipping and hanging onto trees to keep from tumbling down to the continuation of track that tempted Ricky from a few feet below.

After sliding several feet on his backside, Arsenic finally said, "*Sometimes da short vay ist da lung vay, ya know vott I mean? Da hurrier ya go, da beheinder ya get.*"

"Sorry," Ricky replied. "I wasn't thinking."

Now they were sticking to the path, even if it was longer. But Ricky was still leading off and getting further and further ahead.

Arsenic said, "*Slow up! Doan hurry down so quick. I ain't as young nomoah! And too, these shoes doan walk so good. I should'a wore my boots.*"

At the same time, a pack of coyotes started a jam session up the canyon, a bunch of improvising yodelers. Wild sounds ricocheted back and forth across the gap. Ricky felt the short hair stand on the back of his neck.

"Whoa!" he exclaimed and pulled up and waited for Arsenic to pass him. The path was only wide enough for single file. "I'll follow you."

"*Coyotes ain't gesundheitsgefährdend!*"

Ricky stopped. "Ain't what!"

Arsenic stopped and laughed. "*Dat means dere ain't no health risk! A olt Cherman farmah taught me dat vert.*"

A pileated woodpecker hammered out a drum beat on a hollow tree.

They walked on. Arsenic took the lead. They intended to hike down to the stream and walk up the floor of the ravine to the Coudersport Pike and then back to the cabin. A short hike, but tough going.

Arsenic had often lectured Ricky regarding the need to be careful when stepping over a log. Snakes, he said, will slither, or *schlip* as he put it, along a relatively straight line until they reach a snag like a fallen log. Then, they often follow the edge of the log rather than slither over it. Also, a log provides a little cover. Snakes lounge there awhile. When you step over the log from the side opposite the snake, you don't see it and can step right on top of it. It's natural for the snake to defend itself.

Arsenic knew these things, and yet he stepped right over the log across the path, scared the snake, and gave it no time to rattle a warning. The rest was history. It was time to think about effects of rattlesnake venom.

Ricky said, "I should go for help!"

And his grandfather said, "*Yah. Better would.*"

But Ricky's voice showed signs of panic, and so his grandfather added, "*Before ya go, help me get da poison ought my leck. Den ya von't haff'ta hurry up so much.*"

Arsenic knew rattlesnake venom could be *deathly*, and so one had to slow the heart rate to reduce the spread. He needed Ricky's help, and fear was meddlesome in these situations. He settled into a relatively comfortable place and position and asked Ricky to fish a small snakebite kit out of the rucksack he carried on such hikes. Modern science says cutting and suctioning snakebites and applying tourniquets are all useless, but Arsenic didn't always trust modern science.

The old snakebite kit was made of brown rubber and looked a lot like a hot dog. One twisted the two halves which separated to reveal a razor blade, an ampule of germicide, and a tourniquet, and then either of the flexible halves when pinched served as a suction cup to be applied to slits made across the puncture wounds made by the snake's fangs.

With Arsenic's guidance, Ricky scooted up the trouser on the affected leg, broke the ampule, applied germicide around the bite, took the razor blade between thumb and forefinger, and started to cry.

"*Hey,*" Arsenic whispered, "*my leck ya doan haff'ta cut off. Chust a little cut is all.*"

Ricky marshaled his courage, leaned close, and made a cut.

"*Deepah,*" Arsenic hissed between clenched teeth.

Ricky pushed in the blade a little further. Then, as blood flowed, he placed the suction cups on the wounds over and over again.

"*Nauw, dis piece a cloth ya tie right above my knee, an tight I'll tvist it.*"

Ricky complied, and Arsenic used the handle on his hunting knife to tighten the tourniquet.

"*Nauw, back up ta da truck ya got'ta go, on dis trail, an get on da CB radio, an call foah help, o.k.? Heah's da keys. I'll schtay ruich an take a nap til ya get back.*"

Arsenic forced a smile.

Luckily, the only doctor in the little mountain town of Pine Tar still made house calls. He was traveling east on the Coudersport Pike, no more than four miles from Arsenic. He always left the radio on in case of just such an emergency.

"Breaker," Ricky was yelling into the microphone, "my Pop Pop's been bit by a rattlesnake!"

In his earnestness, Ricky had been holding down the button on the microphone and couldn't hear incoming calls. After repeating his message for awhile, fatigue in his finger caused him to let up on the microphone button just as Doc Warren yelled, "Take your blasted finger off the switch!"

"Oh! Sorry! We got big trouble. We need a doctor."

"I am a doctor. Now calm down and tell me where you are, and remember to take your finger off the microphone button when you're done talking."

It took but a few minutes for Doc Warren to pull up behind Ricky and the pickup truck. Ricky was already out, running toward the front of the doctor's car.

"I take it this just happened?"

"Yes Sir. A rattlesnake bit my Pop Pop on the leg. We were hiking down this trail and . . ."

"Which trail, Son?"

"We were hiking down this steep . . ."

"Why don't we go right on down and visit my patient, and you fill in the details later."

Doc Warren recently had a case similar to Arsenic's and started carrying antivenin for rattlesnake bites in his black bag. He also grabbed a splint off the back seat of his car.

Ricky ran ahead, and Doc Warren yelled, "Slow down a tad. We got some time. I'm not as young as I used to be. Me falling head over heel isn't going to help your Grand Paw!"

When they approached Arsenic, his eyes were closed, and Ricky again felt a rush of panic, but Arsenic heard the crunch of pebbles, and his eyes popped open.

Doc Warren saw the tourniquet and said firmly, to be sure Arsenic was awake but not so loudly as to scare him, "I see you believe in the old way of treating snakebite!"

A startled squirrel, searching for nuts within a few feet of the motionless Arsenic, scrambled up a tree and started chattering.

"*Yah,*" Arsenic said softly, "*dis ist vott Pop alvays said ta do venn ya got yoahself bit with a snake.*"

"Well, I got a few tricks up my sleeve. First, let up on that tourniquet. We don't want to kill the leg. Sounds like you're Pennsylvania Dutch. *Bist du schlafferich?*"

With a weak chuckle, Arsenic said, "*Well, no I ain't sleepy, but I'm a little woozy. It's startin ta run tagether in my head!*"

The doctor told Arsenic he needed to "examine" the wound. Actually, he intentionally mispronounced it "*egg-salmon.*"

"*Hey! Yoah Dutch too! Kannst du Deitsch schwetze?*" Arsenic said.

The doctor replied, "*Glei bissel.*"

Arsenic continued, "*Kannst du micka funga?*"

The doctor replied, "*Yah. Wann sie hucka bleibe?*"

Both men laughed while the doctor looked closely at the wound, two punctures with a little incision across each, then he responded. "No. I'm English, but I lived in Reading when I first started in medicine, and I learned to talk *dutchified* English."

Ricky interrupted the discussion, "What are you guys talking about? Is Pop Pop going to be o.k. or isn't he?"

The doctor said, "He'll be o.k."

When asked later, Arsenic would explain to Ricky, from his hospital bed, that he had asked the doctor if he could speak Pennsylvania Dutch. The doctor had replied that he could speak it a little bit, and then Arsenic had asked a sort of coded, insider, question, "Can you catch flies?" And the doctor had given the proper insider response, "Yes, when they stay sitting."

At this point, Arsenic didn't even seem to hear Ricky, as he said to the doctor, "*So, yoah von a dem English, eh?*"

Doc replied, "We don't bite! That's the snake's job. Now, are we sure this was a rattlesnake that bit you?"

"*Vell, rattles it hatt foah shuah, an it vass a schnake!*"

Ricky added, "I saw it too, and it was a rattlesnake!"

"O.k. Now you, young man," Doc said, turning toward Ricky, "you run back up to my car and get my radiophone, it looks like a briefcase, and it's on the passenger seat. Sorry I didn't think of it when we left the car, but you're young and can use the exercise."

Next, he removed the vial of antivenin and a hypodermic syringe from his bag and proceeded to give Arsenic an injection. Then, he placed a small bandage on the bite, put a splint on the leg, and wrapped the whole thing fairly tightly with gauze. By that time, Ricky had returned, and Doc made a call to the ambulance service in Renovo.

With the call complete, Doc said, "An ambulance will be here in about half an hour. We'll have to keep giving you a series of these injections, but I think the worst is already over. I'm glad I was so close when the boy got on the CB radio."

Arsenic responded, "*Yah, me too!*"

The paramedics arrived in about forty minutes, strapped Arsenic onto a stretcher, and toted him up the trail. From his position of repose, Arsenic remarked rather sleepily that the trip up the track seemed a lot easier than the one down.

At about the same time Arsenic was getting a snakebite, Randy, Regan, and James were down on his farm near Reading tending to the livestock. It was eight o'clock in the morning with warm air and clear skies. They were at the rear of the barn standing on the earthen ramp that leads up to the rear doors on the second floor talking to Fat Schmidt, a good friend of Arsenic's.

This morning, Randy had been doing a little horse-trading while Regan and James were freshening up stalls in the barn.

Randy had trained a semi-thoroughbred to pull an Amish buggy that Arsenic kept on the farm. His Pop had actually bought the buggy, a long time ago, from the father of the man to whom Randy was now selling a horse. The fellow's name was Yonnie Kibble.

The Kibbles weren't afraid to stretch the rules about being showy, or *hochmoot*. They loved to own flashy horses. They used them mostly in conventional ways, but Yonnie did race them against other members of his order whenever an opportunity arose. His order was pretty liberal. A lot of people don't know that there is such a thing as Amish horse racing. They can only race them with a buggy or plow attached, never riding horseback. Also, the actual owner of the horse always has to do the driving.

While Randy was down in the *vorbau* of the barn completing the sale of the buggy-trained horse to Yonnie Kibble, Regan and James went upstairs to throw down some straw.

Most of the barn's first floor was taken up by two big rooms containing eight stalls apiece. Hay and straw were pitched down through big framed openings in the floor into a closet-like crib in each room and subsequently carried by pitchfork to one of the stalls in that room.

Fat heard James and Regan working upstairs and knocked on one of the big doors at the rear of the barn, but the men inside thought the sound came from a wookpecker that lately had been stopping by to knock on the upper wall, for what reason no one knew.

When they ignored the knocking, Fat opened the door a crack and shouted in a big "*Halloo!*" Fat had a deep bass voice that seemed to bounce off the floor and resonate through the rafters. The men jumped at the sound.

Three-inch oak planking made the second floor of the barn solid as concrete, and the posts and rafters were squared-off tree trunks pegged together with wood pegs as thick as a man's wrist and braced in places with heavy cast iron brackets fastened to the beams with big hand-forged bolts. On the east side was a pyramid of hay bales, or *heuballen*, stacked thirty feet up into the rafters. On the side opposite the *heuballen* was the *heuhaufen*, a pile of loose hay also reaching the rafters but looking like a small mountain instead of a geometric pyramid. In the center section was the pile of straw bales where James and Regan were working when Fat startled them.

As Randy and Yonnie Kibble completed the sale with an exchange of funds and handshakes, the Amishman had a stern look on his face. Randy watched as the man clop-clopped out the driveway. He had hitched a ride over from his farm near the town of Bird-in-Hand.

Randy walked back under the vorbau to go in the barn, and he heard Fat's shout echo down the shoot from the haymow. He walked back out and around the corner of the barn. Fat's station wagon was parked up in front of James' trailer, up behind the barn. Regan walked in that direction.

There was faint lighting inside the barn and thus James and Regan were squinting in the bright morning sunlight as they came outside.

Fat said, "*It's some warm out today, ain't? I stopped by ta see if ya need any help vhile Arsenic's gone. Kann ich dich hilfen?*"

Fat was facing the farmhouse, and the others were facing away from it. He suddenly aimed his finger at the sky and said, "*Gook mal dough!*"

Everyone looked to where he was drawing their attention, but they were confused for a moment when he added, "*Looks like da sun!*"

Randy'd walked around the back corner and was about to say hello as all looked in his direction and up and so drew his attention toward the sky behind him.

The statement about the sun confused everyone. It was way past sunrise. Yet, when you looked up, there was indeed a big orange sphere rising near Arsenic's house. And, it looked a lot like the sun, but the real sun was above it.

"That's a hot air balloon!" Regan exclaimed after staring for a moment. "And it's headed right for Arsenic's house!" Indeed, a balloon was partially visible on the other side of Arsenic's place, and it looked like it was going to hit either the shade tree or the house.

Just when it looked like the tree was the target, an updraft lifted it up and over. A ludicrous happy face appeared on the big orange sphere and then right below it the words, "Nixdorff Insurance Agency: Agents You Can Trust!" A wicker gondola popped up after that, with a frantic little man running back and forth inside.

For a second, it looked like the balloon might come down in the parking area between house and barn, but another updraft caught it. It almost made it over the barn. It would have, if the gondola hadn't been hanging so far below. The gondola ran smack into the hex sign on the side of the barn and then got drug up the side and over the edge of the roof. But dragging the gondola slowed the balloon to where it could get caught by the weathervane on the peak of the roof. This led to a rapid collapse, and the balloon's ropes got further entangled in the lightening rods, and just deflated, covering about a quarter of the roof in bright orange nylon.

The gondola had started to slide down the roof but was now securely held below the weathervane by the entangled ropes. It was hanging on the backside of the barn, just over the peak of the roof, mostly right side up except for the roof's pitch. The little man had already jumped up to peer over the side. Then, he started screaming.

Arsenic's neighbor to the east, Maggie Stoltzfusz, had seen the big orange object pass overhead and was half way to Arsenic's by the time it hit his barn. The little man inside the gondola was looking over the side and screaming at the time Maggie arrived, and the group suspected something horrible had happened to him.

But he stopped screaming and disappeared down into the gondola just as they ran back from the barn wall to see up over the roof.

Everybody was yelling, "Hang on! We'll call an ambulance! Are you hurt badly?"

The man again peered over the edge and again ducked down inside. They could barely hear him yell, "*I'm o.k. Sorry foah any damitch I done! I'm not hurt t'all!*"

"*Den vhy ya schreamin?*" Fat yelled.

"*I'm fraid a heights!*" the little man yelled back.

Fat said, "*Vee got'a guy fraid a heights flyin who-knows-hauw-high-up, in a balloon. Nauw on da barn roof he's havin an attack off agreeaphobie, or vottever dey call it. Nauw I seen ewerysing!*"

The man's head appeared briefly and then disappeared again. Again, he was barely audible from inside as he yelled, "*I'm o.k. if I doan look dahn!*"

Fat avoided cursing by saying, "*Howdy yashtas!*" Then he yelled, "*Ya shuah ya doan need no medical attention?*"

"*Nah! I'm fine! Ya got a ladder?*"

"*It's hart talkin ta somebotty ya can't see,*" Fat said to the group.

The big balloon was thirty-five feet in diameter, and looked like a big orange juice advertisement, draped over the peak of the roof the way it was. Regan and Fat got a ladder positioned on top of the bank, and James, who was more agile, crawled up on the roof and duck-walked to the gondola. After talking to the man inside, he turned and yelled, "He does seem to be o.k. I guess we can handle it ourselves. The shingles don't look so good up here."

Fat was dizzy just looking up at James. He yelled, "*Talk about agreeaphobie!*"

"You mean acrophobia!" James yelled back.

"*Vottever! Is he comin ought?*"

James yelled down, "He says if he keeps his eyes closed, he can make it. Regan, are you o.k. with crawling up here?"

"Yeah, I guess. If I take my time. Let me see if I've got some other shoes in the truck. These cowboy boots won't work up there."

Randy said, "Let me do it. I've already got sneakers on."

With Randy's and James' help, the pilot moved toward the ladder, not easy with his eyes closed. As he was inching across the roof, Fat and Maggie started laughing. The little guy was wearing a World War I brown leather flying helmet, big goggles, and a clown suit. He even had a big red rubber nose sticking out between the lenses on his flight goggles. He was jabbering on about how he hires out to private businesses for advertising and was headed for the Pennsylvania Dutch Folk Festival in Kutztown. He said he was going to catch the dickens when he failed to show up.

Fat and Maggie walked the pilot down to the farmhouse to make some phone calls. James, Regan, and Randy kept shaking their heads in wonderment. The balloon pilot's name was Denny Drexel. He was a short man, and he resembled W.C. Fields.

While they were waiting for someone to come get the balloon off the barn, Denny explained how he had started his current career. His mother had been a vaudeville entertainer from New York, and his father was a traveling salesman from the heart of Pennsylvania Dutch country. After an attempt at an acting career in New York City failed, because he couldn't lose the Pennsylvania Dutch speech habits picked up from his father, Denny decided to combine the career choices of both his mother and father and became sort of a traveling vaudeville entertainer here in Pennsylvania Dutch country. For awhile, his specialty was birthday parties. He did juggling, card tricks, and a magic act.

After learning to twist and tie balloons in animal shapes for kids, the idea occurred to him to attach advertisements to big balloons and fly them over populated areas for a fee. He had recently taken ballooning lessons and purchased what he called his flying advertisement machine, the one on the barn roof.

Fat pointed out that acrophobia was a serious handicap for a balloon pilot, but Denny said he was getting over his fear.

In a voice that sounded like W. C. Fields with a Dutch accent, the little man said, *"The dumbfound a gettin hung up on da barn roof discombobled and verhoodled me, but I'm o.k. nauw."* He concluded that he was certain he could lick the phobia.

He said that as soon as his helpers got there he would inflate the balloon while the helpers loosened it from the roof so that it could lift itself off. He intended to do some "quick-patch" if necessary while it still had enough air in it to reveal any holes, and then he'd test it. He promised to take them all up for an aerial look at the farm in repayment for all the trouble he'd caused.

Fat said, *"Ya got'ta be nutsed up. Dat balloon von't lift me off da grount!"*

Fat's weight varied between three hundred and three fifty, and so the balloon pilot said, *"Yah! I see vott'cha mean!"*

It was right about at this time that the phone call came through from Ricky informing Randy about Arsenic's snake bite. After Randy hung up, and while he was conferring with James and Regan, Fat said, *"Snake bit! Wow! Vell I tell ya, dat coult'a happen't ta anybotty. Dem things can bite in the blink of a second!"*

As Denny Drexel's workers were removing the balloon from the barn, Randy grabbed some clothing and an overnight kit and was soon on the road back up to the mountains to look after his son and his father.

Right after he said his goodbyes and pulled out the driveway, Fat yelled to James and Maggie, *"Hey! Dey got da balloon air-bored again!"*

Indeed, the big sphere was starting to hover behind the barn.

The little balloonist again extended his offer of a quick ride. All declined, except James.

Denny's helpers kept the balloon attached to a tether to keep it from drifting, and after Denny and James got up in the air high enough to see over Arsenic's farmhouse, James yelled down, "Oh Lord, Maggie. A truck just hit one of your cows on the road that goes past your house!"

The little mountain town of Lock Haven had a pretty good hospital. The ambulance took Arsenic there. One of the staff at the hospital got Ricky situated in a motel right next to the hospital wing where Arsenic was admitted. The staff also helped Ricky get someone to go fetch Arsenic's pickup truck down to the motel parking lot. The two garage guys that fetched the truck also locked up Regan's cabin while they were up on the mountain. Ricky called his father from the motel.

Arsenic Schlank and his grandson, Ricky, had been vacationing at the deer lodge owned by Arsenic's son-in-law, Regan Kutz. The whole family was there for a few days, and then all but Arsenic and Ricky returned home. Ricky wanted to spend a few days alone with his Pop Pop.

The cabin was on a mountain slope right off the Coudersport Pike, surrounded by glossy evergreen bushes that were covered yearly with white and rose-colored examples of the state flower, the Mountain Laurel. A little sign next to the Pike pointed the way into the deer camp. The sign read "Broken Collar Deer Lodge," and an arrow pointed into the woods toward the log structure. Regan had chosen the name many years earlier after one of his hunting dogs broke loose and ran off during a vacation.

Regan was a member of several rod and gun clubs in the Reading area, and each club owned a deer camp up in the Appalachians, but Regan had built his own private deer lodge so he'd have more freedom to invite family and friends without consulting other club members. The structure was located on a little parcel of State Game Lands leased from the Commonwealth of Pennsylvania in the wild north-central part of the state.

It was made of stripped logs that blended with the surroundings. A large roofed porch was built on pillars out in front so that it extended over the slope. This spot provided many opportunities to observe white-tailed deer, elk, turkey, bear, porcupine, and numerous other wild animals. It was well known that one had to be careful when hiking trails around the cabin since timber rattlesnakes were numerous. Arsenic thought about this while lying half awake in his hospital bed in Lock Haven.

Randy entered Arsenic's hospital room after the drive up from the farm. His father was explaining to Ricky why he had not wanted to kill the rattlesnake that bit him.

Randy interrupted, "Hey, there's the venerable survivor!"

Arsenic stopped talking and gave Randy a big grin as he said, "*Vott's wener-able mean?*"

"Old and experienced!"

"*Vell dat I am, ain't? If I get anymoah experience, I ain't gonna be a survivor nomoah. Glei mohl faertzich!*"

"*Glei mohl faertzich*" means literally "almost forty," but when a Dutchman says it, he usually means something like "I'm older than I look!"

It wasn't too long ago that Arsenic had a battle with prostate cancer. At the time of diagnosis and treatment, the disease was thought to be terminal, and the services of hospice were requested. Arsenic was expected to die in less than six months. However, as it became apparent that he was defying the odds, and the cancer was not spreading as originally predicted, Arsenic invested his energy in caring for his wife Peach, who had suffered a stroke shortly after his own cancer diagnosis. He decided he couldn't afford to die, and he dismissed James, the hospice volunteer.

But James had fallen in love with life on the Pennsylvania Dutch farm and also with Arsenic's daughter, Rosa. He did not go away. As a matter of fact, he married into the family. Not too long before the wedding, Arsenic's wife died, and Randy and Ricky moved in with him. Life had been very hectic for awhile, and that's why Arsenic needed a break. Now he was recovering from a snakebite in a Lock Haven hospital. Never a dull moment!

Arsenic used the Deitsch word for farm as he asked Randy, "*Who's in charch dahn at da Büararie?*"

"Don't worry about it. Just rest."

Before leaving Reading a few hours ago, Randy arranged for his brother-in-law James and sister Rosa to look after the farm, with his other brother-in-law Regan and other sister Ruby acting as backup. James had moved Rosa's trailer right behind the barn after they were married, and so they lived right there on the place. James was quickly learning the daily routines and could probably handle things on his own.

Randy glanced at Arsenic's leg where the bandage was peeking out from under the sheet, and he turned to Ricky and said, "Now you see why I got so upset when you caught that rattlesnake last week to make a belt out of it."

"Well, at least I didn't step on it."

Arsenic pretended to take offense, "*Is dat supposed ta mean I'm tollpatschig?*"

Both Ricky and Randy stared with furrowed brow, so Arsenic added, "*Ya know, a klutz!*"

Ricky said, "No, I didn't mean that . . ."

"*I vass chust kitten. Fact is, I shoulda seen it foah I schtepped on it.*"

"Well, I didn't see it either."

"*Ya vass beheint me. Ya voult'a seen it if ya'da schtepped on it!*"

As soon as they stopped laughing, Arsenic looked at Randy and said, "*Vhere ya schleeping, junge?*"

An orderly dropped a tray out in the hall. There was a clattering, a sound of broken glass, and what sounded like cursing. Arsenic looked over at Ricky and grimmaced and then looked back at Randy.

"I moved into the same room Ricky's staying in. They placed him in a room with two double beds. I guess the motel is not too busy right now. Hey! I hope you don't consider it an insult if I make a little money while I'm up here."

"*Hauw's dat?*"

"I got a friend at the university here in town, and I can finagle a chance to get paid to give a short sociology course. We need the money to buy more horses. I'm almost done training all those I brought back from Indiana."

"*Hey, vee're chust proud ya schtill get a chance ta teach once't in avhile. Ain't vee Ricky?*"

When Randy failed to get tenure in the Sociology Department in Indiana, he had returned home to his father's farm near Reading and pursued a childhood passion for training horses. In addition to his academic credentials, Randy had won numerous trophies in dressage and western cutting competition. Cutting is the art of separating out a steer from the herd while on horseback and keeping it separated as long as your quick little quarterhorse mount can dance about and block the return of the isolated steer to his friends. Randy was a pro.

He still taught part-time at some of the small colleges in the Reading area and liked to talk about the sociology of the horse culture, focusing on people who raise, ride, and show horses. Since his family had always boarded horses and staged their own large horse shows and western riding competitions, he was involved with such people his whole life. The farm even had a big indoor arena for winter events.

Randy's friend taught social science at Lock Haven University of Pennsylvania and had been after him for weeks to give a talk to his colleagues. Randy was sure that on short notice he could get scheduled to give a paid workshop.

This University of Pennsylvania was a nice little school founded in 1870 as Central State Normal School, a teacher's college, and renamed Lock Haven University of Pennsylvania, but it shouldn't be confused with the other University of Pennsylvania, the Ivy League one located in Philadelphia. It's still a fine little school though.

Ricky agreed that he was proud of his father for being able to both teach and train horses, and Randy got a smile on his face, as Arsenic added, "*Listen, once't, you two hungry? Let's get a pitsa pie sent up heah so's vee can eat tagettah. Da nurses sett it's o.k allretty.*"

"O.k. and as long as I'm back up here in the mountains, why don't we goof around for a day after you get out of the hospital? Give you a chance to recuperate. You still have to drive your truck back to Reading."

While James was up in Denny Drexel's balloon down at Arsenic's farm, he had been looking over Arsenic's house, looking up the blacktop road that ran next to Maggie's house. Indeed, someone had come down that blacktop road in a pickup truck while James was watching, and just then a cow apparently got through the fence at Maggie's and wandered onto the highway. The truck driver slammed on the brakes, but it was too late. The cow was laid out on its side next to the road. James saw the whole thing and gave an eyewitness report, yelling down from the balloon.

Maggie started to run right over to her place, but Fat insisted on taking her over in his station wagon. Fat swung open the huge side door and started the lengthy process of climbing in. Because of his weight, he traveled in an old station wagon that had the driver's seat remounted toward the rear to make room for his tremendous corpulence. The driver's side door was also enlarged, and the rear seat had been removed to make room for his butchering tools. Heavy duty springs were installed under the vehicle.

Regan and Maggie managed to pile in with him and they drove over to have a look at the cow. James had to wait until the balloon could be brought back to earth, and then he trotted in the direction of Maggie's dairy farm as the little pilot and his helpers started packing up and loading stuff on a big trailer that had a cartoon image of the little guy painted on its side along with the words, "Let me help you advertise."

The truck that hit the cow over at Maggie's apparently made a surgical strike with its oversized rearview mirror, square on the cow's head. It killed it instantly but did no damage to the carcass.

There was very little blood on the road. Since Fat Schmidt was an itinerant butcher, he offered to skin and cut up the carcass for the freezer. This wasn't planned, but the meat was there, and the Dutch don't waste much.

Maggie walked over to her barnyard and got her old Ford tractor which already had a flatbed trailer hooked to it. The driver of the truck, and Regan, Fat, and James managed to tilt the flatbed and drag the cow up onto it, and Maggie drove it back to the barnyard. The truck driver didn't have time to help with butchering, but he offered to pay for all or part of the cow. Maggie just shook her head and said no one was to blame.

"I'd a shooed her off dat roat if I'd a seen, but's too late nauw. I can't be vatchin all da time da clock arount, an I doan ushally have a guy in a balloon standin gart over my place!" She said this for James' benefit and then to the truck driver, *"It veren't yoah fault!"*

Randy gave his seminar the day after arriving in Lock Haven. Arsenic was released from the hospital at noon the day after that. Arsenic suggested they leave right away and stop at the Appalachian Trail on the way home.

"Ya can hike dat trail all da vay from Maine ta Georgia, two thausent miles. I rhett bought it in dis magazine da nurse gift me. Crosses right da etch'a Berks County."

Randy laughed and said Arsenic couldn't do much hiking and maybe they should just move back into Regan's cabin for one more night and then spend a day driving around the mountains before heading back to Reading. They left Arsenic's truck down at the motel in Lock Haven and went back up to the cabin.

The cabin was located in Potter County on a hillside. That evening, the trio barbequed and ate dinner on the big front porch that stuck out on the downhill side, held up by stilts. During the meal, a bobcat darted across the space in front of the porch. Ricky spotted a rabbit first, running for its life, and then the bobcat chasing it. Randy said he had seen something similar once, but it was a coyote doing the chasing that time.

Inside, the lodge consisted of one very big room with knotty pine walls and oiled oak floor. There was a big plank oak table bolted to the floor right in the middle of the room. This served for dining, poker, and even as a workbench during deer season. There were four big handmade double bunk beds along one wall and gun racks all along another. All the wooden surfaces were bare, finished by climate and human occupation, toned by woodsmoke from fires for heating and cooking, by dust, by humidity, by thousands of human touches, and lastly by summer applications of oil soap in preparation for deer season.

After supper, Arsenic was lying on a bottom bunk, resting his leg. Ricky was sitting on the bunk right above him. They were talking to Randy who was seated at the table, carving a piece of wood that he claimed would become a steam locomotive, or a model of one. This led to a discussion of trains.

Arsenic argued that it had been the proliferation of factories and natural resources linked with a web or mesh of railroad lines that won the Civil War for the North. The whole northeast section of Pennsylvania and neighboring states used to be crisscrossed by little railroad lines.

A great horned owl emitted a sort of combination growling-hooting cry from a tree next to the cabin.

Arsenic said there were big passenger trains running straight from City A to B, but the hills of Pennsylvania were also teeming with small railroad companies, or lines, having spurs that picked up milk from farms, and shoppers going to town, and small outputs from little mills and ironworks in communities too small to even appear on a map.

That night Ricky dreamed of Civil War battles that resembled the huge paintings he'd studied in the waiting room of his dentist's office.

The next day the group packed up Regan's truck for the return trip home and began their day of play by driving fifteen miles east of the cabin on the Coudersport Pike into Tioga County to visit a scenic area with the somewhat surprising name of the Grand Canyon of Pennsylvania. Arsenic had been to the Grand Canyon in Colorado when his daughter Rosa was a little baby, and so he suspected this one would be a big disappointment.

But this Grand Canyon turned out to be a pretty astonishing ravine, fifty miles long and up to fourteen hundred feet deep. It was a gigantic gash in the heavily forested Allegheny Plateau, right in the middle of half of the Commonwealth's two million acres of public forest lands. Pine Creek flowed down the length and eventually contributed to the Chesapeake Bay far to the south. Native Americans called it Teeahdotton, or River of Pines.

An elderly couple standing at an overlook next to Randy pointed out a groundhog on the slope below. Then, the old man said they'd been traveling Interstate 80 and stopped for a while in Punxsutawney to visit what he called the Groundhog Day Museum and Zoo. Arsenic said he never heard of it, and the old man, who was a retired and windy college professor, gave a lecture at such a fast clip that Arsenic couldn't interrupt.

Pointing at the groundhog, he began, "The celebration of Groundhog Day on February 2 arose from an old European tradition of using the weather on Candlemas Day, also February 2, and midway between winter and summer, as a predictor of how severe the remainder of the winter would be. If it happened to be cloudy and rainy, winter would end early. The priest leading Mass on this day would bless the candles for use during the dark days of winter. In Europe, they observed badgers as they came out of hibernation, but the closest thing to them in Pennsylvania were groundhogs."

"*Hold on*," Arsenic blurted "*Yoah fershimmled! I din say I doan know nothin bought groundhog day!*"

The Professor seemed to ignore him, but it turned out that he was hard of hearing. He continued, "Punxsutawney is about a hundred miles southwest of here. On the other side of Route 80. It was originally a Delaware Indian campsite named 'ponksad-uteney,' which means 'a camp of sandflies.' The town was right next to the Shamokin path, the earliest known trail to the eastcoast.

"In 1886, the editor of the town's newspaper, the *Punxsutawney Spirit*, declared that a local groundhog named Punxsutawney Phil, perhaps a pet, was the premier weather forecaster in the country, 'Weather Prophet Extraordinare' according to the editor. The idea seems to have stuck and spread, and it was good for tourism in Punxsutawney, especially in early February."

Arsenic was clearly getting angry as he said, "*Ya must think I'm a doom-kupf!*"

Randy quickly stepped in the middle, anticipating hostilities, although as noted, the professor didn't even hear the comment. Randy uncovered the hearing problem when he started to speak and the old man's wife told him to shout because her husband was hard of hearing. Randy shouted, "Aren't the mountains beautiful?"

"You can't see them!" the old man shouted back.

Randy was confused by this comment and asked them to elaborate.

In unison, the couple said, "There's too many trees!"

Randy said, "You mean in front of the overlook here. I think they keep them trimmed back pretty good. So you can see out into the canyon."

"No," both man and wife persisted, "the mountains are all covered with trees."

On the other side of Randy, Arsenic started to laugh, and Randy whispered aside, "Shhhh," and then turning again to the old couple, "Oh, you were thinking like of the Rocky Mountains with rocky peaks and cliffs and such."

"Yeah. That's what mountains look like."

"Well, I guess we could argue that one. But I see your point."

The Appalachians and their Allegheny offspring were once bigger than the Rockies, but they are also much, much older. They are considerably worn down now, and mostly tree-covered, but this two-thousand-mile mountain chain constitutes one of the oldest geographical features still visible on the earth's surface.

As the couple was leaving, Randy tried to distract his father by reading from an informational placard next to the overlook. He read that the canyon in front of them began twenty thousand years ago when a glacier formed a dam and forced Pine Creek, which had been flowing northeast toward New York, to change directions and literally bust its way south through the Allegheny Plateau and on toward the Chesapeake Bay.

"*Dat must' a bin von bick crick!*" Arsenic commented after looking back at the ravine.

Randy also read that an old railroad bed was down in the canyon and had been converted into a bicycle path.

"*Vow! Can ya imachine pedalin dahn da mittle off dat, eh?*"

Ricky was leaning over the rail and his dad cautioned him to be careful.

"I can't see the bicycle path. Uncle Regan says he's going to help me put a motor on that old bicycle in Pop Pop's wagon shed. I might be able to drive it in places like that."

His dad replied, "I don't think they'd let you do that. Not with a motor and all." And then, looking to Arsenic, he added, "It's eleven o'clock. I think we should head down to Renovo and get some lunch."

They drove down a mountain dirt road through Clinton County, sparsely populated with people and densely populated with whitetail deer and other wild animals. The state as a whole registered 274 people per square mile, but Clinton had only forty-three per square mile, and it was close to nine hundred square miles in size. Hunting and fishing were major tourist industries.

The State of Pennsylvania had a deer herd totaling close to 1.6 million, about two thirds the number of people living in the whole city of Pittsburgh. The human population of the Commonwealth as a whole was the sixth largest in the nation, and yet most residents considered themselves rural. Indeed, even the small communities adjacent to or within commuting distance of big cities had so many curvy roads and so many hills, rocks, trees, and bodies of water between homes that even suburbs seemed rural.

Randy, Ricky, and Arsenic spotted a black bear, an elk, and thirty deer along the dirt road down the mountain. Ricky was usually the spotter. He had a Korean gym teacher in school in Indiana, and the fellow had taught the class how to control their attention. He had a little exercise that he called "seeing everything while seeing nothing." It showed the kids how to be fully aware of everything while not focusing on any one thing.

On this ride down the mountain, Ricky found that when he stared broadly into the old-growth forest, the near trees passed through his field of vision faster than the far trees and blurred, and he gained a perspective that enabled him to spot animals deep in the woods even when the car was traveling at thirty miles per hour.

From the back seat, Ricky would yell, "There's something," and Randy would slam on the brakes and back up.

Arsenic would say, "*Hauw'cha schpot dat von?*"

At one point, they came onto a doe with three fawns. It was rare for them to have triplets.

They watched for a few minutes, and Randy was about to resume driving, when Arsenic said, "*Wait avhile yet!*"

He had spotted a coyote coming down toward the deer from the top of the mountain. He pointed. The doe stomped her right front foot three times and the fawns froze. The doe turned to face the coyote. She blew through her nostrils such that it produced a whistling sound. The coyote stopped in its tracks and stared. They stood thus, predator and prey, for half a minute, and then the coyote turned at a right angle to its original path and trotted on around the mountain, avoiding the deer.

Randy said, "Huh! He figured he wasn't any match for that angry momma!"

After they resumed their descent toward the town of Renovo, Arsenic turned in his seat to look at Ricky in the back and started telling him about an incident that occurred when Randy was in high school. A doe had attacked a teenage girl while her class was playing field hockey. He asked Randy to finish the story.

"The girl got between the mother deer and her fawn when she ran off the field to get the ball. The doe panicked and attacked the girl. It ran at her and went up on its hind legs and socked her three or four times with its front feet. It kept punching as she was falling to the ground. My gym class was in the next field playing soccer, and some of the guys saw it happen. I didn't see it myself, but they described it."

"How bad was she hurt?"

"She was bruised on her chest and had a cracked rib, but she recovered pretty fast. It's just lucky it didn't hit her in the face."

Ricky didn't say a word for about a minute, and then he uttered, "I didn't think they'd do that."

Back at the farm, after the truck driver left, James and Regan and Fat hung the carcass from a tripod in a big Quonset hut next to the barn. This was where Maggie did her butchering. There was no pulley system handy, and so the group ran a rope over a rafter, and James and Regan pulled on the rope while Fat basically lifted the carcass with bare hands, from the back of the trailer.

James and Regan didn't think it could be done, but Fat said, *"Chust stay ought'a my road and keep the slack ought'a dat rope!"* And he hoisted it up!

James and Regan were surprised. They really didn't do much. Just kept pulling in slack, then tied off the rope. They couldn't believe Fat's strength. The truth is Fat about lifted the cow by himself. Of course, no one could haul around a body the size of Fat's without having a lot of muscle underneath all that adipose tissue. But it still left a sense of awe.

Folks often teased Fat about his size, but the Pennsylvania Dutch did not consider obesity a sin. The "fat" which gave Fat his name was not soft, but hard like an Olympic weightlifter. He was squarish and solid and stood on the earth as though he had grown out of it. The Dutch didn't even use the word "obesity." A man was "thick, stocky, or stout," and a woman was "plump, fleshy, or buxom." The Deitsch word *fleischig* described the type in a nice way.

Although typically reserved for men, the nickname "Fat" was considered endearing, not offensive. It was fairly common in the area, and it was usually used in conjunction with the person's last name, such as Fat Schmidt, so that one could differentiate that individual from Fat Schultz, Fat Himelreich, Fat Dieseldorf, and so on.

There was a local joke in which the jokester would say to a person, "*Hey, by any chance, do ya know Fat Burns in Allentown?*" And the person would say something like, "*Nah, I doan belief I knowed him.*" And the jokester would reply, "*Ach, fat burns anyplace ya put a fire under it!*"

Fat Schmidt began the job of *obtzeega*, removing the hide to sell to the tannery. Then, he commenced to cut up the carcass into steaks, roasts, ribs and such. When James wanted to help with the cutting, Fat said "no" and he winked at Regan, pointed at James, and said, "*Er hatt zwei linke hände!*" Which means, "He's all thumbs!" And then, "*Er hatt es al hinnersich!*" Which means, "He would get everything backwards." And so, he assigned James the job of wrapping the cut meat for freezing. Regan started carrying cuts of meat from Fat to James.

The truth is that all tradesmen need to protect some knowledge of their trade if their skill is to remain a commodity. Fat made his living as a butcher and was reluctant to show James the techniques.

Maggie went in the house to cook a meal for the workers who were donating their time. She started cooking *boova schenkel*, with *schnecken* for dessert. The *boova schenkel* had to cook for two hours. Butchering the cow would require the remainder of the afternoon.

Since Rosa was attending classes all afternoon, and Ruby was cutting hair, neither of them would be available to help with the cooking or butchering, but they might be able to come for *nachtessen*, the evening meal.

Maggie was using her summer kitchen, a shed attached to the house, equipped with a counter and small wood cookstove. Maggie called the shed her "cookery." The weather had started to warm and Maggie was more warm-blooded, or *varmblütig*, than Arsenic and hated the extra heat from the cookstove in the kitchen. She used the summer kitchen in all but the coldest months. Arsenic did all his cooking in the kitchen. Maggie was making sizable portions of everything, for Fat Schmidt was known for the size of his appetite as well as his body.

Boova schenkel probably has its roots in the pierogi, a pouch of pie dough filled with potatoes or cheese and boiled. Pierogies were Polish in origin. Pennsylvania Dutch culture started out German and this included the Germanic trait of absorbing into itself useful features found in other cultures. Berks County was truly a melting pot, and so was its food. In similar fashion, the Pennsylvania Dutch dialect, or Deitsch, borrowed freely from other languages. It's a spoken dialect, and the rules tend to vary a bit from family to family and neighborhood to neighborhood. Whatever works for communication tends to be fair. Just like the Dutch food, if it eats good, eat it.

Maggie had rolled out eight-inch circles of pie dough and spooned a portion of Pennsylvania Dutch potato filling in the center of each. The dough circles were then folded in half and sealed by pressing a fork repeatedly along the open edge. The potato filling is a Dutch staple made with mashed potatoes, bread crumbs, parsley, onions, and butter. Often it's baked by itself, but true to its name, it can be used to "fill" other things like the dough pouches for *boova schenkel*. These pouches are basically dropped into a previously-prepared beef stew and cooked there for thirty minutes. The fat off the top of the stew is made into a milk-based gravy and spooned on top of individual servings. *Boova schenkel* means "boys legs" in Dutch, and the pouches of dough Maggie was fixing did look a lot like the pudgy little legs of a plump little Dutch boy.

Maggie's dessert, the *schnecken*, was a sort of sweet milky bread dough spread with butter, sugar, raisins, cinnamon, and almonds then rolled up like a jelly roll and baked and sliced to show the swirly pattern of the filling. *Schnecken* means "snails," and each spiraling slice of the pastry does resemble a snail.

Maggie put the finished meal in a warmer on top of her wood stove and headed out to see when the crew would be ready to eat. She yelled, "*Put some elbow grease inta it. Dinnah's rhetty!*" She had called Ruby and Rosa and they were on their way.

"*What does it give foah dinnah?*" Fat asked.

And Maggie said, "*Venn ya get done, ya find ought.*"

Fat said they were "*catched after*" and Maggie helped put the last of the packages of meat in the big chest freezer located in the back of the Quonset hut.

"*Wir sind faertich!*" Maggie announced. "*Es ist die zeit fur essen!*"

On their way to the kitchen, Fat Schmidt said, "*Ich bin hoongerich! I coult eat a horse!*"

Maggie replied, "*I imachin a horse ist chust a average meal foah you, Fat.*" And everyone, including Fat, laughed.

While they were getting seated, Rosa and Ruby arrived. As they entered the kitchen, Regan was washing up at the kitchen sink and he said, "Hey honey!"

Maggie said, "*Ruby, get you and the rest down from the cupboard some glasses an pour everybody from the jug some fresh milk!*"

During the meal, Fat praised the flavor by saying, "*Dis shuah ist schmecklich!*"

CHAPTER 2

After Arsenic, Randy, and Ricky packed up at the cabin and took their morning ride to the Grand Canyon and then down the mountain backroads, they ate lunch in a small restaurant in the mountain community of Renovo near the Susquehanna River. The inhabitants were mostly people of German ancestry brought there by the Philadelphia and Sunbury Railroad before it became the Philadelphia and Erie in 1861.

Arsenic's group sat near the front window where they could look out across the remains of a railroad. This whole side of town had once been a huge switching yard, sometimes called a marshalling or classification yard. There was row upon row upon row of laid track, and roundhouses for switching track, and enormous maintenance shops where whole trains could be pulled under a single roof. One small train was out there now where there had once been dozens. It was adding a few cars before departing for Philadelphia.

During lunch, as though picking up on the topic of discussion at the cabin from the previous evening, Arsenic lamented changes that had occurred in his world and talked about how the railroad yard outside the restaurant window was once filled with steam engines chuffing back and forth as cars were added to a string, or engines were switched from one string to another, until a train was ready to head down to places like Reading and Philadelphia with loads of coal or merchandise from small manufactories and farms. Arsenic said sometimes, on cold days, the yard was like a scene from a nightmare, full of steam and smoke.

"*Schmoke, schparks, an schteam from five to ten locahmotiffs passin each anutter all at once't as dey schtoped and schtarted an schtoped again. Looked like fiah-breathin dragons. Chuff, chuff, chuff, chuff! Dough's vere da days!*"

Originally, transportation of people and goods had been carried out by horse and wagon and canal and river. Like that branch
of the Susquehanna River right close to Renovo. But by 1915,
Pennsylvania had completed 11,693 miles of railway. The golden
age of the locomotive had arrived. And then again by the 1930's, the
truck, auto, and airplane were taking over, and the railroads entered
a long period of decline just like the horse, canal, and river traffic
did earlier. In 1941, the famous Pennsylvania Turnpike opened. It's
ironic that this marvel of engineering with its many tunnels through
mountains was actually started as a railroad, a railroad that ended up
a big highway, like the rest of the nation.

There was a big "kabong" sound from the yard as a car was
added to the string of the train, and the window continued to vibrate
as the concussion transferred from one car to another down the length.
"Bong, bong, bong, bong."

Arsenic continued, *"Deese diesels nauwdays doan make so
much noise an dirt, but dey doan haff da personality a dem schteam
locahmotiffs. Not da muscle needer, ya know vott I mean?"*

At that moment, the waitress came over with coffee refills
and asked if they were on vacation. Arsenic told her about the snakebite and the hospital stay in Lock Haven. The waitress asked if they
heard about the festival celebrating the history of the Piper Cub, at
the Lock Haven Airport.

The Piper Cub was a wonderfully distinctive little yellow
aircraft that was once manufactured in Lock Haven. The waitress
said Lock Haven would be full of those little planes, and they were
going to offer free rides to get the event started. Since the trio had to
go through Lock Haven to pick up Arsenic's truck on the way home,
they decided to stop by the festival.

When Arsenic, Randy, and Ricky arrived in Lock Haven,
the clear sky around the airport parking lot was full of little yellow
airplanes circling overhead like a flock of canaries. Arsenic drew
attention to the far distant horizon where there was a hint of a storm
cloud.

Randy said, "That looks like a cumulonimbus."

"*Vott?*"

"A type of cloud that can produce a storm."

Arsenic was still remembering the college professor up at the Grand Canyon as he responded, "*Vhy not chust say 'schtorm clout?' Sumtimes seems like colletch chust teaches ya moah vays ta say common sense, eh?*"

Randy laughed and replied, "Yeah, in some ways that's true."

And Ricky interrupted, "Hey guys! I don't care what you call it. If it's gonna rain, we'd better get to looking around!"

After walking through the various hangars and tents and having lunch, the skies were still clear around the airport. Ricky bought a sweat shirt stenciled with the expression, "Fly the Lofty Skies of Lock Haven." Then, they came to a tent with a sign announcing free rides in a vintage Cub.

Arsenic insisted that Ricky take a ride, and when he returned, the boy said, "I feel." And he paused, and he swooned, and he concluded, "I don't know how to describe how I feel!"

Arsenic said, "*Dat's life you're feeling. You feel alife!*"

His excitement prompted Randy and Arsenic to take a free ride as well. When it was his turn, Arsenic got a good look at the Appalachian Mountains. The far distant storm cloud was beautiful. It was still in the same place, and it was clear that rain was falling on that faraway place.

Arsenic mumbled, "*Ain't dat beeyoutifall, Peach? Vott vass it Randy call't it?*"

Over the sound of the engine, the pilot yelled, "What?!"

And Arsenic looked a little embarassed as he yelled back, "*I vass chust talkin ta my diseesed vife, Peach!*"

The pilot pointedly raised his eyebrows and quickly focused his eyes forward, concentrating on flying and not saying another word.

When Peach died a few months ago, Arsenic told his grandson he liked to imagine Peach's presence even though he knew she was deceased. He had started talking to her in his thoughts and some-times aloud, which is what spooked the pilot. Arsenic and Peach had been man and wife for forty-three years.

As Arsenic got off the plane, he was wiping his eyes with his big handkerchief. The trio went over and got Arsenic's truck from the motel parking lot, and the caravan of two headed back toward the family farm near Reading. Arsenic said he needed time to think so he asked Ricky to ride with his dad.

Midway into their journey, Ricky was still riding with Randy who was leading off. It was dark and clear. Ricky said it looked like they could drive right into the middle of the big, waxing, bone-china moon that was just clearing the horizon ahead of them. Then suddenly it was drizzling from a cloud directly overhead. Ricky drifted into half-sleep. He stared blankly out the windshield.

The headlights shone on a disabled vehicle pulled off onto the berm of the highway. The rear end of the car was jacked up, and someone had scooted underneath on his back to work on the underside. In the moments it took to approach and pass the disabled car, something fell from its underside and hit the fellow underneath in the face. Maybe a wrench, or a loose part, or just a chunk of dirt. The guy rolled around and grabbed at his eye. Another guy kneeling behind the rear bumper, jumped forward and reached out as though trying to help or console the injured one. And then they were past. Randy didn't seem to notice.

In his half sleep, and in an instant, Ricky's brain registered a story to explain his perception. The guy on his back under the car was the son of the guy kneeling by his legs. A wrench had slipped from the boy's hands and hit him in his face. His father was very upset. The boy was trying to accomplish a repair that his father couldn't accomplish because of his age and the difficulty of crawling under the car. They loved each other, father and son. The son would be o.k. Just bruised.

Ricky looked over at his father who was focused on driving. He was surprised that Randy didn't even mention the events by the side of the road. Ricky didn't mention them either. They were well past the scene. Anyway, he wasn't sure he'd actually seen it all or just dreamed it.

Randy glanced down at the instrument panel and said he needed to fill up with gas. Since Arsenic was following, Randy watched to be sure his dad would see his turn signal and follow into the gas station.

Arsenic pulled up on the other side of the gas pump and started filling his own tank. He said little and looked a bit teary. He faced away from Randy while pumping gas. His pump overflowed and spattered a little gas on his pants. He mumbled, "*Yah, vell.*"

After they had paid their bills, Randy got Ricky to ride with Arsenic, and this time he got Arsenic to go first. He didn't tell him the reason, but he wanted to be sure they didn't get separated. His Pop seemed kind of depressed. Ricky slept the rest of the way home.

Arsenic went right to bed when they got back to the farm-house.

Peach Weidenheimer was born in 1923. She became pregnant during the Great Depression when she was only fifteen years of age. Her father was an alcoholic and her mother was a born-again Christian who spent much time reading the Bible. Peach's early years had been less than happy, and in many ways, pregnancy was the best thing that happened to her up to that point. Her father allowed her to marry Arsenic Schlank and even gave them the wood from an old chicken house to build their first home. Of course, they had to tear it down themselves and haul the wood, which they did.

They named their first child Rosa. She was the one that recently married Arsenic's hospice volunteer, James Christiansen. The Schlank's second daughter, Ruby, was born two years after Rosa, and their only son, Randy, made an appearance three years after Ruby and two years after the beginning of the Second World War. Randy was the first to be born in a hospital. Peach objected to the hospital, maintaining pregnancy was not a sickness, but her doctor insisted and prevailed.

Arsenic's kids stayed close to home. James and Rosa lived in the trailer behind the barn on his farm, although they intended to move to State College near the beginning of next year if James could get permission to begin graduate training in Psychology in the Spring Semester.

Randy and his son Ricky moved into the farmhouse with Arsenic after Peach died. Randy had been married to an accountant, but they divorced while living in Indiana. Randy had been awarded custody of their son, and his ex-wife, Stella, eventually moved to California to take a new job. Randy and Ricky moved back to Pennsylvania to live with Arsenic after Randy failed to get tenure at his university and was forced to seek a new job. He decided to go back to horse training and teach only on a part-time basis. That was right after his mother died.

Ruby and Regan Kutz owned a small gentleman's farm adjacent to the more substantial operation Arsenic and Randy were running. Regan also worked for an Ag company, and Ruby "*fixed hair*," as the locals called it, in the beauty shop in her house. Regan and Ruby spent a lot of time at the Schlank's farm. They hadn't been able to have children of their own and enjoyed helping to parent Ricky. The two were very active in hunting, fishing, and trapshooting clay pigeons. Regan had already taken Ricky on numerous hunting and fishing expeditions and had promised to take him trapshooting when he returned from the deer camp in the mountains.

Maggie Stoltzfusz pushed the kitchen door ajar and yelled, "*Wu bist, Arsenic?*"

Arsenic had watched her walk across the highway. "*Koom rye!*" he said and then added, "*I'm right heah vatchin yoah cawhs foah ya. Get some coffee an sit yoahself foah avhile. I seen dat ya got'a new dawk.*" Maggie loved animals and was always taking in stray cats and dogs.

Since he'd returned from the mountains with his son and grandson, Arsenic's morning routine tended to include parking in the chair by the kitchen window that faced the road. Right after Ricky headed for school and his son went out to the barn, Arsenic would sit by the window and think. He would turn a chair toward the window, prop his feet on the big step-on windowsill, and stare absently out at nothing in particular.

Arsenic's big iron kitchen stove was located in the corner to the left of his position and comforted him on the cool spring mornings while he marked the traffic and the goings-on across the road. There was something very comfortable about that corner near the window. Arsenic called it *gemütlich*. Unlike Maggie, he had no summer kitchen. He and his wife Peach had torn it down years ago. They'd installed a gas stove right next to the wood stove for use on hot summer days when the wood stove was finally shut down.

Maggie Stoltzfusz was Arsenic's closest neighbor. Her dairy farm was located cater-corner across the highway. After Randy commented to her that his dad seemed a little down, Maggie had noticed Arsenic spending a lot of time by that front kitchen window. She'd glance over at the Schlank farmhouse while tending to the chores that took her out close to the highway.

Spring was coming, and life was sprouting everywhere. Arsenic was using the wood stove less and the gas stove more, but he still sat looking out that window for about an hour every morning. Maggie wanted to change that habit.

As she came through the kitchen door, she said, "*I come lookin foah yoah notions on da supchect off milkin machines.*"

Maggie's deceased husband, Raymond, had maintained a dairy herd with the sale of milk providing their only source of cash. Raymond didn't believe in milking machines, but then he was very energetic right up until his death, and he had a full-time helper. Raymond would have thought it outrageous that he and his helper could be replaced by a machine.

When her husband died, Maggie was spiritless for several months and only recently regained her backbone and got the milk business to prosper once again. She recently increased the size of the dairy herd and hired Ricky part-time to help her and her hired man, Amos Zimmerman, with the milking.

Maggie had added a dozen Ayrshire cows from Scotland. The Ayrshires didn't produce quite as much milk as Guernseys or Holsteins, but they were more hardy and survived the Pennsylvania winters better, or at least Maggie's husband had said they did. Also, Maggie thought they were pretty. They were mostly white with an attractive splattering of red or brown, as though someone had flung a bucket of red or brown paint up the side of the cow, most of it landing on her head.

Maggie could just barely keep up with the milking even with Amos, and now Ricky, helping her. She had to either hire another employee or try one of those newfangled milking machines to replace the oldfangled hands, buckets, and stool.

"*Vott's da ulte vay got wrong vith it?*" Arsenic asked.

At first glance, old farmers in the Lutheran and Reformed congregations seemed to shun technology a bit like their Amish neighbors, but in truth they avoided buying new gadgets simply because they were frugal and used the old stuff until it degraded into trash. Even then, useable components of the trash were recycled into other devices. Maggie had been milking by hand, because she didn't want to spend money on a milking machine. There was nothing religious about it.

Arsenic added, "*Dose machines is pretty pricely!*"

Maggie responded, "*I can't keep my chores catched aftah no moah.*"

"*Hauw's Ricky verkin ought?*"

"*Ach, a goot verker he is but a'nutter full-time helpah I need,*"

besights Amos, ya know, nauw's I got moah cawhs. Then too, ya need
Ricky helpin his Pop and you, an a kit needs time ta play too."
          "Vell, I doan know nuthin bought milkin machines."
          "Vell, ya ain't too ulte ta learn! I need advisement!"
          Maggie knew that moping and sulking came easy when your
partner died. She didn't like seeing Arsenic sit around. It wasn't very
Dutchified to do that.
          Maggie was carrying a big tote bag with brown and white
splotches like the hide on her cows, and she'd hand-stitched the slogan
"Milk Ain't Chust Foah Kits Nomoah" on the side. She removed a
stack of brochures from the milking machine company and laid them
on the big kitchen table in the middle of the room. Arsenic dragged
his chair over, and Maggie pulled one of the other pinstriped, hex-
painted chairs, or *küchenstuhl*, away from the oak wainscotting along
one wall.
          After perusing the printed material, Arsenic said, *"A bick*
prodchect is vott dis looks like."
          "Vill ya help me?"
          "Yah vell. Let's haff da company guy come ought'n talk
bought it. Says here dey'll do dat."
          "O.k. I'll jock yoah memory after I get holt'a da guy. You're
pretty vergesslich lately!" She gathered her things and packed her
bag. And called over her shoulder, *"Have'a goot day!"*
          The Dutch have a word, *ormsalich*. It refers to a poor de-
pressed soul who can't get his gumption back. Maggie didn't want
Arsenic to become an *ormsalich*.
          After Maggie left, Arsenic placed his chair again to look out
the front window. He spotted Maggie's new dog running across the
road, apparently following Maggie's scent.
          He pushed open the window a bit and yelled, *"Hey Maggie!*
Yoah new dauk's come lookin foah ya!"
          Ricky's two beagles met the newcomer at the corner of the
yard, and Arsenic laughed as Maggie tried to separate the bunch,
grabbing the collar of her own dog and trying to send the beagles

toward Arsenic's place. Arsenic opened the window and called for the beagles to come home, as a bent-over Maggie waved with one arm and dragged her dog along with the other.

Maggie's farm was similar to Arsenic's, similar houses of Dutch design with three large rooms of living space on floor one and little bedrooms upstairs. Each house had a colossal shade tree on the south side. And although Maggie and Arsenic shared the fear of old folk that storms might drop such big trees on their bedrooms while they slept, each had resisted temptations to cut or top their trees. Spouses helped plant them, many years ago, and the spouses were deceased. The trees had sentimental value.

The Schlank's and Stoltzfusz's farms had different barn designs. The Schlank family settled the area first and laid claim to a section with a better location for a barn.

The back of a good Pennsylvania Dutch barn needs an earthen ramp, or bank, to drive the haywagon and heavy equipment onto the top floor. Also, the front of the barn has to face south to gather warmth in winter.

Well, two hills met between Arsenic's and Maggie's homesteads. One sloped down to the south, and the other sloped down to the west. The Schlank's built on the south-sloping hill, the best place for a barn since the north side could be built directly into the hill, and then the front would face south. The hill itself served as the ramp or bank on the backside. A little bit of soil was dug to fit the first floor into the hillside, but it was easy.

Maggie's husband's family, on the other hand, had to accomodate more to landscape. Their homestead was on the west-facing hill, on the other side of the highway that now ran between the farms. To get their barn to face south they had to build the east end into the hill that sloped west. And so, the barn did face south, but a big gob of earth had to be gouged and moved to the north of where the barn would be, so that it could become the ramp on the backside.

The east end of the barn stuck in that gouged spot in the hill, and thus with the ramp in place in the back, the finished barn had dirt on two sides of the first floor, good insulation but it caused a minor ventilation problem. Normally, stones in the end walls are staggered to produce chinks for flow-through ventilation. Ventilation is important to keep hay and other stored crops dry. Also, if it got too hot in the barn, the hay could catch fire as it fermented. Anyway, the Stoltzfusz barn had to have special ventilation installed on the roof. A big box rose above the peak to gather and disperse heat. It looked like a tiny little barn on top of the big barn. The box even had tiny little hex signs painted on the sides.

Arsenic's great-grandfather helped move the dirt for his neighbor's barn—without a bulldozer. They uncovered a big natural spring where the east end stuck in the hill. That gusher could have stymied the whole project. But old great-grandad Stoltzfusz said, *"Heck an'all. Vee'll chust schtick a schpringhaus in 'da barn!"* And so they did.

It was toilsome getting it in there, what with the flowing water making the concrete run, but they did it. It worked good for keeping milk cool. The spring was channeled into a knee-high concrete tank in the floor. Milk cans placed in this pool were bathed by cold running water until used on the farm or picked up by the dairy truck from the bottling plant.

Overflow springwater from the inside pool ran outside into a stock tank where cattle could drink, and then into a gutter system. It ended up in the meadow below Arsenic's house, where the Schlanks had built a springhouse of their own. There were a lot of springs in the Berks County hills.

Another thing about the Stoltsfusz's barn is that they replaced the classic Dutch *vorbau* with a building expansion, an enclosed space extending out thirty feet in front of the barn wall. The roof for this annex attached up high, halfway between the main barn roof and second floor, to provide pitch sufficient to shed snow and rain.

From inside, a third of the first floor of the barn linked smoothly to the annex in front to form a sort of indoor corral. Where Arsenic's barn had large rooms of horse stalls and a porch in front, Maggie's had much open indoor space for cattle to mill around.

The top floor covered the back two-thirds of the first floor and was held up by posts made from whole tree trunks. From inside the annex, the top floor was a big stage, a hayloft. Only a railing in front, so workers could toss hay and straw down anywhere along the edge onto the ground floor where the cows were milling around. Cows were milked in the area back of the first floor, under the loft, and so they often waited in the indoor shaded area under the annex roof. The cool springhouse with its pool of running water was also back under the loft.

The ground floor extension had big barn doors on each end and the floor was concrete, so Maggie could run her little Ford tractor's front-end loader right across the area and scrape up the *kedrech*, or cow manure, and dump it in the manure spreader parked outside in the barnyard under the eave of the barn, in the place where stillborn calves were superstitiously buried. This burial ritual was supposed to reduce the likelihood that the mother would ever abort again.

While Arsenic's *scheierhof*, or barnyard, was in front of the *vorbau*, Maggie's was on the west end of the barn, next to the west doorway of the building extension. This was another area where Maggie's cows congregated when they wanted to be milked and fed their special treat of silage.

Which brings us to another difference between Arsenic's and Maggie's barns. Maggie had a huge silo attached to hers. It towered over the barn. A big circular storage container where chopped immature plants were packed to exclude air and allow fermentation to develop acids that preserved the moist feed, called silage. Maggie's silage smelled a bit like sweet molasses. Her husband had always mixed corn, sorghum, grass, and soybeans, run through a chopper and conveyed to the top of the silo where the weight of the plants compacted those toward the bottom with sufficient pressure to ensure good curing of the feed.

In fact, the staple food source for Maggie's cows was pasture on hillsides around the barn. Cows were out to pasture most of the day. Nevertheless, the pasture had its limits. Grass could die during drought and was sparse in winter, and so it was always necessary to have a supply of silage. About 400 pounds of blood must pass through a cow's udder to make a pound of milk. That takes a lot of energy and a lot of high quality food. The silage also served as a treat, and the cows were usually eager to participate when it was time to milk. In summer months, the big doors on the ends of the barn's extension were left open, and the cows would gather in the pavilion. In winter, when snow was dangerously high or mercury dangerously low, they often spent the night in the indoor annex. In either case, they were usually there waiting at milking time.

One at a time the cows were taken to a stall under the loft toward the rear of the barn and fed enriched feed while being milked. Milk was then carried by bucket to that place where the barn stuck in the hillside, there it was cooled by the spring discovered when the earth was gouged to make room for the east end of the barn.

Maggie and Arsenic were about to learn from the milking machine salesman that newfangled factory farms rely upon mechanized equipment and extraordinary procedures to ensure high milk production, but the salesman would learn from Maggie and Arsenic that some farmers still live in conformity with nature.

In New Zealand cows spent their whole lives out in the fields, being milked periodically in a small shelter in the middle of the pasture. Costs were low that way, but of course, the United States prefers factory techniques to keep production high, even when it comes to milk. An average dairy farm in New Zealand was producing 7,189 pounds of milk per cow per year at the same time the average cow in the United States was producing 12,147. High productivity!

These things would be emphasized by a film the dairy equipment salesman would show as he tried to talk Maggie into "modernizing" her farm with machines, antibiotics, hormones, vaccinations, and such. Some of that was fine, but Maggie was always interested in whether or not the cows were happy.

A cat yowled and landed square in the middle of the windshield of the salesman's truck, just as he came to a stop next to the rail fence in Maggie's barnyard. The salesman was starting to open his door, and he about fell out when the cat hit.

There was a single cow standing inside the fence. She'd reached through the fence rails and pulled a mouthful of hay out of one of the bales stacked just outside the enclosure. Tousles of hay stuck out on each side of her mouth, and she seemed to be smiling.

The cat had been sleeping on top of the stack, which collapsed when old bossy grabbed the mouthful from the center bale and pulled. This all explains why the cat was upset, but the salesman had not seen the antecedent events and thought only that he had somehow run over Maggie's cat, as irrational as that might be since cats don't usually come flying into a person's windshield, particularly just as the vehicle's coming to a stop.

Although Maggie was inside the house and had no idea what transpired outside, Arsenic had been watching for the dairy equipment salesman from his kitchen window, and he had witnessed the whole episode involving the cat. He was laughing so hard that he had trouble getting his boots on in preparation for the walk across the road to Maggie's place. He was still laughing as he walked up to Maggie's kitchen door where the salesman was still apologizing for his imagined slaying of Maggie's pet.

Arsenic looked at Maggie as he walked up, and he said, "*Ya got a hackles-up look!*"

"*He says he run ovah my cat!*"

"*Nein, die katze hast gespringt! It ain't hurt!*" And in spite of his laughing, Arsenic was able to clarify the events for Maggie and the salesman. The cat was fine; the cow merely startled it and made it jump. "*Let's go show da salesmun yoah dairy set-up!*"

Glancing at the cow next to the fence and the calf beside it, the company rep, Mark Ramsey, admired the size of the calf.

Maggie replied, "*Yah, he's a real grower! Only two veeks uld an look'it da size!*"

As they entered the barn, Mark continued, "You have a pretty good beginning here."

"*Vell sanks. My hussbent's family had it set up venn vee took it ovah.*"

"This area looks like it would make a good parlor."

"*A gute vott?*"

"Parlor! The place where you do the milking."

"*Vell da haus is vhere da parlor is, an I shuah doan milk no cawhs in dere! Dis ist da milich stube, die melkstand.*"

With what could have been interpreted as a touch of condescension in expression and tone of voice, the salesman said, "We prefer the term 'parlor.' Anyway, this is where you milk the cows."

"*Yah!*"

Pigeons were cooing in the loft upstairs. Mark looked toward the rafters, and noticed a dog's skull nailed to one of them. He pointed and said, "What is that?!"

"*A dauk schkull. Die alten beliefed it voot keep cawhs from haffin abortions!*"

Mark grimmiced and shook his head.

Maggie hastened to add, "*I ain't sayin dat's vott I belief. Granpop put it up deah, an it ain't dooin no harm anyvays.*"

The early Pennsylvania Dutch did hold some unusual superstitions with regard to their barns. Legends suggested that the shingles should be nailed on while the moon is waning, or they would leak. Also, they believed the larger the barn a man built, the more good luck he would have. But then, of course, a big barn could be a favorite target for the evil eye of a neighbor, as well as his jealousy.

In Reading, in the year 1820, John George Hohman published an influential German-language magical recipe book filled with spells, procedures, and yes, even recipes. The title was *Der lang verborgene Schatz und Haus Freund*. English translations were later printed in Carlisle and Harrisburg, with one titled *Powwows, or The Long-Lost Friend*.

Hohman was an artist who specialized in *fracturschrifften*, writing and illustrating precious official documents such as birth and marriage certificates. Some say he developed an interest in hoodoo by praying over his documents. He eventually acquired quite a collection of folksy and wizardly information, presented in his book.

For example, a wart might be treated by rubbing the wet half of a cut potato on it and then burying the potato. As the potato rotted, the wart was supposed to fall off. Also, you were not supposed to tickle a child less than a year old, because it might cause it to stutter. And then, of course, there was the thing about burying a dead calf under the eaves of the barn roof, or nailing a dog skull to the rafters. Indeed, the use of a horseshoe for good luck started in a Pennsylvania Dutch barn.

In 1929, teenagers in York, Pennsylvania, were accused of murdering a man while attempting to steal a copy of Hohman's book of Powwows. It was said that the three boys were also trying to obtain a lock of the victim's hair to use for turning around a hex the boys believed to have been put on them by the supposed witch and murder victim, Nelson Rehmeyer. The kids thought Rehmeyer used Hohman's book to learn how to hex people.

The trial got international attention because of the mention of witchcraft, and because it was occurring two-hundred-and-fifty years after the notorious Salem, Massachusetts, witch trials where people were actually burned at the stake.

One famous lawyer, outraged by the stiff sentences handed down at the York trial, wrote articles in the national media saying that education was better than harsh punishment to deter crimes like the one in York, Pennsylvania. The lawyer's name was Clarence Darrow, and he was famous for having defended the high school teacher John T. Scopes, accused of illegally teaching Darwin's theory of evolution to Tennessee public school students. Anyway, Clarence Darrow helped draw attention to Dutch superstitions.

After Maggie explained that she herself was not superstitious, she geared the discussion back toward milking and took Mark into the springhouse on the east end of the barn. The room was filled with the sound of trickling water.

"Come ovah heah, an I'll show ya where da milich gets put."

Mark was duly impressed by the simplicity but felt compelled to insert technology. "How do you get the milk in here?"

"In buckets! Hauw else?"

"We'll set it up so that the claw delivers the milk directly to a milk line using hoses, and we'll put the receiver jar over here, and the vacuum pump over there, and . . ."

"Hold on," Arsenic interrupted. *"Vee doan know vott yoah talkin bought. Vott's dis 'claw' thing?"*

"O.k. I've got the basic idea of your layout here in the barn. Let's go in the house and watch a film I brought from the office."

The salesman got projection equipment out of his truck and followed Maggie and Arsenic into Maggie's kitchen, which had the odor of fresh coffee.

As in most Pennsylvania Dutch farmhouses, the kitchen was the main room in the house. About the same size as a mobile home with partitions removed. A big oak table sat in the middle and pin-striped and scroll-decorated chairs, or *küchenstuhl*, were pulled back against the oak wainscot along the walls. The chairs could easily be pulled up to the table when needed, but they were out of the center walkway until then. It wasn't unusual to see people sitting and talking across the wide expanse of kitchen, because they didn't want to take the time to pull chairs up to the table.

Mark set up the projector on the table and pointed it toward the white kitchen wall. Maggie and Arsenic pulled up chairs and prepared to watch the movie. The projector whirred briefly as Mark got the film threaded.

"*Hold up*," Maggie said as she jumped up, "*got'ta haff coffee*," and she fetched a cup for each of them.

Before restarting the projector, Mark explained that the mechanics of milking by hand the way Maggie had been doing her whole life in no way resembled the natural way in which a calf nurses. Maggie and Arsenic were both surprised and disappointed to hear this, because they generally preferred to do things the natural way and thought they had been doing just that.

The salesman went on to remind the pair that when you milk by hand, you pull and squeeze shut the teat right at the udder with your thumb and forefinger and then close the rest of your fingers on the length to force the milk out. Thus, the milk is forced out by squeezing. Maggie and Arsenic first nodded then showed surprise when Mark said that this is not what happens when a calf is nursing. He said that the milking machine is the only milking technique that actually imitates the action of a real nursing calf. He smiled a big satisfied smile.

"It's true you massage the udder much like when the calf 'bunts' it, or butts against it, to stimulate milk letdown. But the calf's mouth does not close off the top of the teat and squeeze. Rather, it sucks, and the vacuum causes the milk to spurt. The calf does this over and over but not continuously. It bunts the udder periodically. If it were to suck continuously, it could cause swelling and mastitis, the inflammation associated with infection. The bunting helps prevent that.

"The thing I want to emphasize at the outset is that in every way a milking machine imitates the action of a real calf, including the pulsing or irregular sucking action. It is more natural than milking by hand. Stephen Babcock, the man that developed the Babcock test for measuring butterfat content of milk in 1890 . . ."

Arsenic nodded knowingly since he had definitely heard of the Babcock test.

A dog barked outside. Maggie stretched her neck to see if anyone was coming.

After pausing, Mark continued, "Anyway, Babcock argued that milking machines would be harmful to the cow and were unnatural when compared to hand milking. Well, his test for butterfat was ingenious, but he didn't know much about milking machines. He had that backwards. The new milking machine imitates the action of a real calf, including the pulsing or irregular sucking action. It is more natural than milking by hand." Mark smiled another satisfied smile.

Arsenic and Maggie pursed their lips, looked at one another, and raised their eyebrows. Then Mark started the movie, and the projector whirred once again.

In the beginning, the film emphasized the same things Mark had been saying. It also added some surprising information about the history of milking machines. Like the first ones relied on catheters. Tubes inserted through sphincter muscles into teats in order to force open sphincters and allow milk to flow. This typically weakened the sphincter muscle until milk dripped continuously, and it could bruise the tissue and cause disease. Germs and cleanliness were not well appreciated at that time. This is why there had been so many warnings in the late 1800's about the dangers of using a milking machine.

As early as the 1850's, a few companies tried vacuum devices, but they had the idea that you had to put a vacuum cup over the whole udder. Stupid, because it caused extreme congestion and injured the cow. One of the early gadgets even had a pump handle like the one on Arsenic's well. Maggie and Arsenic laughed out loud. And Arsenic blurted out, "*Dat vass a bad idea befoah anybody even thought it!*" And he and Maggie laughed even louder causing the salesman to momentarily pause the projector.

Because of all these early problems, a few technology buffs

watched human milkers and decided to make a machine that imitated a person milking by hand. These were frankensteinian inventions with rollers that pressed the teat from top to bottom and operated with cranks and pullies. They could not compensate for the changing size of the teat as milking progressed, and thus did not milk to completion, and often forced milk back up into the udder and made the cow very uncomfortable, to say the least.

It wasn't until just prior to the 1900's that a vacuum milker was developed that attached to the four individual teats, but even then technicians discovered that there was a risk of causing congestion and swelling. This realization finally lead to the development of a pulsator, which sucked intermittently, and the modern milking machine was finally arriving.

Of course, if the technocrats had spent more time studying a calf instead of human milkers, and if they'd spent less time fiddling with rollers, pullies, and catheters, they would have seen from the beginning how the calf pulses milk from the udder gently as it also massages it!

Arsenic and Maggie started laughing at this point and couldn't seem to stop, so the salesman stopped the film since they were missing the information.

With a smile, Mark said, "What's so funny?"

Arsenic said the Pennsylvania Dutch always knew if you wanted to learn the best way to do something, you needed to study the natural way. Nature always knows best. He said he and his friends were always amazed at the stupid finagling of people who "*vonn'a play Gaud.*"

After regaining the attention of his audience, Mark restarted the film.

At this point, it covered the actual workings of a modern milking machine. To say that a calf simply sucks milk out is to oversimplify a fairly complicated process. Failure to understand the complexity of the process is what led to the failure of many of the early vacuum machines. The calf does not suck continuously with its lungs. The film pointed out that, if we did that when we were sucking on a straw, we would choke. It's more complicated.

Mark stopped the film, took two straws from his briefcase, and urged Arsenic and Maggie to suck some cooled coffee out of their cups. There were slurping sounds.

"Do you notice how you use your mouth and tongue, but you hardly involve your lungs at all? The vacuum action is created in the mouth by movement of cheeks and tongue. The challenge in building a milking machine wasn't the vacuum, the old inventors knew how to create a vacuum, the challenge was recreating that action of mouth and tongue."

Maggie and Arsenic watched each other sucking coffee through straws and suddenly busted out laughing again, practically choking on the coffee.

Feeling like a kid with the giggles, Arsenic tried to act serious, "*Right. Mark. Complacated it is.*"

In similar fashion, Maggie stopped laughing and added, "*It's vonn'a dem sings ya do all'a'time but doan think bought it, ya know vott I mean?*"

Arsenic agreed, and the salesman chuckled, as he handed them two seven-inch long, double-walled, rubber devices that looked like they would fit over a cow's individual teats.

Arsenic and Maggie now raised their eyebrows, looked at one another, then looked at Mark hoping there was some sort of explanation for these suspicious looking objects.

Mark said, "These 'shells' and 'liners,' or 'inflations' as the units are called in the business, are soft and double-walled so that vacuum can be regulated both inside the inner cup, to keep the milk flowing, and between the double walls of the 'inflation' to cause the whole appliance to move in a massaging or pulsating action.

"When air is drawn out from between the double walls, the inner cup expands, and the milk flows, and then when the vacuum between the double walls is released, the inner cup pushes back against the teat, and massages it. This cycle of milking and massaging is repeated once per second, sixty times a minute while there's a constant slight vacuum inside the inner cup. It imitates the action of the mouth of a suckling calf."

Maggie and Arsenic glanced at one another and then back at Mark. They looked bewildered, but Mark simply restarted the film, which went on to cover the other major components of a good milking machine.

There was a shiny, stainless steel "claw" which held the four shells for the four inflations. There was a milk hose or a floor pail, vacuum pumps, pressure gauges, storage systems, and so on. The film ran for twenty minutes more and almost put the audience to sleep, until the last five minutes when it covered the future of "totally automated dairy farming." At this point, both Arsenic and Maggie sat up with looks of astonishment on their faces.

The company that employed Mark had already developed, or was in the process of developing, automated devices that would surprise even the most Promethean science fiction writers. Cows were kept in tiny areas connected by channeling that moved automatically to convey cows to and from milking parlors where robotic milking machines attached automatically to individual cows, weighed their milk output, and fed them accordingly, each cow identified by a magnetic ear tag that was read by the machine.

There were claims that a robot would milk 250 cows in a little over an hour yielding almost 2500 gallons of milk. There were automatic scrapers that periodically scraped manure onto conveyor belts and automatic washers that kept the whole stainless steel and white enamel laboratory-like environment pristine, all controlled by timers.

When Mark stopped the projector, the dog was barking again, but no one moved. Arsenic and Maggie were speechless.

Arsenic finally said, "*Dat schtuff at da ent dere, is dat foah real?*"

"Yeah, you hardly have to touch the cows, and if one isn't producing up to standards as indicated by the machine's records, you get rid of her."

"*Vell!*" Maggie said, a bit too loudly. "*Ya got yoah ideas across't, but dis farm ain't no factory, an my cawhs ain't machines, an deir milk ain't soda pop. I like my cawhs. Vonn'a dem simple machines ya showed at first? Vonn'a dem I could use. But dat's it!*"

Arsenic clapped his hands, and with a big grin on his face, he stared at Mark and wondered if the salesman might just get up and leave.

To his credit Mark said, "I understand exactly what you're saying, and I don't want to sell you something you don't need. With your permission, we'll set you up with two of those basic units so one person can milk two cows at a time, with simple buckets for receivers, and we'll service them for you if you ever have any problems."

As the salesman was backing out of the driveway, Arsenic restacked the bales knocked over while the cow was cabbaging hay through the rail fence when the salesman first arrived. No sooner had he restacked them then the cat jumped back up on the top bale and the cow once again started pulling loose strands of hay in through the rails of the fence.

Maggie invited Arsenic in for another cup of coffee, but he declined, saying he wanted to see if Randy needed help with his horses. They stood for a moment trying to decide if there was anything else that needed saying, and Arsenic turned his head when he heard one of Maggie's bantam roosters crow.

Maggie said, "*Ya know von off dem bandy hens Peach gift me crows chust like a rooster. My Pop use'ta say a hen dat crows ist bad luck but I don't.*"

"*Yah. My Pop sett dat too. I doan belief in bad luck neither. Vell, I'll see ya later. Holler if ya need me.*"

He started to walk away and then paused for a moment and said, "*Ya know, hearin dat rooster puts me in mind off something. Owls, hawks, coyotes, an such bin dune away vith Peach's bandy chickens.*

*S'like dey know she ain't lookin aftah dem nomoah. I bin distracted,
an da mauntins vee bin up in. Vell, dis mornin I ree-liced all da hens
is gone, kill't off, ya know. I ree-liced it's da ent'a da line. Von't be no
moah now da hens is gone. Vell, lebe wohl! See ya later."*

Maggie replied, *"Bis später!"*

And with that farewell, Arsenic walked back down the
driveway and crossed the road to his own place. Maggie noticed he
seemed to be a little more slumped over than he'd been when he first
came over this morning, when he was laughing about the cat.

Within an hour of Arsenic's return home, he was out at the
barn with Randy, over by the pump house. They were discussing a
needed repair on the pump that supplied water to the stock tank. The
electric pump stopped working. Barn swallows were swooping back
and forth above their heads.

*"Dis mornin I had'a pump myself a bucket full, an got ta
thinkin bought hauw hart's gonna be ta pump da whole horse trough
full. Vee got'ta fix dat lectric pump! Amish got da right idea. If vee
never got dat lectric pump, we wouldn't miss it venn it ain't verkin.
But vee did, an I do."*

They were standing with their backs toward the driveway
and were surprised when Maggie yelled, *"Hyah! Got a present foah
ya!"*

They both flinched and turned to see Maggie standing there
with a bandy hen under each arm.

*"Peach gift me dem chickens I got on my farm. Dat time venn
a hen vass kill't befoah she finished raisin'er chicks. She gift me dem
babies."*

A big smile of understanding slowly spread across Arsenic's
face, but Randy just stared blankly waiting for elaboration.

Arsenic said, *"Dat's mighty, mighty thoughtful! Ya shuah ya
doan need'em yoah own self?"*

*"Naw! Ya know bandy chickens make new vons real fast.
Sept venn ya run ought'a hens, like you done!"*

Arsenic detected a question on Randy's face and said to him,
*"I noticed dis mornin dat all yoah Mum's hen's bin kill't off. So dat
voot be da ent a da line. But I mentioned it ta Maggie heah, an she
remembahed dat her's'er part a da same line. So Peach's leckacy
can continue, ya know!"*

Then turning back to Maggie, he said, *"I'll vatch deese real
careful. Til dey get, as dey say, 'ree-stap-lished."* He still had the big
smile on his face as he took the two hens from Maggie.

Within a month, one of the hens layed eggs and incubated
them. One day she walked with the brood up the lane toward the
horseshow arena. Arsenic, working behind the barn, heard a warning
cry from the hen and saw a hawk hurdling toward the family.

The hen's warning caused the little ones to scramble into
hiding, under leaves and into tiny crevices in the gravel road. In an
instant, they were difficult to find even if you walked right over and
looked directly down at the gravel.

The hen, meanwhile, stayed in the open, stared at the hawk
as it dove directly at her. When it was within twenty feet, the hen
launched herself into its flight-path, straight at the predator. They
hit one another with such force that feathers flew in all directions.
The hawk recovered and flew up to the low branches on a nearby
sycamore tree. The hen stood up, shook her feathers and stared again
at the hawk. The hawk flew away.

"Ah Peach, you'd be proud a dat hen!" Arsenic said as he
chuckled and returned to his work.

CHAPTER 3

The following week, Maggie and Arsenic went out to dinner. Randy teased his dad, calling it "a date."

Arsenic said, "*Ach, Maggie's a nachbar. Vee live neighbors is all!*"

Maggie and Arsenic went to a restaurant located in the town called Virginsville. The eatery was in a big, old three-story inn made of grey stones and boasting perfect foursquare construction. It had once been the home of a wealthy German farmer.

Interior space remained in the classic Pennsylvania German *flurküchenhaus* configuration, three rooms on the first floor arranged around a complicated fireplace. From the outside, there was one big chimney sticking up dead center on the roof.

While the upstairs was all bedrooms, the first floor interior space was laid out one room deep on the left and two rooms deep on the right. The left side of the building was all kitchen, the *küche*. The long interior kitchen wall ran the full depth of the center of the building. That wall had an exceedingly large stone fireplace taking up a third of its center section. On the other side of the wall, on the right side of the building, there were two rooms, the *stube* or parlor in front and the *kammer* or living room toward the rear. These rooms shared the interior wall with the kitchen.

The hearth of the huge fireplace faced the kitchen and had tripods for holding cooking pots. The stone masonry to left and right of the fireplace maw had iron doors that opened into the room on the other side of the wall, into the rear of two freestanding iron stoves, one located in the *stube* and the other in the *kammer*. Thus, all feeding of fires and removing of ashes was done from the middle of the kitchen.

There was no mantle on the fireplace, but the hearth was a full twelve feet long and stuck out a foot in front to catch hot embers from either the fireplace or from the little doorways in back that fed stoves in the *stube* and *kammer*. The big hearth also served as a good shelf upon which to set hot pots. The tavern used the tops of the closed stoves in the *stube* and *kammer* for keeping certain foods warm in those two dining areas.

In typical fashion, front and back entrances to the house came through the *küche*. This, along with the massive central chimney, is a disinguishing feature of a true *flurküchenhaus*. All visitors to the restaurant said "hello" to the chef on their way through the kitchen to a table in the *stube* or *kammer*. The chef was also the owner of the establishment.

There was a doorway to the *stube* on the right as you passed through the front door. If you came in the back entrance, there was a doorway to the *kammer* on your left. The *stube* and *kammer* also had a doorway connecting them directly to one another.

There were a few dining tables in the kitchen itself, but these were reserved for special guests. Most diners sat in the *stube* or *kammer*. In summertime, there were also tables and service available on the roofed porch extending across the front and down along one side of the house.

The stairway to the upstairs and basement were to the right of the rear entrance to the *küche*. The stairway had once been outside but now it was enclosed to shelter the stairs from snow and ice in wintertime, and it could be approached directly from inside the kitchen or from the outside.

Kitchen workers had to run down to the cellar frequently, since most of the raw materials for cooking were kept down there along with a good selection of wines. The cellar had a very thick stone arch through its center. This was another of the distinguishing features of a *flurküchenhaus* configuration. By necessity, this arch was designed to hold up the enormous weight of that central fireplace, chimney, and the stoves on the first floor above.

The owner and his family lived in rooms upstairs, reached via the stairs in the back corner of the *küche*. Also, bed and breakfast lodging was available upstairs.

Arsenic and Maggie were seated next to the front window in the *stube* and were joking about all the cabbage they'd eaten. Beef fillets rolled in cabbage leaves and cabbage noodle soup.

"*Sauerkraut's all vee missed, huh?*" Arsenic said.

He was finishing a corn fritter when he said, "*I belief I'll haff myself a cup'a coffee. Ya vonn'a too?*"

"*Yah, vell,*" Maggie replied, and after Arsenic had requested coffee from the waitress, she continued, "*Life's gute, ya know. People complain dey ain't nevah von demselfs a lottery, but dey forget dey von demselfs a life. A chance at life's da biggest chance ya get.*"

Arsenic nodded and agreed, "*Yah. Leben ist gute!*"

The lid on one of the pots on the stove was jiggling. A waiter went over to move it off of the heat.

While they were having dessert, the couple also had a bit of a dispute regarding politics. Arsenic was a Democrat, and Maggie was a Republican. Most psychologists would argue that politics should be avoided if you want to keep peace in a relationship, but Maggie and Arsenic had their own way of keeping peace. After it was clear that they had a terminal disagreement, they simply terminated the disagreement with humor. They were arguing about whether President Ronald Reagan should or should not be re-elected. Arsenic wanted to replace all the Republicans with Democrats.

After a moment of quiet, to reduce the tension, Maggie said, "*Oh heck, voot chust be a different bunch a hogs at the trough, ain't!*"

Everyone in the restaurant turned to look at the couple when Arsenic busted out with a cackle of laughter.

When he quieted down, Maggie said, "*I'll nevah foahget da expression of yoah face venn I sett dat! Caught ya by suprise, ain't.*"

Late in the evening, widow and widower got into a discussion regarding loneliness. Arsenic started it by saying that when his wife Peach died, he felt like "*the loose nut on da end of a bolt.*"

"Yah, I'd chust as soon my hussbent vass schtill alife," Maggie replied, *"but ya got'ta take it as it comes. I miss'im terrible. I'm shuah bought Peach ya feel da same vay."*

"Yah, ya know I hatt cancah, schtill got it, I guess. But, I thought vass me dat vass dyin, not Peach. Da whole sing hatt me ferhoodled venn Peach died. Nevah thought I'd haff ta batch myself, ya know live vith myself alone."

"At least ya got yoah kits yet. Raymond and me nevah hatt kits. Vee vonted to, but cootn't. Raymond's Pop use'ta say, 'Kinder, kirche, küche, dat's a voman's life.' Vell, I hatt da kirche and küche, but missed da kinder."

Arsenic laughed, because Maggie had said this all very fast, and the guttural ending of the words kirche and küche made it sound like she was practicing a tongue twister. *Kinder, kirche, küche* means "children, church, and kitchen." After regaining his composure and explaining his laugh he replied, *"My daughtah Ruby's da same vay. Ruby, an'er husbent Regan can't haff no kits neither. But dey seem happy. I doan know bought Rosa. Anyvays, I guess it's gettin different nauw. Vee got all dees machines ta do farm verk. Vee use'ta need kits ta help on da farm."*

"Yah vell, but ya miss da meanin, sort'a, no kits round in yoah olt aiche and so forth. Halladays'er mighty lonely sumtimes."

"I do appresheeate da kits, but I schtill miss Peach."

They had driven to the restaurant in Arsenic's pickup truck. Arsenic dropped Maggie off at her house and drove over to the parking area between his own house and barn, but then he just sat there thinking.

"Ah, Peach, yoah gone, verloren. Yet I heah yoah voice all'a'time schtill. If dat's vott immortal is, den I guess you're immortal. . . . unsterblich. My idea off heaven is seein you again. But, I can't say I ain't affraid off dyin, chust like ewerybotty else is. I sometimes schtare out benommen, numb. Vonderin vott it'll be like. I only know I look fowott to seein you again."

He pulled a big handkerchief from his pocket and wiped his eyes. A storm had been threatening on the way home from the restaurant, and now sheetlightning was everywhere overhead. Bolts of lightning were jumping from cloud to cloud and often jumping around within a single thundercloud, illuminating it from inside. Arsenic stared. He had a flashback memory of his brother sticking the end of a small flashlight in his mouth and puffing out his cheeks so that they lit up from the inside. Red with lines of tissue and blood vessels. Those lightning-lit clouds reminded him of that.

Then, one of Ricky's dogs barked and Arsenic's mind flitted to a hat that Peach used to wear on those sporadic occasions when they attended church. Arsenic thought the hat looked like a Pekingese dog. The words dog and hat sound very different in English, but in Deitsch, hat is *hoote* and dog is *hoonte*. So, Arsenic would make a joke when Peach came out of the bedroom dressed for church by saying something like, "*Well, I see yoah wearin yoah hoonte again!*" He chuckled at the memory.

Ricky's dogs both started barking now, and the back porch lights came on. Arsenic quickly finished wiping his eyes, blew his nose loudly, put away the handkerchief, and got out of the truck to head toward the house.

As he was closing the truck door, he muttered, "*Ah, Peach, I miss ya!*"

A clear and promising late spring day had big-cloud sailing ships scooting across an ocean of blue sky. Unreal springtime blaze green foliage was everywhere. The sap had risen, and the leaves unfolded.

Regan had been hunting groundhogs in the woods on top of the hill behind his farm. He decided to quit and walk down the southeast side of the hill through Arsenic's place on his way home. He had something important to tell his father-in-law, and he couldn't decide how, and he finally decided to just do it. He could see and hear Randy replanting a pasture in a grazing section down below the barn. So that meant Arsenic would be alone, with Ricky still in school. Good!

As Regan started to hike down the hill, Randy stopped the old two-cylinder John Deere tractor to adjust something on the planter. Arsenic kept the old tractor to use "*chust foah fun.*" As the tractor idled and the fly wheel kept momentum going between somewhat widely spaced firings of the pistons, the sound was "*chickit, boom, boom, boom, chickit, chickit, boom, boom, chickit, chickit, boom, boom.*"

When Regan was about halfway down to where Arsenic was working, Randy finished the adjustment on the planter and was again drilling grass seed in the field. The sound of the tractor working hard changed to "*clack, clack, clack, chick, clack, chick, clack, clack, clack, chick.*"

Randy had to replant the pasture with alfalfa and clover, because it was being overrun by tall fescue. Two of their cattle had developed fescue foot, a debilitating condition. Randy wanted to get rid of the tall fescue.

Arsenic's farm, on the southeast slope of the big hill, wasn't visible from Regan's place, but it wasn't far away. Regan and Arsenic's daughter, Ruby, owned a farm on the southwest slope of the same mound. Thus, they were neighbors though you couldn't quite see one house from the other unless you were up on top of the mound, or up a tree or on the barn roof. While Regan was hunting in the woods on top, he had spotted Arsenic hauling baskets of unshelled corn, or *velshcon*, from his corn crib to the barn.

Arsenic had paused to examine the red paint on the outside of the barn. He was trying to decide whether it needed to be repainted. He concluded that it would be o.k. for another two or three years. It usually lasted at least ten years. The old Pennsylvania Dutch had been mixing their own paints for over two hundred years. The Berks area was full of iron oxide deposits that yielded beautiful red, yellow, orange, and dark brown pigments that were mixed with gum resins from fruit tree sap, boiled linseed oil, and buttermilk, all provided by nature. These paints often outlasted those commercially available.

There was a huge hex sign, eight feet in diameter, on the end of the barn Arsenic was inspecting. It was bordered in yellow and featured two overlapping red stylized birds, or *distelfinks*, on a field of purple. It too had been painted with homemade paint and seemed to be in excellent condition. Decorated "hex barns," as the tourist's called them, usually indicated a "fancy" Dutch homestead rather than an Amish one. The Amish were called "plain" for a reason. They didn't paint decorations all over their barns.

Regan walked up while Arsenic was staring up at the hex sign.

"You expecting some *hexerei*?"

Arsenic chuckled and said, "*Nah. Chust checkin da paint. Dem hex signs doan haff nothin ta do vith hexerei anyvays!*"

"Well the tourists think they do."

Arsenic simply shrugged and said, "*Yah vell!*"

In fact, the arguments connecting "hex signs" and Pennsylvania Dutch *hexerei*, or witchcraft, are a little airy. Some traders told tourists that the colorful, round geometric designs were a way to avoid disease and accidents in farm animals if they were *verhexed* by *hexerei*, such as witches' spells and their evil eye. But the circular patterns just seem to be a form of folk art, not terribly different from the *fraktur* art on official Pennsylvania Dutch documents like eighteenth and nineteenth century birth and baptismal certificates, called *taufschein*. The birds and flowers used by *fraktur schriften* artists are similar to the images on hex signs. Painted kitchenware, or toleware, and painted furniture, also tend to include such images.

"*Herbie Goodhart painted dat.*" Arsenic said, pointing with his nose toward the hex sign. "*He verks dahn at Hank Dienst's body shop in Fleetvoot.*"

Looking up at the sign, Regan said, "I thought Ruby said Jake Zook painted that?"

"*Nah. Not dat von.*"

During the 1940's, Jacob Zook started producing beautiful hex signs in Paradise, Pennsylvania. The early barn art had been painted directly on barns, but Zook made it portable and brought the cost down by painting on a slab of wood that tourists could take back home with them as a souvenir when they visited Pennsylvania Dutch country.

Little hex signs started to appear as logos on products such as pretzel cans. As the popularity of the art form spread, the story that it was a defense against devilry seemed to spread right along with it.

The troublesome woodpecker that had taken a liking to Arsenic's barn showed up again and started hammering within ten feet of Arsenic and Regan as they were talking.

Arsenic looked at the bird and yelled, "*Geh'veg. Get ought'a here!*" And he slapped his hand on the barn wall several times to scare it off.

As the woodpecker flew away, Arsenic looked at Regan again and for the first time noticed that he held a bow and a bunch of arrows.

"*Vott'cha dune? Playin Robin Hoot or cawboys an inchins?*"

"Naw. I was looking for a groundhog to shoot at. I just finished this bow. I'd like to try to hunt deer with it in the fall."

"*I doan see no grundsau?*"

Regan walked closer to Arsenic before he responded. His smoking had finally started to catch up with him, and he was winded.

"I did a lot of hunting, but not much finding! No groundhogs, or *grunsau* as you call 'em." Regan chuckled, and then he used the German word for bow hunting as he said, "I'm ready to give up on this *Bogenschiessen*. Can't hold the bow steady. It's too powerful. Oh well, I had a nice walk."

Arsenic pointed up to the right of the hex sign and said, "*Did you shoot that arrow up dere?*"

Regan looked up and got a perplexed look on his face. "Ah, no! Where did that come from?"

Indeed, there was an old arrow stuck under the eave of the barn roof, to the right of the hex sign."

Arsenic chuckled and replied, "*Ach, dat's bin dere twenty yeahs! Randy did it venn he vass a kit.*"

The bow Regan had made was a reproduction of an antique Welsh longbow similar to the ones English military used from the time of the thirteenth century up into the sixteenth. He had carved it himself, from a six-foot piece of the mysterious yew wood, just like the originals. The arrows also were accurate reproductions, a yard long. Regan had decided to try a truly primitive form of hunting in preparation for deer season this fall.

He could have tried the modern compound bow, which is easy to draw, but it was the appearance of the compound bow with all its pulleys and levers that set off a rebellion in Regan. He was first disturbed when people started using tree stands to hunt deer, sitting on a small platform above eye level until an unsuspecting deer walked beneath and provided an easy shot.

He had said, "In my mind, when you hunt deer, you HUNT. You don't just sit there like a sniper and wait for a deer to blunder into range. These guys don't even walk anymore. They don't know anything about tracking."

Then, along came the compound bow. The Star Wars movies had already popularized fantastic ideas of roughing it by that time, and Regan had described the compound bow as "a contraption Darth Vader would use!" It employs a system of pulleys and cables to make the bow easier to draw back, but a fifteenth-century British archer wouldn't even recognize it as a bow at all.

The ironic thing was that Regan's physician had recently diagnosed the early signs of emphysema, and Regan could neither walk long nor flex his muscles much without showing some early signs of oxygen depletion. Emphysema might in time force him to use a compound bow himself, and a tree stand too, if he continued to hunt at all. The longbow he was carrying required one hundred pounds of force just to draw back the string, and he found that he was having a problem holding steady while keeping the bow at full draw.

Arsenic noticed bramble seeds stuck all over the front of Regan's trousers, and he said, "*Ya got boova lice all ovah yoah-self.*"

As he started picking off the pesky burrs, Regan said, "Ach, I stepped into a patch of them up there. Listen, let's go in the house for a minute. There's something I want to tell you."

After they'd each gotten a cup of coffee from the pot that was always setting on the wood stove, both pulled chairs up to the kitchen table, and Regan chattered on. Unknown to Arsenic, he was trying to avoid talking about the thing he'd stopped to talk to him about.

"This is good coffee!"

"*Yah. It drinks gute.*"

"You often talk about dumb things guys from the city do. Did I ever tell you what happened last deer season up at the deer camp? I took this tenderfoot that works for the same ag company I work for. I took him along deer hunting. It was his first time. We started long before sunup. It was still pitch dark. Had to use flashlights to find our way in the woods.

"Well, I drove up one of those valleys that run between the mountains from up at the Coudersport Pike down toward Renovo. Parked off the dirt road and sent him up one of those steep hillsides on one side of the road, and I went up the hillside on the other. Got situated and figured he was right across the gulley from me. Had my light turned off and was sitting in the dark waiting for the sun to come up. Across the gulley, I see his flashlight come on, and he walks off through the woods a piece, then the light goes off again.

"About five minutes later the light comes back on again, and he walks back in a slightly different direction. Suddenly, I see his light beam start bouncing around on the ground like he's searching for something, and he's getting more and more frantic. Then, the light starts wandering around all over the place like he's walking in circles. Then, that gets more frantic, and it looks like he's really running around. I can't for the life of me figure out what's going on, and I'm starting to get worried. So I head back down my side of the valley and past the car and up his side of the valley to see if he's o.k.

"By the time I'm walking up there, the sun's coming up, and we've pretty much ruined the early hunting. The whole time I was hiking up his side, I could see him continuing to run around, even while it was getting light. Finally, I get to him, and he's real embarassed. 'What's going on?' I ask. He hems and haws and finally confesses that he laid his gun down to go 'empty his bowels' as he put it.

"See, he couldn't find his gun when he came back from doing his business, and that's why he was running around flashing his light all over the ground. It turned out he had headed in the wrong direction when he was finished. He'd never have found his gun. I'd seen his light so I knew roughly where he started and stopped, and I directed the search in the right direction, and sure enough, we found his gun. Of course, since it was light by that time, and because of all the noise we'd made, we just went back to the car and headed to the cabin to wait until late afternoon."

Arsenic was laughing at the story but also curious. "*Ya din come all dis vay chust ta tell me dat did ya? Vott vass it ya vonted ta tell me. Come on. Ought vith it!*"

"Well no. I . . . ah. I feel kind of funny about this, because I'm almost forty-five, and Ruby's forty-four, and I don't know how you'll feel about it, but . . ."

"*Vott da heck, did I miss a birthday, oah vott? Yoah actin mighty strainch!*"

"Ruby's pregnant!"

"*Holy cow flop!*" Arsenic yelled as he jumped out of his chair. "*Dat's fantastical! Hauw lung ya known bought it?*"

"Just a few days. Well, a week really, but Ruby wanted to be sure. So, we had to wait for some more tests to be run, you know? But, we're sure now. Ruby wanted me to be the one to tell you."

"Vell, I think it's bought time! An who cares if yoah foahty-foah oah foahty-vottevah?" Then after a pause, he added, *"Me an Maggie vass chust talkin on dis supchect da utter night."*

"Well, you know my doctor just told me I was showing signs of emphysema."

"Yeah, I know. So, ya qvit smokin and schtart some care takin off yoahself! Hauw far lung's Ruby?"

"Four months."

"Foah monts! Hauw's dat possible? You chust findin ought an all?"

Regan laughed and said, "Well, it's complicated. I'd better let Ruby explain it." Then he laughed again and said, "I'll say this much, we thought she had diabetes."

"Vott?"

Regan laughed again, and sheepishly said, "Talk to Ruby. She'll explain."

As a matter of fact Ruby was explaining at that very minute, delivering an unplanned explanation to some of her regular customers in the beauty shop.

Florence Himmelreich was under the hair dryer and missed the early part of the conversation, but she was the only one present who would truly understand Ruby's situation, because she'd gone through something similar herself.

Ruby had been cutting Margie Hinnershitz's hair, and Margie stopped the process to blow her nose. After asking for a tissue, she said, "I never have a tissue when I need one. When I need one, I don't have one. When I don't need one, I have one in my pocket, but then I throw it away because I don't need it. So then when I need it, I don't have it, you know what I mean?"

After getting no response and finishing with blowing her nose, she looked at Ruby, who was staring off into space.

"What's the matter with you today, Ruby? You seem distracted!"

Ruby had been unusually quiet while cutting, and now she started beating around the bush, telling Margie that she'd been concerned about change of life, and then she got to saying she was also concerned about diabetes, and Margie got off on both of those subjects, and things were getting unnecessarily complicated. Ruby finally decided that it was harder to beat around the bush than it was to get right to the point.

She swore Margie to secrecy, telling her she and Regan had not had the chance to tell her father and siblings yet, but she forgot that Florence could hear some of what was being said in spite of the noise of the hairdryer, and she forgot that Mary Dreibelbeese was getting a therapeutic massage in the attached room with only a drapery in the doorway.

"I'm pregnant!" Ruby finally blurted out.

Margie jumped up from the chair, causing Ruby to nick her ear with the scissors. Hearing the word "pregnant" Florence flipped the hairdryer off her head, almost knocking it over. And Mary came running out of the massage room without a top on, causing everyone to stare momentarily and forget what had actually started the disruption.

Margie finally looked back at Ruby and said, "I can't believe it! I thought you and Regan couldn't have kids!"

"Yeah, so did we!" Ruby responded and then reminded Mary that she was standing bare-breasted in the middle of the beauty shop. Mary's massage therapist came out and draped a big towel around her shoulders. Ruby had also forgotten that the massage therapist, June Schmidt, would overhear the conversation. All four of the surprised women gathered in a circle around Ruby and started firing questions at her. The main question was, "How far along are you; when is the baby due?"

Ruby flopped down in the hair-cutting chair Margie had just vacated, leaving the others standing. "I don't want any of you blabbing this to anyone, but I've been pregnant for four months," she said.

In unison, the four women said, "What?!"

"It's complicated! Yeah, I'd been missing my monthlies, but I thought I was going through 'the change,' you know, meno-pause, 'climacteric' old Doc Klein calls it. I'm forty-four and figured it was about time. Regan and me didn't think about get-ting pregnant anymore. We didn't even bother trying to prevent it. Not for years! Then, I started feeling tired and having to go to the bathroom all the time, and I thought I might have diabetes. Doc Klein did a glucose tolerance test but also did a pregnancy test just as a matter of routine. And he was as surprised as Regan and me that I was pregnant.

"What else can I say. I'm still in shock. We got used to it being just the two of us. I'm happy and confused at the same time. I guess I feel really stupid!"

Trying to rebalance the hairdryer that almost fell over, Flor-ence missed the earlier mention of change of life and diabetes. But, she heard the pregnancy announcement, and as Ruby was explaining the missed periods and tiredness and glucose tolerance and pregnancy tests, Florence kept nodding her head and saying, "*Yah! Yah! Yah!*" Which finally got the attention of the group, and then she proceeded to tell them that exactly the same thing had happened to her.

Florence was seventy-five years old and had a thirty-year-old daughter named Jean. The only other child she had was a fifty-eight -year-old son, and none present had ever given that age difference much thought until this very moment. Indeed, Florence must have been about forty-five when Jean was born, but she was a widow at the time, unmarried! And that's what had dominated the gossip mill. Her husband had died from a premature heart attack, and she did have gentlemen friends at the time of her pregnancy. No one ever really knew the story behind the pregnancy, except that her husband had been dead for two years, and she was unmarried when she became pregnant. Now, Florence revealed that she too had assumed that she was no longer able to have children when she had her daughter. Also, the frequent urination had similarly led her to suspect that she was diabetic. And she didn't really face the pregnancy until she started to swell and the baby moved.

"I vass FIVE monts gone vhen I figgered it ought. So's no reason foah embarrassment in yoah sitchuation. An so far as havin babies so late, I'll tell ya t'vass da best sing evah happen'ta me."

Indeed, her daughter Jean had proved to be exceedingly intelligent in high school, received numerous scholarships for college, and finished medical school. She was currently working in obstetrics.

Florence concluded with, *"Hey! Maybe Jean can delivah yoah baby!"*

Ricky came home from school just as Regan was trying to leave Arsenic's house. Having informed Arsenic that Ruby was pregnant, Regan decided to leave Ruby fill in most of the details when she next talked to her dad. No amount of prodding on Arsenic's part would force Regan to reveal more detail. He just kept saying, "You have to ask Ruby."

In fact, he was just a little embarassed and unfamiliar with this task of announcing a pregnancy, and he was happy to see Ricky show up. Regan had been planning to invite Ricky along with him and Ruby on one of their weekend circuits of the various gun clubs to participate in trapshooting tournaments, and this chance meeting with his nephew provided a good opportunity, and a good diversion.

As Ricky came through the door, Regan said, "Hi, Pardner! How was school?"

Ricky proceeded to tell his Uncle he was worried about an assignment their teacher had given them. He had to write a five-page paper outlining his plans for the future. Like whether he was going to go to college.

"They just want you to think about it," Regan said. "I don't think they'll check up on you to see if you follow through on your plans." He chuckled. "We'll talk about it this coming weekend while you and Ruby and I are out trapshooting."

Ricky's eyes opened wide as he yelled, "Yes!! I finally get to practice wingshooting!"

Since he'd moved to the Reading area to live with his father and grandfather, Ricky'd done plenty of plinking with a good air rifle, but he hadn't had many opportunities to perfect his skill with a shotgun. Sure, he'd gone small game hunting for rabbits and pheasants a few times, but the only time he got to shoot was when he actually found a rabbit or pheasant, and practice was spaced out with little opportunity for feedback, and so Ricky wasn't sure if he was even any good with a scattergun.

Regan had been taking Ricky along to some of the weeknight meetings held by local rod-and-gun clubs, but he hadn't yet had a chance to take him to any weekend trapshooting tournaments. The weeknight meetings generally involved viewing a conservation film and discussing issues related to management of state game and conservation lands. Once in a while they'd turn on the big spotlights and shoot a couple rounds of trap after the meeting. But Ricky had never had the chance to participate

The Reading area's rod-and-gun clubs served somewhat the same function as the golfer's country club. Lots of social life in the bars and restaurants lodged in the club houses. Plenty of recreation on the trap and skeet fields and the rifle and pistol ranges. Also, many of the clubs had a trout stream or bass pond on their property, and they also maintained a lodge up in the mountains for use during deer season in winter or family vacations in summer. During off-months when neither hunting nor fishing were possible, the clubs ran weekly trapshooting tournaments. With spring coming, most members would be out trout fishing, and the trapshooting would slow down, a good time for Ricky to learn trap.

Regan wanted to ensure that the conversation would not return to Ruby's pregnancy, and so he said, "Hey, you won't believe what I saw while I was out walking. During the winter, some guy must have parked on that dirt road on the other side of the hill, the road that goes up to Windy Corners, and he'd hiked into the woods to hunt deer."

"*Yah? Zo?*" Arsenic said.

"This is the part you'll get a kick out of. He used those strips of bright orange plastic ribbon to mark his path. So, I followed the ribbons to his tree stand. It was only a hundred and eighty paces off the road, and he'd tied thirteen ribbons to the branches as he walked. I was doing the math while I walked down here. That's one flag tied to a tree every fourteen steps. Looked like someone was having a garden party. Can you believe that? These guys from the city would get lost at the mall if they didn't have an information booth."

Referring to people from the City of Reading, Arsenic said, "*Ach, nothin dem yankees from da shteddle does saprices me no-moah!*"

Turning to Ricky, Regan added, "Hey Pardner, did you ever hear about the big buck deer that would rustle his antlers around in those strips of bright orange surveyor's tape that he'd find in the woods til his antlers were all draped in orange? All the hunters would see that orange warning tape and think they weren't supposed to shoot at him! He was hiding in the open, as they say!"

"You're pulling my leg!" Ricky said, as Arsenic was unable to restrain a chuckle.

"Yeah, I am," Regan said as he laughed and coughed.

The three turned their attention toward the sound coming from the parking area. Chickit, boom, chickit, boom, boom. Randy was returning from the pasture, and the kitchen window vibrated from the booming of the old John Deere. Chickit, chickit, chickit, boom.

"I'm going to see if Pop will let me drive the tractor," Ricky said. "Is that o.k., Uncle Regan?"

"Sure enough. I'll walk out with you. I have to get on home anyway."

Randy allowed Ricky to practice driving the old tractor for a while whenever he had it running. It was normal for farm kids to be driving long before they got their driver's licenses. Ricky actually got a late start, since he'd lived many of his early years in a college town in Indiana.

Ruby had asked James and Rosa over to dinner to get an opportunity to tell her sister and brother-in-law about her pregnancy. She prepared sauerbraten made with deer meat. To round out the meal, she had potato dumplings, dried corn, hot dandelion salad, with Jerusalem artichokes and souse for appetizers, and with apple dumplings and cherry pie for dessert.

Red wine, vinegar, onions, salt, pepper, cloves, and bay leaves formed the base for the meat marinade, bathing the venison in the refrigerator for three days. Regan must have asked her at least three times, "What's in that container in the refrigerator? Oh yeah, that's right!"

Today, she had removed the meat and cooked and browned it for an hour and a half, and made a wonderful gravy with the strained marinade and flour combined with fresh onions, carrots, and celery.

Early this morning, she had been out in the front yard cutting new springtime sprouts of dandelion for the salad. Only the youngest, newest sprouts were selected, and this was the best time to pick it. You needed to get it before any flowers appeared. Regan had wandered sleepily out on the front porch carrying a cup of coffee and mumbling, "It's a little early to be working on the yard, don't you think?"

She would prepare a hot sweet and sour white sauce loaded with pieces of bacon to pour over the chilled dandelion leaves just before serving them as a salad.

Ruby's potato dumplings were dough pouches a little like Polish pierogis, filled with mashed potatoes, boiled, and then fried. Similar filled dough pouches were featured in the *Boova schenkel* Maggie'd fixed for Fat and and his helpers when they butchered her cow, but *boova schenkel* used Pennsylvania Dutch potato filling whereas Ruby was using plain mashed potatoes.

Ruby started soaking the dried corn the night before the dinner. She would simmer it with milk, butter, and salt. The appetizers of souse and Jerusalem artichokes were purchased at the Reading Farmers' Market, along with apple dumplings. The souse and artichokes were slightly sour. A touch of sweetness was supplied by serving them on a tray with little sweet pickles. The souse had been prepared with pig's feet, pork hocks, and pork tongue, well-seasoned and embedded in a gelatinous block. The Jerusalem artichokes, actually the root or tuber of a type of sunflower, were cut up and pickled. These were popular in the Reading area but relatively unknown in other parts of the country.

The grand finale was to be a choice between apple dumplings and cherry pie, both baked and served hot with vanilla ice cream. Ruby liked to buy her apple dumplings from the farmer's market stand of the Amish family named Schmeiser. Amy Schmeiser had been Amy Dietrich until recently when she married Jake Schmeiser.

At one time, Jake had been "shunned" by his Amish congregation under the *"Doctrine of Meidung."* He was put "under the ban" when he violated the *Ordnung* by becoming an alcoholic, thereby breaking the rule "Do not drink wine nor strong drink, thou, nor thy sons with thee," Lev. 10:9. No one was allowed to eat or talk with him.

Jake had dappled in drink when he was a young adult, during a time of *rumschpringe* or "running around," when young adults are allowed to experiment in English society before they decide whether they want to remain Amish. Jake had returned to the order and been baptized but then backslid at a future time. This was unacceptable to the order since changing your mind after taking the vow was like abandoning your spouse after taking the marriage vows. They would turn their backs toward him whenever he appeared. Rather than leave the area, Jacob had lingered on in the fringes of the society.

And then a fall from a farm wagon paralyzed Jacob from the waist down, and he quit drinking and was eventually taken back into the congregation when he repented. No one thought he would ever marry, but Amy fell in love with him.

The couple needed to sell baked goods and hand-made clothing, since Jake couldn't work in the fields. Amy's baked goods were elegant. She would pack her cored apples with cinnamon candies, brown sugar and nutmeg before wrapping them in pie dough. Ruby claimed they were better than any she could ever make herself. Besides, the Schmeisers needed the money.

The cherry pie Ruby made herself using cherries she'd picked and pitted and frozen the previous summer, picked from a tree right behind their house. She'd used an antique cherry pitter or stoner that her grandmother had given her. It was made of cast-iron and had a patent date of 1917 stamped into it. As Regan cranked it and she inserted fruit, the pits fell out one opening and the slightly scrunched cherries fell out another opening. Now the frozen, pitted cherries were being put to use.

Ruby'd just placed the desserts in the oven and started getting dressed for their company. James and Rosa Christiansen were due within the hour.

Ruby's sister and Arsenic's former hospice worker were married only a few months earlier. Rosa was still working at the factory that made breaker points for auto ignition systems, but she'd been accepted at Penn State University to work on a Bachelor's Degree. She always was a reader and practiced yoga and acting and felt out of place in the factory. She'd served notice that she was quitting so she and James could move to State College in the Fall.

James was going to become a clinical psychologist. He'd just been accepted into the Psychology Department's Graduate Program at Penn State. In a way, his interest in psychology started while he was still an infant. His father was killed during the Korean War. He called his childhood "confusing" and developed the life-long interest in psychology. He worked in a factory up to the age of thirty-one, but then quit and went to college.

When he and Rosa married a few months ago, James was thirty-five years old, and Rosa was forty-five. Arsenic said, "*Bettah late den nevah!*"

Ruby offered the invitation to dinner to celebrate the career moves of the couple, but she also wanted to make her own announcement.

Regan surprised the couple when he opened the front door before they had a chance to knock. His greeting was excessively animated and immediately followed by the announcement that he had quit smoking, hadn't had a cigarette in a week.

"Cold turkey!" he said, his voice unnecessarily loud.

Very rapidly, he added, "It's easy! I'm already over the worst of it! Just takes willpower, you know! Have to hang in there! I got it all figured out!"

This was a bit disconcerting, as Regan was normally steady and calm.

He added that he wanted them to know right away in case he acted strange during dinner. James and Rosa could see where that might be a problem. He was already talking so fast that they could hardly understand him. As Regan turned toward his wife, the couple looked briefly at one another, smiled, and winked.

To Ruby, Regan said, "Tell'em Honey!"

"Later, Babe!"

"No, I mean about my smoking! How I quit!"

"I think they already got the idea. Come on in, you two. How about a glass of iced tea while I finish up here? Would you get them some tea Regan?"

"Sure thing! Ruby makes the best tea! She puts in lemon juice and orange juice! Don't ya, Babe?"

"Yep, I do. Remember to breath deeply, Honey. Rosa, how's work now that you told them you're quitting?"

"Oh, fine. Everybody's real proud of me. They say they always thought I should go back to school. It's real flattering. I'll miss them. I'll especially miss my boss."

"You mean 'the obstinate bullhead?'" James added with a chuckle.

"That's exactly what I'll miss. His 'rants.' He always reminded me of Pop. Of course, State College isn't far away, so I'll always be able to come back and visit Pop for my 'bullhead-fix.'"

Everyone laughed and then Ruby said she and Regan wanted to congratulate the two of them on getting into school, and she said they had a present to give them after dinner. Regan added that he too was proud of them and wanted them to know that his college years came second in terms of being the best years of his life.

"My best of the best, of course, are the years with Ruby. Including now! Tell 'em our news, Honey."

"No, you tell them."

"We're going to have a baby! Well, Ruby is, and me I guess, kind of!"

Rosa about fell off her chair, and James jumped up and shook Regan's hand as he said, "I'm really happy for you, Buddy. And I'm afraid that, in the long run, you're going to work a lot harder as a parent than I have to work to earn a Ph.D.!"

That got everyone laughing, and Rosa went over and hugged her sister.

After dinner the group went out on the deck for coffee and dessert. A night bird was singing a repetative song and Ruby commented that she loved the sound of a whippoorwill.

Regan said, "That's chuck-will's-widow."

James and Rosa said in unison, "What?"

"You don't usually hear them this far north, but it's a relative of the whippoorwill."

"Huh," said James, "How can you tell the difference?"

"The song of this one goes 'dah, DAH, DAH.' Higher at the end. And a whippoorwill goes 'DAH, dah, DAH.' Softer in the middle."

James stared at him for a second and said, "I'll take your word for it."

And Rosa said, "No. I hear it. You're right!"

Ruby looked at James and raised her eyebrows. "Regan and I have been over this before. I can't hear the difference either."

Regan seemed to have calmed down a bit, and he was lighting some candles designed to repel the mosquitoes, which were bad this year. He and Ruby talked about the changes a child might make in their lives. Ruby was planning to continue her hair dressing after the child was born. The beauty shop was really part of their house so it would be easy. Regan was excited about having a hunting and fishing accomplice. He said he didn't care if it was a boy or a girl.

Then, James and Rosa both discussed their career plans. They used this as an opportunity to inform Regan and Ruby that Arsenic was going to help them out financially. Rosa was concerned that Ruby might resent the special help given to her sister, but Ruby seemed genuinely happy that the family was being a family, helping one another.

Ruby said, "Pop just co-signed on a bank loan so that Randy can buy some new colts. He seems to be making a go of the horse training business." Then she glanced at Regan and added, "Let's give them their present!"

And Regan ran in the house.

James and Rosa were surprised by the size of the box Regan carried out on the deck. After fumbling with the wrapping for awhile, the first thing they saw was a picture of a new Apple computer peeking out from the side of the box.

"It's one of those new ones! They just developed it," Regan

said. "They call it the Macintosh. That's why I wanted Ruby and me to get it for you. I like McIntosh apples." Then he laughed loudly.

"It uses a little thing for pointing at the screen, they call it a 'mouse!' And there are pictures on the screen that you point at when you want it to do something for you. They call those pictures 'icons.' They say you don't have to know anything about computers to use one. It's a whole new idea."

Both James and Rosa issued a well-mannered protest, saying it was too expensive. Ruby dismissed this and replied that she was proud her sister was going back to school. She wanted to give the couple a good start.

Regan added, "You two can pay us back by giving Ruby some free psychotherapy!" And he laughed while Ruby scowled.

Then, after reconsidering and looking at Regan, Ruby herself laughed and added, "Maybe we can go together!"

After a little discussion of what it would be like to return to school, Regan changed the subject and expressed an interest in purchasing an old hand-carved horse from the merry-go-round building that James' mother purchased in a defunct amusement park, to remodel into a circular house. He began by asking whether they had sold everything that had been in the old "Carsonia Park" building.

James was confused for a moment since his mother had nicknamed the place *The Distelfink*.

"Oh, you mean *The Distelfink*. No, my Mom's pretty much gotten rid of everything that was left in the building she bought."

"That's too bad. I was hoping to buy that old merry-go-round horse you found in there when she bought it. I'd make it into a big rocking horse for our kid."

Very little was conserved from Carsonia Park after it was closed in 1950. Most of it had been leveled and converted into a housing project known as Pennside. Some said the carousel had been bought privately and sent to Texas for repairs, but no one seemed to know if that was true. One of the old hand-carved horses from the merry-go-round had been left in the round building James' mother purchased to remodel into a home. It had probably been set aside for a repair that never occurred, and it was lying under some rubble in an attached shed.

Carsonia Park was built in 1896 to increase the use of Reading's trolley service on weekends. The trolley and "trolley park" were built by the United Traction Company at the end of one of the company's trolley lines. The trolley was the only way to get to the park. In the beginning, it was just an outdoor picnicking, swimming and boating area, but rides were quickly added to increase its attractiveness. The carousel, or merry-go-round, was one of the first rides built in the park. Then, over the years, there was the Pretzel, Jack Rabbit, and Thunderbolt, Dodge Em bumper cars, the Caterpillar, a Hupmobile Speedway, a Strato Ship and Airplane Ride, a Castle of Mirth, the Cuddle-Up, Shoot the Shoot, and a big old ferris wheel and the Circle Swing. The International Miniature Village, a lovely work of folkart, is said by some to have been moved to "Roadside America," a popular roadside attraction still visible in Shartlesville.

"Ahhh!" James thought for a minute and looked at Rosa as though he wanted her opinion, which she couldn't give because she didn't know what he was thinking.

Then, to Regan he added, "That's different. I think you just gave me an idea for a baby gift for you and Ruby! Mom stuck that horse in the garage she built after the house was finished, and she was just saying recently she wanted me to help clean out the garage, because she needs more space for supplies for her cleaning business. That horse might be our gift to you and your new baby!"

Rosa added, "That's a really good idea, Sweetie. Are you sure she'll let you have it?"

"No! You can't!" Ruby interrupted. "Those things are worth a lot of money!"

"Ha," James said, "so is a Macintosh computer!" He gave a conspiratorial wink to Rosa as he replied, "I'm sure I can get Mom to sell it to me at a reasonable price!"

While the group was enjoying a second cup of coffee, Rosa commented on some of Ruby's houseplants and that led her to say, "Tell 'em about your cactus, James."

Regan and James had been discussing computers, and upon hearing his name, he said, "What was that you said about me?"

"Tell 'em about your cactus."

"Oh. o.k. When I was moving into Rosa's trailer, after we'd moved it up behind Arsenic's barn, I accidentally broke off a cactus while moving it, and it was laying on its side, broke off for a few days before I noticed it. So I used some popsicle sticks to prop it back up, hoping that it would form new roots, which it did. But, here's where it gets weird. In a few days the side of the cactus that had been facing up while it laid on its side got buds all over it, baby cactuses. Probably thirty or forty. Looked like warts, you know. All Rosa and I could think of was that while it was laying on its side, broke off and dying, it got the impulse to put out babies all over that side that was still facing upward. And when I stood it back upright, it just followed through with it's plan. Like it thought it was dying and those babies were its last chance to survive. And when I stood it back up, that impulse just continued. If we're right about what made the buds appear, it's weird because it makes you wonder if plants have some kind of intelligence."

"They do. They do have intelligence," Regan said.

The others looked at him questioningly.

"Last spring, a year ago, I pruned that apple tree down by the pond. It's a McIntosh apple tree. Well, last fall I was mowing the lawn, and an apple fell out of the tree, and hit me square on the head."

The others continued to stare.

"Don't you see? That tree was vengeful! Punishing me for cutting his branches in the spring."

The stares of the others turned from questioning to concerned.

"Heh. Heh, heh, heh. Ha, ha, ha. Really had you going!"

And then he started to cough. And then, "God! Do I need a ciga-rette!"

"Now, now, Honey. Breathe deep!" Ruby said, and then, "Ricky told Regan you got two dogs for pets. How's that working out?"

"Great! James is spoiling them, of course. They're black Scotish Terriers, already full grown. The old couple we got them from wouldn't give away just one. They had to stay together. They're brother and sister."

James added, "I read that Scottish Terriers used to be hunt-ers. The owner would send them down in burrows to dig out foxes and such. They're so lionhearted that they wouldn't quit even if the fox was winning the battle down in the hole. So, they were bred for short stout tails so the owner could grab ahold of the tail to pull them out of the burrow if they seemed to be losing a fight down the hole. And their coat is so wiry and skin so tough that the other animal had trouble biting through it."

Rosa winced and said, "We like them because Itty, that's the boy, is a gentleman, and Bitty is a lady. Isn't that right James?"

"Well, yeah. They have great personalities. I'd say they're eccentric, but then, so am I."

CHAPTER 4

"**Researchers** determined that people in the Reading area consume nine pounds of pretzels per individual per year, compared to six pounds in Chicago, and four pounds in New York City." This information was revealed by an anchorman on a local TV news broadcast to fill the time until the commercial began.

During the commercial, Arsenic told Ricky that Reading was the Pretzel Capital of the World.

Ricky seemed unimpressed, "You can buy pretzels all over Indiana."

"*Oh yah! Nauw ya can! But my Pop vass buyin hot soft pretzels from guys vith handkarren, ya know, pushcarts, on Penn Street in Reading long befoah ya could buy dem anyvheres else. Alzo, dey hatt hot roasted chestnuts in paper cones rolled from old newspaper, but dat's a nutter schtory.*"

The guy on television came back from the commercial and finished off his pretzel shtick by pointing out that the oldest pretzel factory in the country was built in the town of Lititz in nearby Lancaster County in 1861 by Julius Sturgis. He added that in 1935 the Reading Pretzel Machinery Company developed the first automatic pretzel twisting machine, which is one of the reasons you can buy pretzels all over the country now, like Ricky said.

Indeed the guy on television pointed out that the popularity of the pretzel nationally, with sales of $121,000,000 a year, was largely due to mechanization, factory production, and national distribution of pretzels from the Reading area. Pretzels were so important in the area, that locals had them delivered weekly directly to their home doorstep, just like milk.

The news guy switched over to sports now. Baseball. The Philadelphia Phillies. Ricky kept glancing at Arsenic, hoping he'd say something else about pretzels or Reading in general. He was interested in learning more about his new home, now that he'd left Indiana.

Arsenic took cues from Ricky's inquiring glances and from the sports announcer. He said, *"Course da city coult a bin call't Baseballtown, too! Besights Pretzeltown."*

He looked back at the screen, and then back at Ricky, *"Some claim it's really da cough drop capital, or da candy capital, or da potato chip capital, or da pasta capital. But baseball's got a higher claim."*

Indeed, this was true due to the avid devotion and organized practice of baseball in the Reading area dating from the middle of the 1800's. One of the country's few original minor league teams was based in Reading in 1883.

Amazingly, Arsenic managed to swing the conversation back around to pretzels. The minor league team located in Reading in 1907 was, according to Arsenic, called "The Reading Pretzels." The Pretzels won their league title in 1911, but lost the post-season series to Trenton. Reading history records the fact that George "Jake" Northrup tossed a perfect nine-inning game on June 14 of that year.

Arsenic reminded Ricky that the pretzel was even featured when Arsenic's oldest daughter, Ricky's Aunt Rosa, married James Christiansen.

Ricky's Dad, Randy, was in love with a divorced equestrian who boarded her horse on the Schlank's farm. Sabrina Plochmensch was her name. Her father and mother, Richard and Esther, owned Plochmensch's Pretzels, one of the larger pretzel factories in the Reading area. Randy introduced the parents by inviting Sabrina to bring her mother, father, and kids to his sister's wedding reception.

Sabrina's two children liked Randy and got along very well with his son Ricky. Arsenic liked Sabrina and her kids and was hopeful Randy himself might "tie the knot" again. He also loved Plochmensch Pretzels.

One of Richard and Esther's gifts was a pretzel that Richard had special-made in his factory. It was three feet wide and weighed fifteen pounds. When James and Rosa unwrapped it, Richard came to the front of the audience and gave a little speech and required the newlyweds each to grab one end of the pretzel and pull until it broke and separated. He explained in his little presentation that this had been a tradition in his childhood in Germany. He said the member of the couple that ended up with the largest piece got to make a wish. Rosa got the largest piece.

Richard went on to argue that the traditionally knotted pretzel and its involvement in wedding ceremonies is what gave rise to the expression "Tying the Knot" as a synonym for "getting married."

Arsenic told Ricky that was a lot of *scheiss dreck* which he translated as "poop." He said tying the knot had to do with the old custom of tying the right hands of the bride and groom together with a piece of ribbon to symbolize their union.

Ricky was still in the mood to hear more about Reading. The guy on television said something about a railroad derailment, and Ricky said, "Reading's famous for its railroad too. Ain't, Pop Pop?"

Arsenic nodded.

"Is that train that runs through Fleetwood part of the Reading Railroad?"

Arsenic nodded again. Then said, *"Da Reading Railroat hauled schtuff all over from little towns like Fleetvoot, vitch is vhere dey use'ta make da Fleetvoot Cadillac. Dat's hauw da Cadillac got da name Fleetvoot, from da Fleetvoot Body Works."*

Ricky said, "The kids in Indiana where we used to live thought the Reading Railroad was a name made up by the people that made the board game called Monopoly. And they pronounced it 'ree-ding' instead of 'red-ding!'"

Indeed, the Reading Railroad's familiar to all who played Monopoly. Some are surprised to find that it was a real company. Some wonder why such a "little" company was picked for the board game.

The truth is "The Reading" was a perfect symbol for the game of Monopoly, a game where you can try to force opponents into bankruptcy. You might say the game is about the rise and fall of a corporation.

The Reading Railroad started small in 1833, a little ninety-four mile stretch of track used mostly to haul anthracite coal. But the founders rode high on the Industrial Revolution until, in the 1870's, the Reading Railroad was the largest corporation in the world.

Then, there were the days of ruthless competition, like playing ping-pong with a paddle in one hand and a switchblade knife in the other. Some said J. P. Morgan, one of the best players, helped knock the Reading down to size by calling in loans at a bad time. At that point, the company practically went under and had to specialize once again in pedaling coal, as it had when it first started. It was still the biggest carrier of anthracite coal in the world.

Nevertheless, the company's persistence in tying up capital in anthracite-rich real estate and numerous other diversifications again messed up its finances. It was forced into receivership and reorganization several times. In 1971, it declared bankruptcy. In 1976, it sold out to the federal government's Consolidated Rail Corporation, or CONRAIL. It had a complicated business history, and one might argue it represented both the upside and downside of the real-life game of Monopoly.

Arsenic tried to explain some of this with Ricky giving rapt attention, and then he added, "*Venn Peach an I vass raisin a family, da railroats carried coal from da coal fields dahn ta Reading vhere dey hatt lot'sa iron. Dey used da coal ta make schteel an sent it on da Reading Railroat ta Philadelphia along vith cloth, cigars, beer, and vhiskey, made in da Reading area. Good times dey vass. Lot'sa factories. Lot'sa chops. Easy ta support a family in dose days.*"

Spring was turning into summer on this beautiful morning. Temperatures were in the mid seventies and rising. Showers were forecast for late in the day, but at the moment the weather was beautiful, and the equestrians were out in force.

A big bowlegged local businessman, who somehow managed to mix Pennsylvania Dutch with what Arsenic called "Texican," was riding past the arena as he shouted to Randy, "*Vell, y'all haff yoself a gutten tag.*"

Randy stifled a laugh, because he knew the guy wasn't aware of how funny his accent sounded, and then he replied, "Yeah, you too!"

Randy and Ricky were practicing a form of rodeo competition called "cutting." They were in the outdoor ring up the hill behind the barn right next to a big indoor arena used for winter competition. They were going to practice until Randy's girlfriend and her two kids got there to go on a trail ride with Randy and Ricky. With his dad's help, Ricky was practicing cutting with a little herd of five cattle.

One of Ricky's schoolmates, a girl about his age, was seated in the bleachers cheering him on.

Cutting requires the horseman to separate, or cut from the herd, one or two steers and keep them separated as long as possible, an extremely difficult task since the herding instinct of cattle is paramount. They don't like being alone. Also, once a particular steer has been separated out, the rider is supposed to drop the reins and let the contest come down to a confrontation between two animals, the steer and the horse, without guidance from the rider.

The Schlanks preferred Quarter Horses for this sport. They're quick on their feet, and able to block attempts of an isolated steer to return to his brethren. Scores in competition are based mainly on the amount of time horse and rider keep an individual steer separated from its herd. The Schlanks raised both Quarter Horses and cattle specifically for this purpose.

In the late 1600's, Quarter Horses were run in races in Virginia and Rhode Island on quarter-mile tracks, and that's how they got the name Quarter Horse. Westerners later found them to be exceptional for herding. They were compact and strong but very agile, able to change direction quickly. It was this early herding that led to the popular cutting competition in which Randy excelled.

The Schlank farm had been in Arsenic's family for three generations. In recent years, their chief sources of cash consisted of boarding, breeding, and training horses; staging periodic horse shows; and offering small rodeo-like events that focused on cutting competition.

Ricky's friend in the bleachers was named Beaner. Beaner was afraid to ride, but Ricky was slowly getting her interested.

Randy saw Sabrina pulling into the parking area down at the barn, and so he headed down to help her saddle her horse and the two ponies her kids rode. He herded the cattle along with him to return them to pasture. He didn't want Ricky to practice unless he was there to coach and protect him.

Ricky got down from his horse and went to sit with Beaner in the bleachers. He tied his horse to the whitewashed wooden fence surrounding the ring. The white lime and water composition was flaking off and needed to be redone that summer, a job for Ricky.

After putting the cattle out to pasture, Randy tied his horse next to the outdoor water tank in the barn's *vorbau* so it could drink while he helped Sabrina. The ponies were in the largest of the eight stalls on the left side of the barn. They roomed together. Sabrina's horse was in one of the eight stalls in the right-hand section. The tack room was in the pump-house. Everything in the stable area had the smell and look of maturity and seasoning. Wear and patination. All surfaces and objects had a cured and matured look visible all over Pennsylvania Dutch country. Rounded and burnished by touches from man and beast. Knots and grains highlighted by varnishes of body oils.

The horses were taken out on the *vorbau*, in the shade. Saddles and other tack were carried from the pump-house. Sabrina worked on her Arabian gelding with chestnut coat while Randy saddled the two gray ponies that looked like bookends. He was very quick after so many years of experience and finished about the same time as Sabrina did.

Sabrina's children, Michelle and Michael, were helped into their saddles. Michelle was nine years old, and Michael was eight. They were about the same height. Both kids had blonde hair and were slightly overweight like Sabrina. Arsenic called their look, *saftig*.

Both Sabrina and the kids were proficient riders and liked riding on the trails around the farm.

"Come on, let's go!" Michelle yelled to no one in particular and started trotting into the parking area between house and barn and up toward the horse ring.

Randy got his Quarter Horse and took off the bridle which had a bit placed in his horse's mouth. He had been using the bit while he helped Ricky work with the cattle. He replaced it with a hackamore that involved only a loop of rope around nose and mouth. More comfortable although providing less control of the horse. Trail rides were casual affairs.

The three tried to catch up to Michelle. Then paused as Michael tried to goad his horse into starting. Michael was yelling, "Wait up!" But the pony just stood there. Michael called his pony "Charlie," because he had the irritating habit of stopping unexpectedly on the trail as though he'd gotten a charley horse. He was stubbornly refusing to move right now, and Michael was yelling, "Charlie's got another charley horse!"

Michelle was yelling back, "Very funny! I'm going up to talk to Ricky and Beaner!"

Sabrina's and Randy's horses were relatively short, about fifteen hands up to the withers or shoulders. Anything below fourteen is a pony, so they were short. At four inches per hand that's five feet. A big race horse can go to seventeen hands.

Randy's Quarter Horse had heavy muscles, a deep, broad chest, and a short, wide head. Sabrina's Arabian was less muscular with a smaller head.

As Michelle rode up to the horse ring, Beaner was about to

leave. Ricky was going to go along on the trail ride, but Beaner had to go home and clean her room. After she and Ricky talked to Michelle for a bit and said goodbye, Ricky mounted his Quarter Horse with Pinto markings, as the rest of the group arrived.

They headed up toward the family cemetery on the edge of the old oak woods that looked like a green beret and capped the big hill behind the farm. In reverse direction, they rode on the same trail that led Regan to the Schlank's when he first decided to tell Arsenic he was going to be Grandpa once again.

When they got to the cemetery, Ricky pointed out the graves of his relatives to Michelle and Michael.

"Hey Pop. Who were Israel and Magdelena Schlank?"

"They were your great-uncle and great-aunt, brother and sister to your Pop Pop and Great-Uncle Valentine and Great-Aunt Ellamanda. They died close to the same time, near the end of the First World War. In the influenza epidemic in 1918."

Sabrina said, "That would be awful. To lose two kids almost at the same time."

Randy added, "Pop talked about it a lot when I was growing up. He called it 'the grippe.' He used it as an example of how people can't control and fix everything, or 'play God' as he put it. Twenty-five million people died in that one epidemic, or pandemic. No one ever knew where it came from or where it went. It popped up a few more times in the 1920's, then it just stopped. There for awhile Pop said it looked like everybody in the world might die. But then it just stopped.

"The funny thing is they never talked about it in school. I knew a lot about it because of Pop, but when I'd ask about it, even the teachers, didn't know anything. It was like our culture didn't want anybody to remember that sometimes the wonders of medicine can't protect you from nature. To this day they don't know what happened. Twenty-five million people worldwide!"

Sabrina cleared her throat, "Ah hem," frowned at Randy and said, "well, kids, let's get going. We're supposed to be having fun!"

They followed the trail down into the woods off the opposite side of the peak of the hill into a low damp place. It was so shaded and moist down in this gulley that the trees seemed to sprout from pyramids of moss. There were big oak trees and undergrowth full of birds. The group stopped and sat their horses.

Randy looked ahead to where the trail took a turn to the northeast. In the fall, at this time of day, it would be cold down in this gulley, but then when you got to that turn to the northeast, the sun would hit you square on the back and feel warm like an unearned gift from God. Randy smiled.

Sabrina was a birder and could identify many of the species. She was a member of the National Audubon Society and had schooled her children in bird identification, and they in turn were schooling Ricky.

"Hey, there's a scarlet tananger," Michelle whispered loudly.

Sabrina said, "That's right, Honey. That's the male, scarlet body with black wings. The brightest red you'll ever see on a bird. See if you can find the female."

"She's in that same bush. A little higher up."

Her brother, Michael, started to laugh, and said, "That's a different kind of bird. Maybe a warbler."

"That's what the female looks like, you ninny!"

Sabrina intervened, "She's right, Michael. Not about you being a ninny, but about the bird."

"But Mom, it's a totally different color, and it's a bright color like a male!"

"I know, Michael, it's strange, but it is the female. She's just as bright with her greenish yellow feathers as he is with his red ones. You can hardly believe it's the same species."

Ricky stayed out of the main discussion, but when the others couldn't hear him, he said to Michael, "Hey, I thought it was a different species, too!"

The trail wound its way down the west side of the hill. At the edge of a cornfield they spotted a doe and her fawn. The fawn looked newly born. It was unsteady in its balance but frisky nonetheless. They rode on.

They reached a blacktop road that came from the south. They would follow it a short piece to Regan's main driveway which came into his place from the west. Then, if they continued down the driveway past Regan's pole barn, it would turn into more of a tractor path and lead back to Arsenic's.

They traveled only a short distance south on the blacktop before they came onto a mother racoon and three babies. All killed by a car on the road. The bodies were so widely spaced that it appeared more than one hit-and-run was involved. Randy explained that the babies keep coming back to the mother's body even after she's been killed and eventually they get hit by other cars traveling the same highway.

The kids sat their horses and stared in silence. They knew. They all knew what that would be like.

Ricky said, "That isn't fair!"

"No, it isn't fair," his Dad replied.

"They deserve better!" Ricky added.

"We all deserve better," his Dad said.

They rode on.

As the summer unfolded, Ricky started chugging about on backroads around the farm on a motorized bicycle his Uncle Regan helped him build. He and Ricky had worked on it for several weeks. They'd mounted a reconditioned lawn mower engine on one of those old-fashioned heavyweight bicycles with wide balloon tires. The gasoline engine rode on a bracket over the rear wheel, and a broad radiator belt off an old tractor transferred the power to the axle on the wheel beneath it. The pedals were also left in place. The idea being that when the engine had trouble pushing the bike up a steep hill, Ricky could provide a supplemental boost by pedaling in the traditional manner.

No one was certain whether he needed a driver's license to drive this contraption on public roads, and everyone had forgotten to check into the matter, and so Ricky just got into the habit of exploring less-traveled roads. This was not unusual as it was a rare occasion when a sheriff's deputy bothered a young farm kid out in the country, no matter what he was riding. It was a very rare occasion when one even saw a sheriff's deputy out there.

Ricky was an imaginative kid who loved to build new things out of old parts. He would travel to the various dumps looking for discarded paraphernalia to use in his latest inventions. He called it "dump-fishing." A basket over the front wheel, attached to the handlebars, enabled him to carry stuff home.

One of his inventions was a big live trap intended to catch a raccoon that kept raiding the corn crib on the farm. It was a box trap with a sliding drop-down door in front, held up by a string that ran up through a pulley and down to a releaser inside. The weight of the door hung on a stick the size of a pencil slipped under pegs on each side of the rear of the inner wall, balanced delicately in front of some bait. If a raccoon crawled in the box and reached for the bait, the stick would slip out from under the pegs, and the door would fall shut and latch behind him. To date, Ricky hadn't caught any raccoons, but it still looked like a good design.

He was currently working on another device for trapping squirrels. This gadget used a box with a hinged top. When a squirrel stepped on top, it would fall through and the spring-loaded door would slam and lock above it. Once again, corn kernels served as bait. The trap worked good, but trouble was that research and development trials indicated squirrels could chew out of the wooden box.

His Pop Pop suggested he search for an antique milkbox made out of double layers of steel. Arsenic explained that these originally had insulation between the layers of metal to keep milk cool in summer and above freezing in winter. Squirrels would not be able to chew through those metal walls.

Everyone used to have such a milkbox setting on their back step or porch for door-to-door delivery of milk by the local dairy's "milkman." That's when they used glass bottles instead of plastic jugs, and you'd put the empties back in the milkbox to be picked up by the milkman at the same time he delivered some that had been refilled after sterilization at the dairy. When everyone started shopping in supermarkets, waxed cardboard containers became the norm for awhile, and then of course, the ubiquitous plastic bottle.

Most of the old backstair milkboxes ended up in dumps along with reusable glass milk bottles. Ricky hoped to find one of those boxes for his trap, and Arsenic told him to look for some of the bottles with the dairy's logo painted on them. Arsenic said Ricky could sell the bottles to get cash, or *ferdeen schpendin money*, for store-bought hardware needed for his inventions, the parts that he couldn't find in dumps.

Arsenic told him the most valuable of the old bottles were one's shaped like an hour-glass and designed to catch cream that rose in the bottle. People would pull the paper cap off and spoon out the cream for use on fruits, cereals, and in sauces, and then drink the milk left in the lower portion of the bottle. Or, they could shake the bottle, then pull off the cap, and drink very rich, creamy milk. Arsenic also said the old reusable soft drink bottles painted or impressed with trademarks were valuable as well.

It wasn't that the Dutch were stingy or money-grubbing. They merely valued independence and freedom. That's why most of them migrated here from Germany in the first place. The culture of that loose collective called "The Pennsylvania Dutch" warned that dependency could be abused. Be not too conformed to the world. The borrower is slave to the lender. The Amish, of course, made such sentiments a centerpiece, but all the Dutch knew the value of financial independence and freedom, and they knew the economic forces that would steal away these luxuries.

Randy once commented that the Amish seemed to avoid conformity to the world but still conformed to each other. Randy said he didn't want to conform to anyone. But then, of course, conformity is a relative thing. In any case, all the Dutch seemed to agree that the borrower is slave to the lender. Randy carried it a bit further and said the employee is slave to the employer, which is probably why he kept switching careers.

Anyway, on the subject of "dump-fishing," in the era preceding trash collection, practically every house had a favorite dumpsite, often in abandoned quarries and gravel pits. Some good dumps were on the mountain behind Maggie Stoltzfusz's dairy farm.

Ricky often had to dig below the surface layer because the stuff on the top was often shot up with bullet holes made by people doing target practice from the lip of the dump.

A narrow blacktop road ran right next to Maggie Stoltzfusz's farm and up the mountain, locals called it the macadam. Elsewhere, macadam was an unpaved road, and tarred macadam was tarmac or asphalt, but in this place, tarmac or asphalt was macadam and an unpaved road was a dirt road. Anyway, if Ricky drove out Arsenic's driveway and straight across the main highway, he could go up the macadam into a secluded area with little traffic and lots of dumps.

About a mile above Maggie's, the road split left and right. Locals said, *"the macadam gives a fork at the top."* If Ricky took the right branch of the fork, he rode along a ridge that overlooked Maggie's and Arsenic's farms, and further off in the distance, to the west, he could even see his Uncle Regan's place. If he took the left branch, it headed on top of a ridge north toward Reading, past the homes of some wonderfully eccentric hill people.

The first time Ricky went up the right side of the fork to the highest point, he was amazed to discover that he could see the Pagoda atop Mount Penn, above the city of Reading. He could look straight at it, about ten miles in the distance. So the mountain behind Maggie's was about as high as the Pagoda. The amazing thing to Ricky was that when he was looking up at the Pagoda from the center of Reading, it seemed to be sky high, his Pop Pop called it *himmelhoch*, at least a thousand feet above the city. So Ricky was surprised that he could look straight at it from above Maggie's, which meant the mountain right there across from Pop Pop's place was as high as Mount Penn. Unbelievable!

Well, there were a lot of good dumps down the right fork, but the lefthand branch of the fork led to a whole lot of other types of adventure. The hill people. Down that left branch of the macadam there was a middle-aged fellow called "The Airplane Spotter," because he was always looking skyward. His neck had been broken as a child and never set properly, and so he stared forever skyward. This reminded the neighbors of a World War II Civilian Defense Corps airplane spotter looking for enemy aircraft. They used to joke that all he needed was a white metal helmet with the old "CD" logo on the front

Because of his handicap, "The Airplane Spotter" couldn't get a driver's license but managed to pedal an old bicycle around the neighborhood, a bicycle he bought from an Amish man. If a neighbor was out in the yard, he'd invariably stop by to tell him a joke, which was fine, but he also walked around a lot at night. Neighbors would sometimes gossip, "*he's up ta no good.*" Overhearing such worried comments, The Spotter would confide in his one friend, his pet goat, "*It ain't true, Christine, no matter what they say. I ain't up ta no good!*"

And then there was a very old man and his wife, Jake and Lizzy Burnable, who kept a very old Model T Ford truck in service to ride around the neighborhood selling fresh produce. Originally, it had been a big flatbed truck, but many years ago, Jake built upon the bed a canvas-sided shed. You could go up the steps at the rear of the truck and walk down the center aisle with piles of fresh produce displayed in frames on either side atop slanted counters, like a little grocery store. Additional produce was stored beneath the counter displays. The canvas sides were rolled up in good weather to yield a traveling, open-air, roadside stand, wherever Jake pulled off to the roadside.

Jake drove the truck. Lizzy rode in back. She sat just behind the cab with an old 1903 McCaskey cash box next to her. People flagged the couple down if they needed anything and talked as they walked up the center aisle picking up stuff until they reached Lizzy, and paid, and headed back out. If you got there and somebody was already shopping, you had to wait outside until they finished, because the aisle was a bit constrictive. The old man stayed seated behind the wheel while his wife played the shopkeeper. Sometimes a husband would stand by the driver's side door chatting up Jake while his wife shopped. Everyone in the area knew the Burnables.

And then there was an old eccentric woman who lived in the last house on the left, on that left fork of the road. She claimed to be a faith healer who had, in fact, died in 1819. She was destined to play an important role in Ricky's life.

The very first house on that left fork, belonged to the parents of Ricky's best friend Beaner, the girl who watched him practice cutting with the cattle before he went riding with Sabrina and her kids. "Beaner" was actually her nickname, and it wasn't clear where it came from. She was a skinny, freckled, redheaded girl, full of spunk just like Ricky, and about the same age. Ricky had heard her mother say she was "full of beans," so maybe that's where the nickname came from.

Beaner and her family were not eccentric. Ricky figured that's why they lived in the first house, near the fork. Beaner's father was a non-union plumber and an all-around handy person who kept his prices low and never lacked for work. He drove a big panel truck labeled "*Deets the Handeeman*" on the door. He helped out on the Schlank's farm when they had a big project they couldn't handle by themselves.

Ricky first met Beaner when she came over with her dad, Ralph Deets, while he did a job at the farm. They also attended the same school and rode the schoolbus together, so it was an easy alliance to slide into. Since she lived close to the Schlank's farm, they would often meet after school and go out riding on their vehicles. Beaner had a little scooter her older brother passed down to her when he was old enough to buy a car.

The kids loved to explore the bouldery cliffs off on the right side of the right branch of the macadam, right above Maggie's dairy farm. It was a lovely spot and typical of Berks County, which is peppered with beautiful cap-rock cliffs similar to those above Maggie's. The famous Appalachian National Scenic Trail runs through similar cap-rocks all along the northwestern edge of the county.

Everyone in the neighborhood referred to the cliffs above Maggie's as "The Rocks," or *Die Steine*. Sometimes you'd hear Arsenic vexedly tell Randy, "*Dem kits're up'in Die Schteina again!*"

The Rocks were huge and nearly vertical, in places, overhanging dangerous cliffs. The overhangs formed shallow little caves along the face. Ricky and Beaner liked to play in the little caves. Swallows were always swooping about, apparently near the nests they'd build under the overhang of one or the other of the boulders.

The kids had been advised to stay away from the rocks, because a boy had fallen there in the 1940's, and the tale had him killed. The parents of both kids told them the same grisly story about the search for the boy and the finding of a body partially eaten by animals. The story didn't keep the kids from the cliffs, because they suspected it was specifically designed to make them take the advice seriously. Kids their age tend to be contrary. But the story was at least grisly enough to make them cautious while they played up there, which was no small accomplishment in its own right. Nevertheless, they did have one small mishap, or Ricky did, which turned out to have no big consequence, other than the fact that the kids became friends with the eccentric old lady who lived down the road from Beaner, in the last house on the left, down the left fork of the macadam.

⤜ ✳ ⤛

Late one Saturday morning, Ricky and Beaner were walking down toward the forbidden cliffs when they flushed two very strange birds from the ground, almost stepping on them. Two reddish, brownish, whirly, helicopter-like birds flushed with a whirring burst of showiness, right near the kids' feet, then went straight up in the air, then out thirty or forty yards, and right back to the ground next to each other. Both kids jumped.

"That's a mating pair," Ricky said after calming down.

"A mating pair of WHAT?" Beaner barked, trying to recover from the startle.

"Woodcocks! Uncle Regan calls them timberdoodles. He used to hunt them, but says he decided they're too pretty to shoot. They're really cute. About the size of a pigeon, but they're ROUND, round body with a big round head and very big round eyes. And their beaks are about three inches long, shaped like big tweezers coming right out of the middle of the big round head. They walk real funny too, close to the ground with a little bobbing motion, like they're taking two steps front and one back. They look like something from another planet."

Ricky laughed, but Beaner didn't, still suffering from the surprise burst of feathers.

They walked on.

As they approached a big elaborate spider web across their path, Beaner swung a branch she was carrying and absentmindedly knocked down the web.

"That spider's going to have to spend the rest of the day trying to rebuild that!" Ricky commented as they walked past the remains of the web.

"What else he got to do?" Beaner barked.

After a moment's thought, Ricky replied, "Yeah. I guess you got a point there."

"Watch out!" Beaner yelled.

They had come to a sharp drop off, and Ricky was looking back toward Beaner as he walked toward it. They stopped at the edge of some stone cliffs.

Colossal trees on top with fists of roots clinging to great shapes of rock. Surfaces full of pockmarks. Spaces like city streets between boulders. Crevices carpeted by moss and ferns.

The kids started to go down between two big rocks but came to a small drop-off near the bottom. Beaner wanted to retrace their steps. Ricky decided they could climb down one of the slanted bumpy stone faces. In spite of Beaner's counsel to the contrary, he went on and slipped.

It wasn't really such a huge drop-off. He was lowering himself facing frontward, his back to the rock, over the edge, stepping with his heels, from bulge to notch to bulge, on the weathered stone, toward the ground, while sliding his back along the rock. He was about halfway down when his left heel slipped out of an indentation with moss in it, and he fell, or slid, on his back, four feet to the ground, not far, but there was a bit of an overhang near the end, and it propelled his feet outward. He landed square on his backside.

The wind was knocked out of him. He sat there gasping as one does when the nervous system loses its rhythm and can't remember whether it's time to inhale or exhale, and it tries to do both at the same time. Beaner had waited at the top, but when Ricky fell she scrambled up around rocks and down sloping crevices to where he was sitting and gasping.

Suddenly, an old woman appeared, startling them both. She put her hand on Ricky's back and started murmuring. Ricky found himself trying to understand what she was saying and thereby forgetting the fear that was worsening his predicament.

"Yea, zoe I valk s'rew da valley off death, I fear no eebil . . ."

She was praying!

Ricky'd been about to panic for lack of air, but the gentle repetition of verse and delicate touch and distraction calmed him to where he could breath normally again.

As he relaxed and breathed, the thought flashed through his mind that sometimes just breathing is good enough. He looked to the side, and the old woman flashed her big blue eyes and smiled as she said, *"Ya hatt me verried. Til ya g'schnowf'd!"*

Ricky's brow looked puzzled.

"*Til ya breathed, ya know! Nauw, ya look luftich.*"

Ricky still looked puzzled.

"*Ya know, nauw ya got da breath a'life back. Oh, nevahmind,*" she laughed.

When Ricky was able to get up, the old woman looked him over and said "*Du bist ferroontzled,*" and she brushed dirt off his back, took another look, and said, "*Nauw, ya look gabootzt.*"

She laughed.

Ricky still didn't understand half of what she was saying but he got the gist, knew it was Dutch, and knew she was helping him. And, sometimes just breathing is good enough.

She smiled again, this time with a cute version of the primate smile, broadly exposing upper gums and teeth. She had beautiful teeth.

Ricky couldn't help but laugh.

Noticing a scratch on Ricky's nose, Mary said, "*Ist deiner naws gebrochen?*"

Ricky looked puzzled again, and Mary gently placed a finger on the tip of his nose and moved it slightly side to side.

"*Gibt das schmerz?*"

Ricky looked puzzled, and Mary said, "*Does yoah nose hurt?!*"

Ricky cautiously shook his head and said, "No."

"*It ain't broke den.*"

Ricky shook his head no again.

The three stood there for a moment, and then Beaner broke in, "You're the woman who lives down the road from us. Where'd you come from?"

"*Like you. From Gott!*" And her eyes twinkled as she gazed toward the heavens.

"No, I mean . . ."

"*I know.*"

And now she laughed, a warm gentle chuckle, as she showed

Beaner the contents of an old leather haversack, or *toote* as Mary called it, hanging from her shoulder.

"I vass back by dat letch, pickin dis. Ginseng! Fill't my toote! Ya make tea ought'a vit. It doan grow so good in my garten so's I got'ta pick it vild, ya know."

A squirrel was walking down the slope of a leaf-covered space between the rocks. He finally heard the talking when he came out of the crevice and scrambled back the way he'd come, chattering all the while.

They watched him retreat, and then the lady continued, *"Foah lot's a schtuff ginseng's gute. Makes ya verstandig, ya know, makes ya think better! Maybe it's som'a dis ya should drink befoah ya climb around da cliffs again."*

Ricky said, "I fell."

"Yah. I know. I saw." And the old woman smiled her smile and looked at Beaner as she added, *"Er kam auf einen sprung here-inkomm!"*

Beaner looked puzzled so Mary added, *"He chust dropped in! Glooked bad in da face, but seems better now."* And she laughed again.

The old woman was tall. Her childhood friends had called her Alpine and Rangy. She stood straight-up but without ramrod stiffness. She looked and sounded like an aging version of the mannishly attractive old actress, Marlene Dietrich.

She was at once ageless and very old. A shock of grey hair framed bright blue eyes. Her skin was seasoned with wrinkles, fine and numerous, like soft, expensive leather. Deeper creases, or what Dutch call *roontzel*, appeared next to each eye when she smiled. Her pithy beauty must have been really striking in youth. Her expression was serene, almost saintly.

"I grow erps like parsley, sage, rosemary, and thyme. 'Kräuter' my Mum call't em. Grow wetchtaples too, carrots, spinach, beans. In my garten. Go ought sometimes pickin vild erps. Goot vons grow in da voots bottom off dese'here cliffs. Such as ginseng. My name's Mountain Mary."

Beaner looked skeptical as she responded, "MOUNTAIN Mary, eh? Who are you really?"

Mary laughed and said, *"Wass ich nicht weiss macht mich nicht heiss!"*

Beaner looked puzzled.

"What ya don't know von't hurt ya!" Mary added.

"Yeah, right!" Beaner replied.

Beaner's skepticism came from the fact that Mary had a dubious reputation in Beaner's neighborhood. She was eccentric, but that was normal enough. The problem was that she called herself a "holy woman." The neighbors said she claimed to be the faith healer who lived in the hills around the Oley Valley near the end of the seventeen hundreds. Mountain Mary actually died in 1819. This woman was obviously not really that Mountain Mary, although it was said that her real name was, indeed, Mary.

"Yah, I practice braucherei. Powwows!" Mary said.

"Yeah, right!" Beaner said again, thinking about the stories her parents had told her.

A woodpecker hammered on a distant tree and then gave its chuckling call.

Ricky hadn't heard the stories about Mary, and so he proceeded as though she was exactly who she said she was.

"What do you do?" he asked.

"Help people. Heal em, or help em heal demselfs. Make em feel better anyvays. Drop up my place an visit sometimes! Right dahn from Beaner I live."

"How'd you know my name?" Beaner blurted out.

"We live neighbors doan vee? Vhy vould'nt I know yoah name!"

"Come on, Ricky. We'd better get on home!"

"Yeah, I guess, Beaner." Then, looking back at Mary, Ricky said, "Thanks for your help. You might'a saved my life! I'd like to come visit sometime."

"Gute! I'll teach ya bought braucherei. Powwowing. Only

simple schtuff. Vee powwowers ain't suppose ta talk bought it. Least-vays I'll teach ya bought erps an roots an schtuff in my garten."

"Come . . . on . . . let's . . . go!" Beaner said and pulled on Ricky's arm to speed him along as they walked toward Beaner's home. She couldn't wait to tell him the "truth" about MOUNTAIN Mary!

On the way back to where they'd stashed the motor bike and scooter, Beaner said, "I tell you she's crazy! Crazy!"

"Seemed nice enough to me."

"I didn't say she was 'evil.' I said 'crazy!' She thinks she's a woman that died almost two hundred years ago. Wouldn't you call that crazy? The funny thing is she does have people come visit her for help, like when they're sick or sad or something. My pop says they're probably as crazy as she is."

"Well, I'd like to go visit her sometime."

"Why?"

"Well, she made me better!"

"You just had the wind knocked out of you, you ignoramus!"

"Yeah? How do you know I didn't have heart stoppage or something, and maybe she saved me?"

"What in perdition is 'heart stoppage? You ARE a *glutzkopf,* you ninny!"

Ricky started chasing her at that point, but she outran him.

CHAPTER 5

During the week that followed the encounter with the old woman up at the cliffs, Ricky decided to tell his father about the character he encountered up behind Maggie's. He was curious about Mountain Mary and the "powwowing" thing too, or *braucherei*, or whatever it was called.

When he told Randy about the incident, his dad dug out a book he'd purchased in college when an English professor gave his students the assignment of writing a term paper about their ethnic heritage. Randy said he hadn't covered powwowing in his paper, but he was pretty sure it was mentioned in this book about the history of the Pennsylvania Dutch.

Father and son settled down on the couch in the front room. The book's index led them to a big section on powwowing. Randy read aloud. The book said the label was originally pow-waw in the Narraganset Indian language and pau-wau in the Massachusett dialect. Indians used the word to refer to their medicine men. The book speculated that the Pennsylvania Dutch had adapted it to refer to their own medicine men, and women, who were also called *brauchers*.

"So she's an Indian!" Ricky said excitedly.

"No. They just used the word, or probably people outside the Dutch culture used it, because the faith healers reminded them of witch doctors. Anyway, it talks about their technique here."

In their faith healing, the book said Pennsylvania Dutch pow-wowers often lay their hands on a patient's body and repeat verses from the Bible subvocally.

"Hey," Ricky interupted again, "that's what Mountain Mary did, when I had the wind knocked out of me, up at the cliffs! It worked!"

"Maybe it just calmed you down. Got your breathing rhythm back where it belonged, when you relaxed."

The book added that Christians always respected the power of words and had elaborate rules regarding blasphemy, or misuse of words. The word for cursing, *fluchen* in Pennsylvania Dutch, referred both to blasphemy and to damning or calling down evil on somebody.

Randy read silently for a second and then said, "Huh! It also says here that the laying on of hands, called the 'imposition of hands' in the Christian church, is rooted in the Old Testament and emphasized in the New Testament as an instrument of healing."

"See!"

"Wait a minute!"

"What?"

Randy laughed and said, "It mentions Mountain Mary here. It says she died in 1819. Would you say that woman that helped you up in the rocks was over a hundred and sixty years old?"

Ricky was a little confused as he replied, "I don't think so. That's pretty old."

Randy laughed again. "Yeah. I'd say she's not the woman they're talking about here in the book." He read silently again, and then added, "This is pretty interesting though.

"It says Mountain Mary was called *Barricke Mariche* in Pennsylvania Dutch or *Berg Maria* in German, and she was born in 1749 in Frankfort, Germany, and lived to be seventy years of age. Her father was killed during the American Revolution in the Battle of Germantown, near Philadelphia. Mary and her mother and two sisters fled from Germantown to that section of the Oley Hills called Pike Township in honor of the plentiful species of fish found in the area's streams."

Randy stopped and thought for a second and said, "I didn't know there were really pike in Pike township!"

"Keep reading!"

"In 1747, Lutherans built St. John's Church not far from the area where Mary would eventually make her home. The church came to be called Hill Church, and soon thereafter a village of the same name was formed. Mountain Mary Road and Hill Church Road still intersect just down the mountain from where the remnants of Mary's home and gravesite are located."

"Can we go there sometime?"

"Sure, I've been through there a lot. Your Uncle Regan shoots trap at a gun club down there. Hey, listen to this. It says the first census following the American Revolution classified Mountain Mary as 'head of household,' since she cared for her sisters, but it also classified her as 'Abbess' suggesting that she might have had religious followers or a church of her own, or at least the census taker thought she did. Some people in Pike Township claim she was a Herrnhuter. That was a religious group that had a mission in Oley."

"Herrnhuter?"

"Yeah. It says it was a reform movement that John Hus started a hundred years before Martin Luther supposedly started the Reformation."

Randy stared at the wall for a second, then added, "So much for what they taught me in Sunday School about Lutherans being the first. It says here The Unity of the Brethren formed after Hus was burned at the stake in 1415, and it is the oldest organized Protestant denomination in the world. This eventually started the modern Moravian Church."

"What about the Herrnhuters?"

"Yeah. Sorry. It says the Unity of the Brethren built a town called Herrnhut on the estate of Count von Zinzendorf in the kingdom of Saxony in Germany. That's why some people called them Herrnhuters. Says they sent missionaries to Berks County. It even says that Zinzendorf himself visited Oley in 1742 and held services and baptized both settlers and Native Americans. The town of Bethlehem, Pennsylvania, was founded by him. And his daughter, Benigna, started the first girls' boarding school in America, which later became Moravian College. It ends by saying Zinzendorf was the only European noble to ever have held meetings with Indian leaders on their own turf. Zinzendorf died in Herrnhut in 1760."

"So that woman up in the rocks is a Herrnhuter?"

"No. It's not that simple. They're not even sure this Mary in the book was really a Herrnhuter, but that's beside the point. It's not the same woman as the Mary you met up in the rocks. Remember, Mountain Mary died a long time ago!"

"Oh yeah."

"It says here Mary, this Mary, knew the value of numerous roots and herbs and generally believed in good nutrition. Her garden, *der gartenische du Maricha,* was cultivated with fruits and vegetables used in her healings, and it was as legendary as her faith."

"Whoa! This woman I met wanted me to come see her garden!"

"I don't know about that, but I do know it's not the same woman they're talking about here!"

"Yeah. That's right."

The subject came up again one evening near the end of the week during dinner at the farm. Fat Schmidt had stopped by to visit in late afternoon, and Arsenic invited him to eat with them. Randy was preparing oyster sandwiches. Seafood was easily available in this part of Pennsylvania, with both the Delaware and Chesapeake Bays nearby. Arsenic had wanted crab cakes, or *crap cakes* as he called them, but Randy and Ricky outvoted him, and they were having oysters. Fat was happy to eat whatever they were having.

After dessert, Ricky told again about the encounter with the old woman, and the name she'd given herself, and what he and his dad read in the history book.

Randy nodded.

Arsenic knew the folklore concerning Mountain Mary. He said she was holy, *heiliger* he called her, and added that her real name was Mary Young, or Mary Jung. She was friends with the Indians, he claimed.

Ricky chimed in, "The book Pop and I were reading said she got along great with the Indians."

"Da Inchins got ta Oley first, ya know. Dey hatt sree vil-liches, vith teepees and huts ya know. Dem Inchins call't it 'Olink!' Dat means 'kettle' in da Inchin lankwitch. Oley's got mauntins rount, ya know, like it sits down in a bick kettle, sort'a."

Arsenic continued that the woman up on the hill, down from Beaner's, is a different woman, but he said he knew a little bit about her, too.

"Dat voman up dere nex'ta Beaner helped lots'a people vith kronkheit, sickness ya know. Like Mauntin Mary done too. I hatt a frient, arthritis he hatt, vent avay venn he visited dat voman up on da hill. Heck, da Christian Scientists belief in dat kind'a thing."

The group at the kitchen table stared at Arsenic, wondering why he brought up Christian Science.

Arsenic was arguing that faith healing is not such an oddball practice. The Church of Christ, Scientist, often called Christian Science, founded in 1879 by Mary Baker Eddy, places full confidence in devine healing. In the 1930's, an era Arsenic remembered very well, the church had grown to a membership of about 350,000 with 2,500 branches in more than 50 countries.

Arsenic shrugged and said, *"Anyvays, faith healin ain't such a dumb ideah! Off course, da real Mountain Mary died a long time ago."*

"Yeah. That's what the book said."

"Ach, I doan know. I figered Mauntin Mary vass chust a nickname dat voman up on da hill used. Like Fat here's got a real name. Though I don't know vott it is."

As an afterthought, he added, *"Dere ain't many powwowers left nomoah."*

Fat Schmidt said, "*Ya sink dis voman up on da hill coult help me loose veight?*"

The group stared at Fat now. They were surprised by the question. Arsenic responded, "*Ya vootn't be Fat Schmidt nomoah if ya vassn't fat! Vott made ya bring dat supchect up?*"

Fat confided that he was still embarrassed about getting stuck in the portable outhouse at James' and Rosa's wedding reception. The fiberglass portable privy had a lip around the door that allowed Fat to easily slide in, but kept him from sliding out. They'd been forced to cut out a wall in order for him to escape. That was after the portable building had nearly fallen on a group of people trying to pull Fat out through the doorway.

"*Ach,*" Arsenic said, "*dem toilets is mate too schmall!*"

Fat persisted, "*Vell, dat ain't all, I get it so in my back lately. I'm sinkin maybe it's my veight dat's painin my back.*"

At ten o'clock the following Saturday, with Beaner reluctantly in tow, Ricky knocked on Mary's door and yelled, "Mary, it's us, Ricky and Beaner! Are you in there?"

Mary had been out back, and she appeared to the left of the house, shoulders back, hands on her hips, and said, "*Vell, vill ya look who's heah! Da mauntain climmah! An his frient Beaner!*"

Ricky laughed and said, "You mean 'mountain stumbler!'"

"*Vell, ya fall gute, an ya get up gute! Come on back heah an see my garten.*"

The kids were surprised by a big bass voice coming from the other side of the house as a man yelled, "*Vell, got'ta be goin! Nex' veek see ya I vill, and vee can pray it up again!*"

Ricky was surprised to see Fat Schmidt emerging from the opposite corner of the house and sheepishly hurrying toward his station wagon parked in Mary's driveway. As he was opening the car door, he yelled, "*Hyah Ricky! Sorry I can't schtay. Got verk ta do.*"

Ricky waved as Fat pulled out of the driveway.

Mary came toward the kids on the near side of the house and led them in through the front door, with Beaner hanging back a little and looking wary. Ricky sniffed a little wisp of herbal smoke, and Mary noticed.

She pointed to the little incense burner next to the front door and said, "*Sometimes I burn erps in dat raucher. Fix da schmell in heah, ya know? Some folks call it a pott-pouree.*"

"It smells good in here!" He looked at Beaner, who just shrugged.

The furniture in the front room seemed totally out of place given the plain, almost run-down, exterior appearance of the building. The furniture was very old, once elegant French Baroque that, in its day which was long past, would have made King Louis XIV quite comfortable in one of his sitting rooms. Curved fronts, rich carvings and lots of tortoiseshell and ebony inlays on high-backed shapes, upholstery that had been dark maroon and plush was now looking tired and a little dusty. The kids stared at it.

"*I brung dat fernitcha vith me venn first I moofed in heah. Fat Schmidt seen it venn he come in, an he says, 'Vhy dat's Elderly American,' an I says, 'No, Fat, dat's French!'*"

Mary put her hands on her hips and gave the kids one of her wonderful smiles and then one of her quirky special looks, concurrently focused and dreamy.

The kids just stared at her, so she said, "*Let's go ought back an I'll show ya hauw Mary's garten grows.*"

As they entered the kitchen, Ricky noticed a *Himmelsbrief*, or Letter of Protection, in a frame on the wall next to the door. It was a sort of prayer drawn up official-looking, and Fraktur-style with colorful borders. It was believed by some of the old Pennsylvania Dutch to provide protection to the household. Ricky made no comment but thought to himself that it looked like his grandmother's baptismal certificate.

They went out through the closed-in back porch, which

seemed to serve as a summer kitchen. The kitchen itself was furnished very plain and practical compared to the front room, and the summer kitchen was even plainer. The backdoor had a spring on it and slammed loudly behind them.

On the walk to a section behind the house where the herbs were planted, Mary said, "*Folks in Oley talked bought Mountain Mary's garten all da vay ta Philadelphia, an folks from far vay come foah healin. Dey'd come sayin dey hert bought 'der gartenische du Maricha.' Neighbahs call't her 'Barricke Mariche.' Some called her 'heiliger' cause she kenned the Bible by heart, vert foah vert, front ta back, insight an ought. Chust like me.*" Mary laughed and pointed to her herb plot.

Mary didn't notice that Beaner had tugged on Ricky's sleeve, and as he glanced toward her, she had a grimmace on her face, was pointing at the right side of her own head, and making little circles around her right ear with her index finger. Ricky held his finger across his lips and made a "Shhhh" sound.

First, Mary showed the kids some senna, licorice, and boneset plants, explaining how to distinguish them from surrounding vegetation.

She said senna tea worked well for treating constipation, and licorice was good for heart flutters. "*Dat boneset's vott I vass burnin in da front room, in my raucher. Schmell dis.*"

She broke off a leaf from the licorice plant, pinched it, and held it up so Beaner could smell it.

"It smells like cough medicine," Beaner said as she wrinkled her nose.

"*Speak a da heart,*" Mary said as she ignored Beaner's comment and pointed out a foxglove plant saying that it was the opposite of licorice, stimulating the heart rather than slowing it down.

Then, there was *nuxvomica*, Mary called it "logan," which she referred to as another "heart medicant," and added "*ya can't knowtche dat too much, ya know fondle it. It dies easy if ya touch it.*"

Ricky almost tripped over a wheelbarrow full of manure, and

then he covered up the misstep by quickly reminding Mary that she hadn't told them what boneset was good for besides smelling, and Mary said it was a *"tonic foah da hot times."* She said in summer it reinvigorated the patient and encouraged perspiration.

Next, came liverwort and wolfbane, noting that the latter made a good lotion for treating cuts and bruises, *"an ya got'ta keep em from kratzen, ya know, scratchin da itchie places."*

She indicated a spotted hemlock plant, which she described as a remedy for pain and said it worked when you rubbed the juice on a sore spot. Lastly, she indicated a nightshade plant and said it could be used for *gichtra*, which she translated as "convulsions."

And finally, mint. She said this was good when your *bauch* hurts. *"Ya know, bellyache! Dat's all da erps I got."* Looking at the kids, she added that she often picks wild *krauter* as she had been doing that day when they first met.

They were all quiet for a moment, which seemed to start a squirrel chattering in the top of the tree next to the garden.

Mary added that she would like to find some poppies to make a more powerful *"schmerz medcine, foah bad pain."*

A woodpecker hammered out a rhythm.

She added, *"Dayah's poppies rount heah, but only some keint's gute foah pain, an I can't find dat keint rount heah."*

She concluded, *"All dis medicine verks best if ya pray, an if da sick person weisz wie zu beede."*

"If they what?" Ricky responded.

And she replied, *"I mean dey folla da Bible an underschtand da power off prayah. Dey belief in it, ya know!"*

Next, they got a tour of the vegetable patch. A rabbit hopped away as they drew near.

Mary explained that she rotated her crops, even on this small patch, by the rule of over-then-under. She laughed and called it *über-unter-über*. This meant that in any particular section of the plot, she would plant crops which yielded fruit from under the ground, such as turnips, carrots, sweet potatoes, and beets, in the year after planting ones that bore fruit from above ground, such as tomatoes, peas, and beans. This procedure would be repeated each year. She explained that the former would "fix" damage done to the soil by a planting of the latter. And thus the soil was continually, and naturally, renewed. Between these rotations, during winter months, she would apply manure obtained from her own cow and from the next door neighbor's sheep. She explained that she was now getting a bigger yield from the soil than she did when she first started cultivating the little patch.

Indeed, as Regan pointed out when they were cleaning up his fish kill, most Pennsylvania Dutch farmland increased its yield with use, due to crop rotation and application of manure, something the Dutch had been doing for over two hundred years. Their farm plots were among the most productive lands in the United States. This reflected a cultural propensity to conserve and improve, rather than use up what God gave them. Mary referred to such wasteful wearing out or depletion as *abnutzen*.

Finally, Mary described how she was grafting fruit trees. It involved affixing or sticking, *angestecken* Mary called it, a branch from one tree onto the trunk of another.

She invited them back into the kitchen for a cup of tea.

Seated at the table in the kitchen, Beaner started to relax a bit. Mary had inquired about Ricky's family, and he was telling the two about the death of his grandmother, his Gammy.

"I ran away from home in Indiana because my Pop wanted to move to Europe for post-doctoral study, and I didn't want to go live there. I made it all the way to Reading. Pop Pop and Gammy talked my Pop into letting me stay with them while he was in Europe. Then, while he was on the way over to Europe, his plane got hijacked and my Gammy died. Both about the same time."

"Hijacked?" Beaner blurted out. "How'd he survive?"

"It's complicated. I'll tell you about it another time. The thing is that he was o.k., but then he got a call from my Uncle Regan telling him his Mom was dying. It changed things. He flew back here in time to talk with Gammy before she died, in the hospital. But something changed in him, and he quit his job in Indiana and the post-doc in Europe, and he moved back on the farm with Pop Pop and me. He still teaches now and then, but mostly he trains horses for resale."

Mary said, "*Tell me moah bought yoah Gammy. I'm thinkin I knowed'er. Knowed som'a her freundschaft anyvays.*"

"Her name was Peach Schlank, and she was a wonderful person. She met my Pop Pop, Arsenic, because they lived close by and would visit on Pop Pop's parents' farm."

"*Nah, her family name I vass vunderin bought, bafoah married she vass?*"

"Weidenheimer."

"*Ach! I knew I know'd her!*" Then, Mary hesitated as though she carefully considered her next words. "*I knew her Pop venn dey ran a wotts haus ovah tort Allenton.*"

"Ran a what?"

"*Wotts haus. Gasthaus. Rasthaus. Ya know, a hotel. A road-house!*"

Beaner interrupted and acted as though she might have caught Mary in a lie, "I thought you said you lived in the Oley Hills? That's a long way from Allentown."

Mary was thoughtful. She seemed surprised by the question. As she stared off at the space over Beaner's head, she said, "*Yah vell, I sett Mauntin Mary lived near Oley, but I din say I vass DAT Mauntin Mary. Dat ain't my real name. I'm Mary, but I use't Mauntin for callin myself cause it chust fit me, ya know vott I mean?*"

Ricky sensed the tension, and so he changed the subject, "Tell me about my Gammy. What kind of kid was she?"

After a pause during which Mary seemed to gather her thoughts, she said, "*Vell . . . like I sett, I know'd er Pop. He vass a bad man an yoah groszmutter an yoah mum's bruders hatt a tough time. I know'd'er bruder Heinrich better'n her. A good man he vass an held da family tagetter. Deir Pop vass soffen most often!*"

"He was what?"

"*He vass drunk! Sorry ta tell ya dat, but's true.*"

"I know. Gammy told me that. Gammy hated alcohol because of that!"

"*Dat's gute. Alcahol makes people verrückt! Dat means nuts. I shoult say it made her Pop unzurechnungsfähig!*"

"What!"

"*Dat means really, really insane! I sink yoah Mum's Pop vass vonn'a dem dat should not drink alcahol at'all, ever. But he drank a lot an offen!*

"*I rememper she hatt a freund named Sarah Bieber, who married Jacob Hinnershitz venn she growed up.*"

"Yeah!" Ricky said. "Jacob and Sarah Hinnershitz were good friends with Gammy and Pop Pop while Gammy was alive! I guess they're still good friends with Pop Pop."

"*Vell, real nice people Sarah vass. Yoah groszmutter alzo. Tame people.*"

Ricky said sadly, "Gammy used that word, 'tame.' She said tame people were good people. I miss her real bad." And a tear crept onto his cheek, embarrassing Beaner.

Noticing Beaner's reaction, Mary said, "*Hey, sad ist gute, Beaner. Helps ya grow. Makes ya schmart. Doan be shamed a sad feelins!*

"*Verst thing ist ta go berserker! Angry, ya know? Anger gets ya geschtuck so's ya can't grow up. Real bad anger gets ya in trouble.*

"*If ya get schtuck like a little kit dat got his toy busted, ya vonna get even. Revenge. Do ya vonn'a get bettah, oah ya vonn'a get even? Dat's da qvestion. Can't haff it both vays. Doan get mad, get sad, den foahget it, get on vith sings such as dey are.*"

Beaner suddenly looked a little sad herself as she mumbled, "I get mad a lot."

"*Vell ya ain't mad nauw, are ya?*"

Beaner shook her head no.

"*Yoah sad, ain't?*"

Beaner slowly shook her head yes.

"*Ya can't get mad and sad at da same time. Sad puts ya in touch with Soul. Christian Scientists call God Soul. Sad puts ya in touch with Soul, and Soul is God. Sad makes ya grow vhile mad gets ya schtuck. An yoah zu scheen a kint, too beautiful a girl, ta schpent yoah life gestuck.*"

Beaner got a little smile on her face, but then seemed to get angry, and she stood up and said, "I gott'a go home! You comin, Ricky?"

"I'm going to stay awhile. I'll catch ya later."

Beaner left, letting the door slam behind her.

Mary chuckled and said, "*She remeints me off myself.*"

Ricky said he didn't understand Beaner. "She can be mean sometimes! You're not mean."

Mary thought for awhile and then said, "*She's chust dick-koepich. Ya know schtubborn, cantankrus. Sometimes a person'll be pesky foah reasons dat got nothin ta do vith you. Maybe dey ain't feelin gute, oah like I sett, dey're tryin not ta be sad, so dey get mad instead.*

"*If ya can be nice to such a person, even venn dey're schlecht, dey'll rememper yoah kindness. Freundlichkeit can earn ya real fri-ents venn a person ain't actin nice, cause offen dey know dey ain't actin nice an dey feel bad bought it but can't schtop it. If ya doan let it make ya mad, an keep be'an nice ta dem, dey'll be grateful. I'm shuah Beaner's got her own schtory ta tell. Chust like you an me.*"

Impressed by Mary's knowledge, Ricky said, "You called yourself a powwower when we first met. Do you mean like when Indians have a meeting or a celebration?"

"*Naw! Dat's wrung. Dat ain't vott it means. Vhen da dumb English come ovah heah, dey saw Inchins, gettin in a circle, an talkin, an dancin, an dey ast em 'Vott cha dune?'*"

Here Mary paused to consider the difference between the

sound of a V and a W, and then continued, "*Da Inchins pointed an sett, 'pau-wau!' Da English thaught dey sett 'powwow,' an dey thaught dey vass talkin bought da get-tagettah, da meetin, talkin, dancin, an such like dat, but dey vass pointin ought da leader, da 'pau-wau.' It means 'da von dat dreams.' Dey vass sayin, 'Ya got'ta ast him. He's in charch.' Dis pau-wau vass vott some called a 'medsin man' oah 'medsin voman,' I mean 'woman.'*

"*Dutchies dat practiced healin vass later called 'powwow-ers.' I like ta call myself a 'braucher.' Dat's vott I am. Brauche means 'need,' an I help people vott's in need, ya know vott I mean?*"

Beaner's father, Ralph Deets, was down at Arsenic's barn helping Arsenic and Randy fix the pump that delivered water to the large stock tank, inside the barnyard, in front of the *vorbau*, against the stone wall of the pump house. Horses were watered at the tank before stepping up on the dry concrete *vorbau* floor to be unsaddled and curried and returned to their stalls.

The trio was installing new washers on the pump. While they worked inside the pump house, Ralph asked Randy what he thought about the woman who called herself Mountain Mary, the woman their kids were visiting. Randy said she seemed harmless, and Ralph nodded in agreement.

They worked in silence for a few moments, and then Ralph continued, "My wife's grandfather, before he died, he once saw her out in her yard when he came over to visit my wife, and he asked if we knew who she was.

"My wife says, 'Yeah, she's a cuckoo. She thinks she's a woman who's been dead for a hundred and sixty-five years!'

"Then her grandfather said, '*I'll tell ya who I sink she is. If I'm right, her name ain't Mauntin Mary, it's Dutch Mary!*'"

Ralph stopped talking at this point and looked over at Randy as though he'd revealed some deep, dark secret.

After awhile, Randy broke the silence by saying, "So? Who, may I ask, is Dutch Mary?"

Ralph said, "A prostitute!"

And with that, Randy flinched, and the woman on the hill stimulated discussion of yet another local legend. Another Mary. This one had questionable credentials but again a generosity of spirit.

Ralph related the legend that maintained that there was once a prostitute named Dutch Mary working in Reading. She was in a disgraceful occupation, but managed to achieve some grace and respect in the community. She's said to have owned a successful bordelo, and the story had it that she was very kind to poor people during the hard years of the Great Depression. Everytime there was a holiday in the city of Reading, during the Depression, Dutch Mary sent her employees through the poor sections of the city distributing baskets of necessities and sometimes welfare vouchers to people in need. These were always given in such a manner that they seemed to come from a charitable organization.

Dutch Mary supposedly instructed her employees to accept food stamps and welfare relief checks for services rendered by her employees. If checks were signed, Mary's girls cashed them in for baskets of produce to go to the customers' needy families. The goods included essentials like shoes along with basic foodstuffs. If checks were unsigned, they were simply given back to the family. Ralph said his wife's grandfather claimed Mary threw in a little extra, depending on whether or not she was having a good year.

Since one would suspect that proper families would reject such charity, if they knew the source, the ladies who delivered the goods supposedly left the impression that a reputable charitable organization was providing it. The legend included the detail that the women were always dressed in prim and proper business suits and driven to the homes of their benefactors in taxi cabs that waited for them outside while a delivery was made, and then took them on to the next site.

After listening to Ralph's version of the legend of Dutch

Mary, Randy reflected a minute, looked at his father, and said, "Pop, do you know anything about this?"

Arsenic put down the socket wrench he was using, leaned back against the wall of the pump house, and slid down to sit on his heels. The temperature was always between sixty-eight and seventy-two degrees inside the stone pump house, like a cave, and comfortable. Articles of tack such as halters, bridles, reins, and saddles, were stored in the pump house on hooks and saddle trees covered the walls. These gave the building a pleasant smell of leather and horse.

"*I know who Dutch Mary is, but I don't know any connection betwixt her an da voman lives da roat a little down from Ralph, sept both're freigebig.*"

The last word made Ralph and Randy wrinkle their brows and give Arsenic a bewildered look.

Arsenic broke it down, "*Frei!*"

Randy said, "Free!"

"*Gebig!*"

Ralph said, "Giving!" And Randy added, "Giving freely!"

"*Right!*" said Arsenic. "*Chenerous! Big hearted! Anyvay, die alte Dutch ain't so wunnerfitsich.*"

Arsenic paused, then said, "*Dat means dey ain't so nosey, ya know, as folks nauwdays.*"

Ralph said, "I know what *wunnerfitsich* means!"

"*Anyway, if a voman says her name's Mauntin Mary, vee chust call't her Mauntin Mary. Nauw, I know da real Mauntin Mary's bin dett a lung time. So, dis Mauntain Mary ain't dat Mauntain Mary. But I sink people can call demselfes vott dey vont. It's deir life, ya know vott I mean?*"

Ralph said, "I was just repeating what my grandpaw said."

"*Dere ya go. Dat's hauw carrytale verks. Sumbotty knows half a schtory an tells sumbotty dat adds a nutter half an tells sumbotty dat chainches da first half an so on.*

"*A family guy I knew durin da Great Depression use'ta say 'vann es geht ihm schlecht, Dutch Mary hilft ihm.' Dat chust backs up vott ya sett bought Dutch Mary helpin ought people vott's in need.*

   "From vott da kits tell me, dis Mauntin Mary voman up on da hill is mighty helpful too, but dat doan mean she's Dutch Mary. Mauntin Mary vass helpful too and she's dett. Dat din sound right. Anyvays, I doan know who lives dahn from Ralph. Verstehen sie?"

   Then, Arsenic winked at the other two and continued, *"Anyvise, vee got plenty ta pull at avah own noses. Vee ain't saints, ya know. Let's keep spek-you-lation bought connections betwixt Mauntin Mary an Dutch Mary ta avah selfes. I know folks in Reading said Dutch Mary disappeahed from da shteddle sometime aftah da Depression. She 'retired' ya might say. Could be dat's her livin up dere, I doan know, but dat's her business, ya know vott I mean?"*

   Ralph nodded sheepishly and added, "Yeah, I think my wife's grandpop would've agreed to keeping the rumors down. He seemed to have a lot of respect for Dutch Mary too."

   The three returned to their work in silence, each thinking his own thoughts.

   Ricky and Beaner got into the habit of dropping in on Mary when they were out gallivanting on their scooters. Both of their families would later come to appreciate the special skills of the woman who called herself Mountain Mary, regardless of who she was. She helped Ricky and Beaner recover from a grim incident which, in the end, seasoned both kids in a good way, with Mary's help.

CHAPTER 6

On Sunday morning, Ricky walked the tractor path connecting Regan's and Arsenic's farms. He was headed toward Regan's. Ruby, Regan, and Ricky were going trapshooting. Actually, Ruby decided to quit until after the baby was born. She was going along to watch and visit with some of her old trapshooting partners.

As Ricky arrived, Regan and Ruby were busy doing something with a cage. As Ricky walked up, Regan was pulling his sweater off, stating that he didn't want it to get tangled in the cage's wires. There was a crow in a small cage, and they were in the process of transferring it to a large cage on the end of a big shed near the house.

Regan reached into the cage and grasped the crow in his two hands. It looked wise as it gazed into Regan's eyes, and then it looked carefully at the hands restraining it, at one finger in particular, and then it clamped down on that finger with its beak.

"They sure got a strong bite," Regan said.

They waited, both staring at the crow, waiting for it to let go so they could complete the transfer.

"Are you o.k.?" Ruby asked after awhile.

"He didn't break the skin," Regan replied. "Not yet anyway!"

They continued to wait.

Regan finally said, "I believe you're going to have to pry his beak open. I don't think he's going to quit. We'll be here all day. Besides, it's starting to hurt!"

Ruby pinched the lower bill between two fingers of one hand and the upper one between two fingers of the other hand and slowly pulled to give Regan some wiggle room. Regan pulled his finger out as Ruby took over restraining the bird with her two hands.

"Keep your fingers away from his beak," Regan said.

"Don't worry. I saw what he did to you. Any blood?"

"No. He didn't break the skin, but I don't believe I could have pinched myself that hard with a pair of pliers."

Ruby laughed, and Ricky just kept in the background, staring in wide-eyed wonder.

Opening the door to the big cage, Regan said, "Put him in on the floor and jump back, and I'll slam the door."

After the door was closed, Regan said, "Let's give him some food and water," and then noticing Ricky for the first time, he explained, "Hey Ricky! Ruby saw this guy hopping across the yard. It has a broken wing."

"Hey Ricky," Ruby said. "Do you think we should keep him as a pet?"

"Yeah, I do."

"We're ready to head for the gun club," Regan interjected. "The truck's already loaded. I'll finish up here."

Regan climbed in behind the wheel of the pickup, and Ricky climbed in the passenger side.

Ruby paused to give the crow some corn and water.

She came over to the passenger side and said, "*Rutsch* over!" And so Ricky ended up in the middle of the bench seat.

As they got underway, Regan spoke his thoughts. "You know, my Pop used to take me crow hunting when I was a kid. I don't shoot them anymore."

Ricky said, "How do you hunt crows?"

"With an owl as a decoy."

This got Ricky's attention, and he looked at Regan with surprise and asked, "An owl?"

Regan stopped at the stop sign by the main road, and while he waited for a car to pass, he looked at Ricky and smiled and nodded and said, "Yeah. He kept a great horned owl as a pet. Used it to hunt crows like the one Ruby and I just put in that cage. He'd put a leash on the owl's leg and sit it on top of a little platform he'd built in a clearing in the woods. Crows attack an owl when they find one in the daylight. They're enemies. They gather in flocks and harass it. My Pop called it 'flocking,' but in college I learned that it's called 'mobbing.' I guess they want revenge, because the owl picks them off at night and raids their nests too.

"My father and I would hide in a blind close to where the owl was sitting and shoot the crows with a shotgun when they mobbed the owl."

Ruby interjected, "I used to like that owl. When we were dating," then looking at Ricky, she added, "I'd come over to his parents' farm, you know, and I was always fascinated by it. This owl had long beautiful eyelashes."

Ricky showed surprise again, at the notion of eyelashes on a bird, then he looked back at Regan as he said, "I don't see how he caught a live owl."

Regan concentrated on making a sharp left turn onto route 73 and then glanced over at Ricky and said, "He'd trap one. He'd set a metal muskrat trap on top of that same platform we used for hunting the crows. He wrapped terry cloth around the part of the trap that's designed to clamp down on a muskrat's leg. That was so it wouldn't hurt the owl's leg. Then, he'd set the trap overnight on the platform and lay a soft rabbit skin over it. An owl would dive at that 'rabbit' with his claws sticking out in front, and when he hit the skin, the trap caught him by the legs. The soft rabbit skin and the wrapping on the trap kept it from breaking his leg."

"I thought it was illegal to catch and keep wild animals like that."

From her seat by the window Ruby said, "The Pennsylvania State Game Commission used to pay a bounty for killing an owl in those days."

"Yeah," Regan added, "I think it was five dollars, or something like that. They used to pay a sort of bounty for shooting crows, too. If you'd send in two crow's feet, that you cut off a dead crow, they'd send you a shotgun shell. If you were a good shot and didn't miss, they'd basically be buying your ammunition for you."

"That seems stupid," Ricky said. "There aren't that many crows and owls around."

"Well, there were in those days. They don't do it anymore."

"What did he feed the owl?"

"Road kill. And crows."

"Dead crows that he shot?"

"No. He'd put wounded ones in the pen with it. The owl and crows would just live in there together, for weeks sometimes, until the owl got hungry. Then, you'd hear the crow squawking."

"Yuk!" Ricky exclaimed.

"Yeah. I don't go along with that now myself. But attitudes were different in those days. And there weren't so many people and so many houses. I don't judge those people." Regan chuckled then and said, "I guess you could say they didn't have habitat destruction and pollution to keep animals under control in those days so they had to put a bounty on them. Anyway, let's change the subject, my Pop was actually a pretty nice guy."

Ruby entered the discussion again as she followed her own train of thought and said, "This owl would eat bones, hair, everything, when he was eating an animal. Then later, he'd regurgitate the bones, and hair, and feathers in pellet form."

Ricky interrupted, "What's re-gur-gitate?"

"Throw up, barf, upchuck," Regan said with a laugh.

"Yuk!"

Regan continued, "The great horned owl is one of the few animals that will eat a skunk. The owl my Pop caught stank like a skunk when he first brought it home."

"I remember that," Ruby said.

"Mostly they eat mice and squirrels. I read someplace that they'll kill four thousand mice in one year. There aren't any predators that bother the owl, except people, and other great horned owls. They'll kill and eat each other even. They're pretty ferocious."

At a later time, Regan would give the crow that he and Ruby had caught to Ricky to keep as a pet. It never did re-acquire the ability to fly more than a few feet and couldn't be released back into the wild. Arsenic would become very irritated with it, because it was very impish and would fly up on his clothesline and pull out the clothespins, letting the clothes fall to the ground. It seemed to enjoy annoying the old fellow.

It was a good day for trapshooting. Very little wind, temperatures around seventy-five. Bright sun. Low humidity. Beautiful! Regan, Ruby, and Ricky sat in the truck for awhile and watched a squad of guys shooting.

Then, Reagan asked Ricky if he'd feel insulted if he asked him to start with a light gas-operated 20-gauge Remington 1100 automatic shotgun. This gun was less powerful than a typical trap gun but produced very little recoil when fired. The boy could concentrate more on the target and less on the kickback of the gun.

"I'll do whatever you think will help me shoot better!"

It was common for shooters to miss a target by jerking or flinching as they pulled the trigger, before the gun even fired. This conditioned reflex anticipated the recoil. A funny way to prove this to a shooter's is to give them an unloaded gun that they think is loaded. Have them "shoot" at a target. They'll jump or flinch as they pull the trigger even though nothing went "bang." This sort of reflex flinch makes the gun jump off target. Regan didn't want Ricky to develop such a bad habit.

The three went around to the back of the pickup as Regan opened the tailgate entry to his camper top. He removed the gun from its case and handed it to Ricky, as he said, "I've got a present for you. Not the gun. This."

He handed him a little plastic case such as would hold sunglasses. Ricky layed the gun back on the tailgate and took the case. He opened the hinged top to reveal a pair of blaze orange Winchester shooting glasses.

Regan said, "We'll be shooting at blaze orange clay pigeons, and those glasses make them stand out and radiate against the green background. It's one of the 'tricks of the trade.'" He winked.

Ricky put them on and looked over at the targets flying out on the nearest trap field where a group was already shooting. He was surprised and said it looked like there was a light inside each target.

Ricky said, "Much gratitude, Sir!" Just like that. And Regan laughed.

Regan convinced the man managing the club that day to allow he and Ricky to have a whole trapfield, or shooting range, to themselves. Normally five people shot as a group. Having just he and Ricky together allowed Regan to call a halt whenever necessary and counsel the boy regarding his technique. He wouldn't be bothering any other shooters in the group. Ruby watched from behind Ricky and offered advice of her own from time to time.

Normally, one person stands at each of the five shooting positions, or stations, located in an arc sixteen feet behind the sunken trap house. The person releasing the targets by remote control is standing a little behind this arc.

You can only see the roof of the traphouse, and a tiny bit of the back wall. The birds or clay pigeons are like little Frisbees made of clay and black pitch and painted orange on top. A spring device, called a trap, flings them out the front of the sunken traphouse at about fifty miles per hour at randomly varying angles. They fly out a slot on the front of the traphouse and go up like a quail lifting off the ground. With a solid hit, you get a little cloud of black and orange dust hanging in the air.

Shooters fire in turn, station one to five and back to one again. When it's his or her turn, the shooter shoulders the gun and yells

"Pull!" The clay pigeon is launched. After every shooter has fired at five, the person releasing the targets yells, "Change stations!" Each shooter moves to the right, to the next station, and the person on the last position, station five, comes round to station one. They continue this way until each shooter has fired at twenty-five.

Since you fire at five from each station, and there are five shotgun shells to a row in a standard box of twenty-five shells, you always know it's about time to change stations as you get to the last shell in a row in your box

A shotgun fires a little over an ounce of lead pellets that spread as they leave the muzzle. The circle of pellets is thirty inches at twenty-five yards. People think it's easy to hit a moving target with that many pellets—until they try it themselves.

The main problem is to keep swinging the gun when it fires, or you'll shoot behind the target. Shooters stop or flinch and jerk the gun when they pull the trigger. The fact is it takes awhile for those little pellets to get to where the target is, and you have to get ahead of it and keep swinging after you pull the trigger in order to hit it.

Regan explained this. Getting-ahead-of-the-clay-target he called "lead," and don't-stop-swinging he called "follow-through."

Ruby added that Ricky would have to find his own way of doing all this. She said she preferred to start behind a target, then speed through it and allow the acceleration and momentum of the swing to create lead and follow-through. Regan said he preferred a sustained lead, staying ahead of the target the whole time, until he saw the cloud of black dust.

Both Regan and Ruby were exceptional shooters, and so both techniques seemed to get the job done. Regan admitted Ruby's way was easier for most people when they first learn, so Ricky decided to use that one. He hit seventeen out of twenty-five targets, a very good score for a beginner, especially since he was shooting such a small gun.

At this point, the trio decided to head for the clubhouse and get something to drink while they discussed Ricky's first round of trap. As they were going though the door, Ricky carried his gun rested back against his chest, careful to keep the muzzle pointed safely at the ceiling. Regan asked him to lower it, so that the muzzle pointed at the floor. After the guns were in a rack, and they were seated at a table, Regan said he wanted to explain why he asked the boy to lower his gun.

"When I was sixteen, I went hunting early on Thanksgiving morning and got back just about the time the family was getting ready to have a big Thanksgiving dinner. Everybody was standing around discussing the seating arrangement, and some of the food was already on the table. I walked in the kitchen door and headed for my room to put my gun away. I was carrying my gun up high like you were just a minute ago."

Ruby started to laugh as she remembered the story.

"We had this big round fluorescent light in the center of the ceiling in the kitchen, pretty much right over the table. I walked close to the table because of all the people standing around. Well, the end of my gun barrel slammed into that big fluorescent light."

Ricky cringed.

"Boom! The bulb exploded. Glass flew all over the place, all over the table, all over the food already on the table. Boy, did I catch the dickens. Thanksgiving dinner was late that year, and we had less food. My family was ready to run me out of town."

Ricky said he would remember that story, and probably wouldn't make the same mistake. He asked for feedback on his shooting.

Regan said, "You shoot real quick."

Ricky looked serious and asked if that was bad.

"No, no, not at all. You shoot like Ruby, and she's won a lot of championships. It's just a different style. Sometimes they call it 'instinct shooting' and it goes good with that technique you used for lead and follow-through. You just let your natural instincts take over. It'll be real important for you to be psyched up before you shoot. If you get rattled when you're shooting like that, it's hard to recover, and it can ruin your score. I'll give you a tip. Usually you're shooting with four other people and you can recover from a miss while the others are shooting. The trick is to visualize, you know imagine or picture, shooting the other four targets, in your mind, before it comes around to your turn again. Imagine doing it perfectly. Smoking every one of them."

"Smoking?"

"You know, hitting them dead-center. Turning them into a cloud of black smoke! Let's shoot on a full squad this time. You hit seventeen. You're ready for the big time. Also, you can shoot one of my big twelve gauge shotguns this time."

Regan and Ricky signed up on a squad along with three friends of their's who wouldn't mind the distraction in case Regan had to give Ricky feedback during the round. It turned out that Regan didn't have to say a thing. Ricky was a natural and hit twenty-two of the twenty-five targets.

While they were resting and watching another squad shoot, there was a bit of startle and confusion. One of the shooters had rested his gun barrel on the ground between shots, and it got clogged with mud. When he fired at his next target, the end of the gun barrel blew up and the whole barrel fell off the gun's action. Everybody was surprised, but no one was hurt. On the way to the car, Regan said he'd read that things like that could happen, but it was the first time he actually saw it.

"Wow!" He added after a moment's thought, "That gun was a classic Ithaca single-barrel trap gun. Probably worth four or five thousand dollars! Not anymore, eh?"

On the way home from the gun club, Regan swung around through Boyertown, Gilbertsville, and Pottstown and up the Phila-delphia Pike with the intention of cutting between Mount Penn and Neversink Mountain on Perkiomen Avenue and then north along the base of Mount Penn toward Pricetown and home. Mount Penn and Neversink Mountain cross like a T, and a little valley cuts through where they cross. The road runs through that valley, and it runs through a borough called Mount Penn.

As they were passing right to the south of the mountain named Mount Penn, just below Reading's landmark Japanese Pagoda, Regan pointed out the opposite side of the car, to the left, and said, "You know, there used to be a big resort up there on Neversink Mountain, and an inclined railroad that ran on electricity generated right there on the Schuylkill River. It was the first electric railroad in America operated by waterpower. Used one of Edison's new electric generators. That was in 1890!"

"That's not much of a mountain compared to the one your deer camp's on."

"Well, that's true, but then you could say the same thing if you compared the mountains where the deer camp is to the Rocky Mountains out west. There's always a bigger mountain I guess.

"Anyway, in the old days people would take shorter trips for vacations. For one thing, transportation was slower. At least you could catch a trolley from Reading over to Neversink and up to the resort on top for a getaway weekend. See there weren't any cars and darn few roads at that time. Travel wasn't easy. People still hike and bicycle up there on Neversink. There are a lot of public trails in those woods, from the old days."

Switching his gaze to the opposite direction, up toward the Pagoda, Ricky said, "What about Mount Penn? Did they vacation up there?"

"Oh yeah. There were two resorts up there. And a gravity railroad."

"What's a gravity railroad?"

"It was a model for the roller coaster you ride out at Dorney Park."

"Pop Pop says there used to be a roller coaster right down from the Pricetown Road. In a place called Carsonia Park. Pop Pop calls it the 'Jack Rabbit.'"

"Well, yeah, that's true. They tore that down around 1950.

"Anyway, this gravity railroad on Mount Penn would run trolley cars up to the top of Mount Penn, about thirteen-hundred feet, and then the trolley would just coast, you know 'roller-coast,' down the ridge to the north on top of the mountain and then zigzag east, and then south toward that Carsonia Park you just mentioned, then down a slope in back and around into Reading again. Just like a roller coaster in an amusement park, but it went slow and went right through the woods. Some passengers stayed at one of those hotels up there, but if you stayed on the railroad, it was a five-mile coaster ride around the mountain."

"Was that really the model for the roller coaster?"

"Yep. Well, wait. The 'first of the first' you might say was another gravity railroad over west of Allentown. I think it was the second railroad built in the whole USA. It was called the Mauch Chunk Switchback Railway, and it used to coast down from the coal mines to the Lehigh River, carrying coal to barges that ended up in Philadelphia. It had some of the steepest drop-offs in the world for a gravity railroad. That must have been a lot like a roller coaster. And when the coal business got in trouble, they used it to carry passengers who wanted a joy ride. It was another closeby vacation thing to do. They said it attracted as many people as Niagra Falls. Imagine flying down the mountain on a train."

"How'd they get back up?"

"Mules would pull the cars back up. At least that's how they did it at first. Later they set up steam engines and cables at a couple places along the line to pull the train back up."

"How did the mules get back down?"

Regan laughed and said, "They'd ride down on the train, then they'd hitch'em up to pull it back up to the top."

Ricky said, "Ahh! You're pulling my leg again!"

"No! I'm serious. Isn't that true, Ruby?"

Ruby looked at Ricky and shrugged and said, "That's what I was always told."

"This area's pretty famous for roller coasters. The Philadelphia Toboggan Company is the oldest manufacturer of wood coasters in the world. They started in 1904. One of their most famous leaders and designers was named Herb Schmeck."

Ricky stared at Regan and asked, "How do you know all this?"

Ruby interrupted, "Herb Schmeck was a relative of his!"

"Yeah." Regan said, but he was again looking up toward Mount Penn, off to their right. "Just imagine coasting five miles through the woods up there. Quiet, except for the sound of the wheels on the rails. 'Click, click, click, click.'

"You know that road up there that people call Skyline Drive, with all the pretty overlooks of the city of Reading? Well, that used to be the railroad bed. They had a couple bad accidents in the old days. One at a place they call cemetery curve."

Regan was leaning forward and looking up through the windshield toward the top of the mountain and veered into the lefthand lane as they were approaching the Pricetown Road.

"Honey!!" Ruby yelled.

Regan said, "Sorry!" And corrected his course.

Ricky jumped when Ruby yelled, but now he was leaning forward as Regan had done and looking up toward the Pagoda. "Wow!" he said. "I've been up there. It's pretty. So that's what they'd see from the trolley. Wow."

When they finally returned home from the gun club, Regan turned off the engine and stared through the windshield as he said, "Oh my God!"

A startled Ruby responded, "What's wrong?"

Regan pointed at the pond, visible from the driveway, and simply replied, "Look!"

There were white objects of all sizes floating in the Kutz's farm pond. The pond was an acre in size and about a fourth of the surface was full of floating white things.

"What is it?" Ricky asked.

"Fish!"

"But . . ."

"There's been a 'fish kill.' Maybe there was an algae bloom."

As he said this, Regan was already halfway out the truck door, which he slammed, and practically ran toward the pond. He stopped at the edge and started coughing, as Ricky and Ruby caught up.

"I should have put lime in it. I always put lime in it. But I've been putting it off. Now look at it. Oh, I'm so sorry."

Regan said this last as though he was talking to the fish, and he was barely audible as grief affected his breathing. When he turned, his eyes were moist.

"Nine years they've been healthy, and one screw-up did this."

"I'm so sorry, Honey," Ruby muttered as she wiped a sympathetic tear from her own eye and then squeezed Regan's arm.

Ricky was agape. "Were they poisoned?" he asked while staring at the floating white objects.

Regan regained his composure and responded sadly, "No, Ricky, I just think they suffocated. See how some of the smaller fish are still sucking at the surface, like they're trying to get oxygen? I have to get the aerator."

Ruby said, "What do you mean? What aerator?"

"That paddle wheel I bought at auction a couple years ago. It hooks on to the back of the tractor."

Indeed, Regan had purchased a paddle wheel that looked like a miniature version of the wheels that propelled the old river steamboats. He bought it at an auction held at a fish hatchery that was going out of business.

"Oh, that!" Ruby said. She had been opposed to the strange purchase, but relented when it went for a very low price. Now, she was glad he bought it. If they could save the little fish, the pond might regenerate.

Regan had the paddle wheel attached to the power takeoff on their big all-purpose tricycle-type tractor in short time, and he headed toward the pond. He backed down a slanted berm, careful not to mire in the mud, and lowered the paddle wheel halfway below the surface of the water and locked the hand brake. When he engaged the power takeoff at the rear of the idling tractor, the wheel slowly turned, splashing like a steamboat but going nowhere. The splashing started the water moving in little waves throughout the pond and provided a source of oxygen.

Ricky was standing on the axle behind the tractor seat. Regan turned his head and said, "We'll leave it run all night, or until it runs out of gas, I guess. I'll get some friends to help get the dead fish out in the morning. We don't want them rotting in there, or it'll definitely be the end of all of them. Even the little ones."

They got down and went in the house where Ruby was fixing dinner. Regan got on the telephone and called around to get help removing the dead fish the following morning.

"Hey James, I had a fish kill on my pond. Any chance you could help me clean them up? It's a pretty big job."

James responded, "Can you count on an abacus?"

"What?"

"It's something a guy in the factory used to say. I'll be happy to help. An abacus is . . . wait a minute," James held his hand over the receiver and talked to Rosa, "Rosa says she'll come along and help. When are we doing this?"

"Tomorrow morning. Let's say seven o'clock."

"Sounds good. Maybe I'll stop over in awhile and have a look at the job."

"Thanks. Oh, by the way, I know what an abacus is."

Next Regan called Valentine, Arsenic's brother. Valentine was a truck farmer, dealing in fruits and vegetables, produce. He sold it at the large Reading Farmers' Market on Saturdays. Sweet corn, cabbage, cauliflower, eggplant, peppers, broccoli, lettuce, collard greens, raspberries, strawberries, and apples. He could use the dead fish to fertilize his vegetable patch.

Arsenic and Randy were tied up in the morning but they'd come over as soon as they finished their work, to see if their help was still needed. They were giving the horse stalls in the barn a thorough cleaning.

Arsenic said, "*Vee're already busy still in the morning manuring ought.*"

Manuring out is what the Dutch called a thorough cleaning of the barn. It was done every two months. They had the daily freshening routine, forking wet spots and feces into the old wooden wheelbarrow and sprinkling fresh straw in place, but once every two or three months, the stalls were completely cleaned. Arsenic said they had to "*fork the stalls empty.*"

The whole operation required at least half a day. Daily freshening slowly filled the manure spreader parked next to the stone wall in front of the *scheierhof*, and a load of manure could be emptied up in the fields every few weeks, mechanically strewn as organic fertilizer. However, manuring out would fill the spreader at least twice by the time they finished the job, and at least one load had to be spread on the fields to empty the spreader and make room for more.

They were actually ahead on the cleaning schedule, but Tex Martin, a guy who boarded horses at the barn, had commented that the odor was pretty strong in his horse's stall.

A Dutchman is deeply embarassed by any suggestion that his barn is dirty. And so Arsenic emphasized that he and Randy had to finish cleaning before Tex came back. "*Wir müssen foadijch sein vor Tex zurück kommt.*"

The evening before the big fish cleanup James came over to Regan's to look at the pond. Regan, Ruby, and Ricky were finishing dinner. James joined them for a cup of coffee and a piece of pie as they moved to the patio and discussed the events of the day. He was amazed that so much devastation could occur in just the short time the group had been out trap shooting. Regan speculated that the fish were already starting to appear on the surface before they left for the gun club, but they just hadn't noticed them. He explained that most fish kills occur early in the morning, when oxygen levels in the overall pond are at their lowest.

"The algae grow fast when there's nutrients in the pond. I think it was overstocked, and I was feeding the fish every other day. Anyway, when the algae bloom so densely that sunlight can't penetrate, they start to die, and the decay uses up what little oxygen there is. So, not only are the algae not producing oxygen, but they're using it up as they decay. It just happens really fast at that point, like dominoes falling over, and the fish are caught in the middle. I wish I'd noticed that the water was murky.

"Another thing, it was really cloudy a few days ago. The sun hardly shown at all. I bet that was the straw that broke the camel's back. Started the algae dying."

James mentioned he'd learned in college that a pond is essentially a closed system, very finely balanced. He said they did a demonstration experiment in his college ecology class. And yes, it happened quick. As the algae died off, they removed oxygen from the system instead of putting it in.

James added that the instructor in the class drew an analogy between a pond and the earth itself, which he described as the biggest closed system of all.

"It's like we're walking a tightrope. One slip, and it's all over fast. Sometimes it takes a long time to develop, like that algae growing, and then you reach a point where the system can collapse, like a house of cards, in a short time. My instructor said it's like a balancing act.

"My instructor was a devout Christian, and he loved to point out references to nature in familiar Bible verses. Like in the 23rd Psalm it talks about green meadow grasses, quiet streams, and dark valleys where we have no fears and where we have plenty to eat, and so on. He said nature was the original house of the Lord, and we were supposed to watch over and protect it, not abuse it."

After a little contemplation, Ricky looked over at Regan and asked whether something like what happened to the pond could actually happen to the whole earth, and Regan said he was afraid it was possible. Working for a big agri-business company, he related the phenomenon to modern farming practices.

"I shouldn't be saying this, because I work for the big ag companies, but the old Dutch didn't use so many chemicals on their fields, and I believe their fields stayed more fertile. During the Great Depression and Dust Bowl years, when the soil in this country was about played out, this land around here that the Dutch had been farming for a hundred years was more rich and fertile than when they first started farming it. They'd actually improved the land by farming it.

"The old Dutch lived a little more in conformity with nature instead of fighting it. My grandfather used to say, '*Gottspäle ist Gotteslestrung.*' I think that means 'it's blasphemous to play God.'

"The old Dutch used fertilizers that were natural, like manure, like those dead fish out there that your Uncle Valentine's gonna haul away.

"Another thing, they tried to fight insects naturally, like by dusting the plants with pulvarized limestone that you find all over this area and which is good for the soil. Or sometimes they'd dust 'em with ashes from the woodstove. That sort of thing, combined with crop rotation, nitrogen fixing, and contour tillage did the job, maintained the balance.

"These big corporation farms dump tons of chemical fertilizers and insecticides on the fields. Sure, in the short run, it works great. But next year comes around and the soil's damaged and needs even more and stronger chemical fertilizers and insecticides. And then more the year after that, and more, and more, until the soil's organically dead and just there to hold the plants up, no better than sand. All the nutrients come from chemicals which are nothing but powder and liquid, no real topsoil anymore. Lots of stuff to wash into our water supplies. How long can we keep fighting nature like that before the system collapses?"

Regan paused and then said, "Don't tell the company I work for what I just said!"

Ruby interjected, "You got him going, Ricky!"

"But it's true!"

"I know Honey. You know I agree. I'm just teasing."

"I know," Regan reflected. "Tomorrow your Great Uncle Valentine will recycle those fish, and I'll put pulvarized limestone in the pond, and we'll start over again.

"You did good at trap shooting today, Ricky! You're already a good shot. Maybe you can start competing on the circuit this winter."

The following morning Valentine showed up before Ruby and Regan were through with breakfast. He took a cup of coffee and walked down to look at the pond. He'd driven his old pickup truck and planned to put the dead fish in back to haul them home. He'd hired three high school kids who would be waiting at his place to "plant" a fish or two at the base of each sweet corn stalk and throw a shovel full of dirt on top.

Ricky came over to the Kutz's with James and Rosa shortly after Valentine got there. The three walked toward the pond to talk to him. The paddle wheel aerator had run most of the night and pushed the floating carcasses over to the opposite shore, essentially raking them together. Valentine surveyed the task.

When Ricky, James, and Rosa walked up, Valentine said, "*Gonna be a dreckig chop!*"

Rosa looked at her uncle and smiled as she said, "*Yah vell, Vallie, ist ein dreckig welt, ain't!*"

Valentine just nodded solemnly in agreement and walked down closer to the shore.

James leaned close to Rosa and asked, "What'd he say?"

"It's a dirty job."

"Yeah, that's for sure! So, what did you say back?"

"Well it's a dirty world, I said! Pop would have said it's *verschmutzt!*"

James raised his eyebrows and said, "Ohhh-K!" Then, he turned toward shouted greetings coming from Regan and Ruby, who were headed down from the house to start the work.

It took three hours to clean up the dead fish and another hour to dump five hundred pounds of lime in front of the paddle wheel, which Regan restarted after filling the gas tank on the tractor. Valentine left for home as soon as the fish were loaded.

Regan couldn't forget the experience of dealing with two hundred and fifty gallons of dead fish. They'd used fifty-gallon plastic garbage cans with wheels to transfer the fish to Valentine's pickup, and they'd filled them five times.

James commented on the size of one of the dead bass, and Regan replied, "A lot of those would've been record size if caught in a bass tournament. The biggest bluegills look like exotic fish you expect to see on a corral reef in the ocean."

Indeed, the biggest bass were so big their weight added as much to their width as to their length, and their mouths were huge.

Regan had been feeding them throughout the past nine years, and he vowed not to do that anymore. He said it looked now like one more example of why it's not good to interfere with natural processes.

"If I ever catch another bass out of there, it'll be wild and it'll have made it on its own!" Regan said this after pouring the last of the pulvarized limestone in front of the paddle wheel.

The size of the fish did not surprise him. He'd used the pond to practice fly fishing for years. He always used a barbless hook and threw back what he caught after examining it. He told friends that those fish were his pets, and his pained reaction to their deaths seemed to support that claim.

Regan had been excitable all morning. *Schooselich*, the Dutch called it. Having quit smoking made it especially hard to bear. At one point, he shouted, "Oh no! Where's my sunglasses? They must'a fell in the pond. Oh, nuts!"

Ruby was pointing at her eyes.

"Something wrong with your eyes, Honey?"

"No! Your G-L-A-S-S-E-S!"

"Oh, I've got them on," and he got right back to what he was doing, not seeing the humor in it. This was very uncharacteristic of Regan, who normally had a wonderful sense of humor.

After the last of the lime had been spread, the group sat on the shore on lawn chairs that Ruby hauled down along with a bunch of those tall, colorful, aluminum glasses and a big matching pitcher of iced tea.

Right then, Arsenic and Randy showed up, and Regan teased them about missing all the fun.

"*Vhere's Vallie?*" Arsenic inquired.

"He left as soon as the fish were loaded. They were already covered with flies, and Valentine said it was hard enough getting his workers to help with such a '*dreckig chop!*' Said he didn't want to risk losing his helpers."

Regan paused to laugh and cough, apparently regaining his sense of humor.

Arsenic mumbled, "*Dis chop could'a not bin more dreckig denn da von vee vass dune. Vee're both verschmutzed. 'Manury' ya know.*" And he wrinkled his nose.

Regan continued, "Vallie said if the fish were covered with maggots, he'd never be able to get the kids to do the work!"

Randy laughed at that and said, "Pop, you remember how Jacob Zimmermann handled the fly problem out on his farm?"

Arsenic laughed and nodded.

Randy continued, "There was this old guy lived on a farm

out near Dryville. We used to visit him when I was a teenager. He's not living anymore. Anyway, early in the summer, he'd dump a pile of dead carp out in a field some distance from his house and let the flies lay eggs on 'em.

"He'd let the maggots eat all the meat. They'd run out of food and start swarming, a big mass of maggots. We came to visit him one time at the end of this process."

Arsenic wrinkled his nose as he inserted, *"Dis is vonn'a dem sings ya got'ta see ta belief. Dees maggots vould'a fill't a vheelbarrah. An dey vass movin avay from da fish bones, hungry foah moah meat, like a bick livin octapus, oah sumthin like dat. Crawlin on top'a von anutter dey vass, like a bick, rollin, oozin monster! Aaaah, I vish I hat'n't seen it! It schticks in my head! Such a verschmutzung! Makes me kutz!"*

"What's *kutz* mean?" Ricky asked.

His Pop said, "In German, *kotzen* means vomit!"

"You mean re-gur-gitate," Ricky replied.

His Pop laughed, and noticing disgusted and disbelieving looks on all the faces, he continued, "It's true what Pop said. I've thought about it a lot. I honestly never dreamed that so many maggots could be in one place at one time.

"Anyway, Jacob had this big bag of rock salt, like you use to melt ice on your sidewalk in winter, and he throws hands-full of the stuff over the mass of maggots to kill them. They literally BOILED when he did that. A rolling boil! It just mixed the salt all through them, and right before our eyes, the pile got smaller as they started bursting and turning into water, I guess, and they soaked into the ground. You know how slugs die and disappear if you put salt on them!"

Rosa said, "Yuk! I don't know about you, Randy, but I never tortured slugs when I was a kid."

"No! It's not to torture them. I've read books that recommended killing them that way. Isn't that true Pop?"

Arsenic shook his head yes and said, *"Yah. Von off my books had'a footmark on dat supchect."*

"A what? Nevermind. Anyway, you all are getting me off the subject. Jacob claimed that by giving such a big bunch of flies a chance to reproduce in one spot, and then killing all the offspring while they were massed like that, he actually cut down on his fly population for the whole summer. You know what a big problem flies are on a farm."

After some discussion, everyone agreed that it seemed doubtful such a thing could actually reduce the fly population. They also said they'd never forget the description.

CHAPTER 7

Samuel Kunkel was the son of an auto mechanic. His father owned an automobile repair shop along the Pricetown Road. That's how he met Ricky and Beaner. Beaner had a malfunction in her scooter, and she and Ricky pushed it out to Kunkel's Garage for a repair.

The garage was located in an old stone quarry right off the berm of the road. The quarry was a big yellow and brown gouge in a steep hillside, and the big blue pole barn that was Kunkel's Garage stood toward the rear wall of the dig.

While the kids were pushing the scooter across the parking area in front of the repair shop, Samuel's dad was poised, with wrench in hand, next to a long green sports car with its hood open. It looked like an alligator was about to swallow him. Samuel, himself, was in the driver's seat turning the wheel to and fro, as he pretended to drive.

After Beaner explained the scooter problem, Samuel's dad said he'd look at it as soon as he finished the sports car which required a new headlight which he had to pick up at a parts store in Fleetwood. Samuel said, "Can we go along?" Apparently including Ricky and Beaner as though they were old friends. They got acquainted on the way to Fleetwood.

Samuel's friends called him Chicken-Wing, and so that was how he introduced himself. He was on the slim side with long arms.

In the course of their conversation, Chicken-Wing told Ricky and Beaner about a very big old tricycle his father had equipped with a lawn mower engine on the little step where a passenger used to be able to stand right behind the seat. It was belt driven. They could try it out after returning to the garage.

The auto parts store was located across the street from the train station. There was a Coke machine on the platform attached to the old station. As Chicken-Wing's dad paid for the headlight, he asked for extra quarters in change. The group headed toward the station platform to buy Cokes to drink. Then, they sat on the platform with their feet dangling over the edge. He gave a quarter to each kid to stick in the old-fashioned top-opening, chest-style Coke dispenser.

The Coke bottles were setting in cold water in the bottom of the chest, and you had to slide one by the cap along a track to a little locked hinge that would release when you dropped a quarter in the slot. Then, you could pull the bottle up past the hinge which clanked and relocked until you stuck in another quarter. You had to use the old towel hanging next to the chest to wipe off the bottle drenched with ice water. The customer did most of the work, and patience was required. The customers were in no hurry. Lots of acquaintances stopped by when they were in the neighborhood just to drink a coke and chat with whoever might be hanging out on the platform.

Four bottles were withdrawn before they sat and dangled their legs and talked.

A big old sign said Reading Railroad. Ricky told the group about the train yard up in the mountains.

Chicken-Wing's dad said this here railroad was a spur connecting Reading, Philadelphia, and Lehigh Valley. The Reading was once the largest corporation in the world.

"They used to make Cadillac cars right here in Fleetwood."

Ricky laughed and said his Pop Pop had told him that. He told again about his schoolmates in Indiana thinking the Reading Railroad existed only on the Monopoly Board. "They thought that's where the name came from."

Chicken-Wing's dad confirmed what Arsenic had told Ricky earlier. "The guy from Germantown who invented the Monopoly game borrowed the name of this local company for good reason. It represented the type of thing he wanted to show."

Indeed, it was 1935, the Depression was going on, a lot of people blamed the crash on cutthroat monetary games, banking, commerce, monopolies. Germantown was right between Reading and Philadelphia, right by the railroad line.

"Yeah!" Ricky said. "That's what Pop Pop said."

Before they returned to the garage, they gave their empty bottles to the station master and got a nickel for each.

When they got home, Mr. Kunkel commenced to work on the scooter. Every now and again, a truck or car roared by out on the road in front of the garage.

Chicken-Wing took the kids out back where they started the engine on his motorized tricycle by pulling a cord, and then they took turns riding circles in the parking area.

After awhile, they sat on some old tires at the edge of the parking lot.

Chicken-Wing told them about his two great uncles, *die groszonkel*. They lived together in an old log house at the foot of Mount Penn. He said his dad's uncles were lots of fun, and they lived right next to a trout stream that was guaranteed to yield a stringerful. They made arrangements for a future visit to this interesting place. Chicken-Wing said they could get there on back roads from his dad's garage.

About this time, Chicken-Wing's dad announced that Beaner's scooter was again functioning properly. He said the carburetor needed adjustment. Easy job. No charge.

Chicken-Wing's *groszonkels* were Billy and Harvey Kunkel. They were past middle age. They'd reached that age where the inner child reemerges, directed this time around by the wisdom of experience. Rather than working at life, they played at it. Chicken-Wing's dad called them *schpielerich*, which meant they fiddled around a lot. They were bachelors.

Up until two years ago, they lived with their father in the

house where they were born. Now, it was just the two of them. Pappy, as they called him, had a heart attack one bright summer morning just as the rooster crowed. The two brothers inherited the log house and Billy's woodshop.

Their mother had died during the birth of what would have been their younger brother, but the baby also died within a week of birth. Right there in the big log house.

Their father raised them under strange circumstances. He was a school teacher, although he had only nine years of education himself. He'd taught in a little one-room school only a mile from his home. After their mother died, Pappy's older sister moved into the house and took care of Billy and Harvey in the daytime for three years while Pappy was teaching. She was a good, loving substitute for a mother and actually babied them a little too much. Pappy also was very tender at home, and this contrasted greatly with his demeanor at school.

When Billy reached five years of age, and Harvey reached six, they started to attend their father's one-room school. Pappy wanted them to be in the same grade so they could help one another. Pappy's sister moved to Reading at this point to care for their mother.

The contrast between Pappy's at-home and at-school de-meanor is illustrated by one of the *groszonkels*' favorite stories about Pappy and his teaching.

As noted, Pappy was pretty tender at home, but it was standard for those Pennsylvania German one-room schools to have a gruff male teacher. There were eight grades in one room, and the building was often a mile or two from any home sites. The teacher was on his own. It took an authoritarian approach to keep things under control. The male teacher's authority was absolute, and there was no school board to interfere. Pappy learned to act tough pretty fast after he started teaching.

The brothers illustrated their Pappy's teaching approach by describing the way he would start each new school year. Whether this description was accurate or not no one ever knew. Other students didn't seem to talk about it much outside school. Billy and Harvey had kidded their dad about it, because they knew he was really a push-over.

Billy would start the oft-repeated story thus, "*Aftah everybotty's inside, on dat first day, ya know, Pappy shout's, 'SIT,' an Pappy had a big shout*!

"*Everybotty sits down qvick vith some endin up on da floor in eagerness to avoit da front off da room. Pappy gets dis all sorted ought, an tells'em nauw dat's deir seat foah da rest off da yeah. Den he schtarts talkin bought hauw learnin, takes concentration. He used the vert fe'staunden, vhich means understanding. He said he wanted alvays aufmerksamkeit, vhich means attention. He schpoke half Deitsch and half English, as did da kits. Anyvays. he tells'em everybotty needed ta be qviet and pay'tension.*"

Then, Harvey would pick up the story.

"*Pappy's talkin from beheint his desk all along, which is up on a little platform. Venn he gets ta da topic off troublemakers, he says ta rememper alvays dat he's in charch, an he points ought a big block a voot mounted between da winders off ta da side'a vhere he's sittin. It's a voot plaque, hung on da vall, an's got da immich off Chorch Vashington carved in it. Da olt kits knew vott's comin here, so dey vatch da young vons ta see deir reaction.*

"*Nauw Pappy opens da drawer on his desk an pulls ought a little twenty-two calipre revolver an takes aim at old Chorch an fires off von shot, vhich hits Chorch schmack-center in da eye.*

"*Everybotty chumps venn da little gun goes off.*

"*Pappy says, 'O.k. Chust vonn'a schtay in practice. Let's get schtarted on da lessons nauw!'*

"*Everybotty's sittin schtraight-up like schtatues, and da olt kits're tryin ta keep from laughin cause da young vons chumped so much venn da gun vent off.*

"*Pappy nauw talks bought hauw da lessons vill be run each day an so forth.*

"*He nevah hatt much truple from any kits aftah dat first day.*

"He vass tough at schule, but he vassn't mean at home. Nevah.
He vass chenerally happy as a wet hen."

And then finally, Billy would end the story.

"His aim vass perfect. Right in da eye, yeah aftah yeah.
Nevah missed. Dat's hauw come Harvey dere's such a gute shot.
Pappy learned him. Every summah Pappy had' a fill in ole Chorch's
eye vith putty so as ta get ready foah da next schule yeah, an so as ta
give da bullet a place ta schtick vhen he repeated his act da cummin
yeah."

Billy always praised their Pappy's teaching. He said they learned well their *lesen, schreiben, und rechnen*, or as Harvey phrased it, *readink, writink, an rithmetic.*

But education in those old one-room schools only went on for eight years. When a kid was ready for ninth grade, he either quit or went to one of the big borough schools. Pappy insisted that Billy and Harvey try this, but both dropped out after a month.

They both spoke a mixture of English and Pennsylvania Dutch, or Deitsch, and their English was heavily accented. Also, Harvey had a habit of making up his own words. For example, he called a lot of the city folk that he encountered, *shucksters*. This word he seemed to construct from a combination of s*hyster* and *huckster*. *Shucksters*, not a bad description of a lot of city folk.The other students called the brothers the "DD's," meaning "Dumb Dutchmen." They had several fights over this, as well as enduring numerous other insults, and then they dropped out of school and stayed home.

The brothers were deeply disillusioned by their high school experience as were many of the early Pennsylvania Dutch. They expected rural decency and compassion but frequently encountered cruelty and coldness in "the big city."

The disposition of both had originally been toward good-natured optimism. But neither quite got over the discovery of petty selfishness and malice in the world outside their backyard. Billy became indignant, idealistic, and dogmatic, and he talked of what should be rather than what was. He was forevermore easily affronted.

Harvey simply became terminally disenchanted. He went out very little, and he was shy.

Thus, except for one attempt to leave the area, both brothers grew old in the company of Pappy in the old log house. And then Pappy was gone.

Billy was the more adventuresome of the two. He was sixty-three years old and looked like Gabby Hayes, the old sidekick of Roy Rogers, the cowboy movie star. His unkempt gray beard stuck out in all directions and blended in with the matching tufts of gray hair that stuck out in all directions from under his red crackeled leather ball cap. He was what Harvey called the household's "bread-earner." He made money by selling his woodcrafts and by digging graves at a nearby cemetery.

When they were still in school, both kids tried their hand at earning money, but Pappy put a stop to the project. They had started to run a trapline before going to school in the morning. The problem was that one or the other of them would periodically show up at the schoolhouse smelling like a skunk. A few drops of that stuff sure can permeate a one-room schoolhouse. Anyway, Pappy put a stop to the enterprise.

Billy drove a car that his brother called an old flivver, but Billy thought it was beautiful. It was a 1940 Ford. Classic car enthusiasts were always trying to buy Billy's car from him, but it was his first car, he said, and it would be his last. He kept the black coupe polished with a shiny coat of wax and only drove it over to the church when there was a grave to dig or to a grocery store located in a little valley town about four miles down from the house.

Only once in his life had he tried to move away from the Oley Hills. He wanted to move to Pittsburgh to get a job in the steel mills. He had a cousin there who would help him get started. He was eighteen years old. He drove his new car on the newly completed Pennsylvania Turnpike, but he never made it to Pittsburgh. His experiences on this trip made him turn back and never move away from home again.

The turnpike originally followed the bed of an unfinished

railroad. In the 1880's, the South Penn Railroad Company made considerable progress constructing a line from Harrisburg to Pittsburgh and then in 1885 the project was abandoned. It just sat there for fifty years. Partially completed tunnels, roadbeds, and bridges. Then, in 1934 President Roosevelt was convinced to use part of the roadbed as the basis for a four-lane highway.

This was the Depression Era, and Roosevelt was seeking public projects to put the poor back to work. He spared no expense to make the project elaborate enough to employ many people. This was to be the model for the nation's interstate highway system. The road was to have no crossings of any kind, no stop signs or street lights, no sharp curves or steep grades, bridges over all the gullies and cuts, and tunnels through all the mountains, a wide strip of lawn separating double lanes of oncoming traffic, and lots of space to pull off to the side when necessary. There were plenty of tables and benches in nice tree-studded picnic areas evenly spaced along the roadway, and there would be ten fine service plazas with very fancy restaurants. It opened in 1940, just in time for Billy to drive to Pittsburgh.

The trip went bad right off.

Firstly, there was no speed limit when Billy used the turnpike. Human behavior soon demonstrated the need for one, but the fact that it was then set at seventy miles per hour gives one a general idea of how fast cars were traveling before the limit. Pretty fast for old 1940's cars and trucks with suspension systems that could sway side to side if you turned the steering wheel too quickly. Billy wasn't used to driving so fast.

The second of the trials and tribulations associated with this trip concerned the fact that the highway had a lot of tunnels that were poorly lighted when Billy took his trip. There were so many tunnels that many called the Turnpike the tunnel highway. The road would narrow from four lanes down to two as it approached each tunnel. Some of these were nearly a mile long, and they had to have ventilation fans to keep carbon monoxide fumes from asphyxiating the travelers. Billy thought, "Lord if you had an accident in here, you'd ricochet wall to wall, down the shoot, and out the end."

Thirdly, there was an unexpectedly large volume of traffic on the road when it opened, in part because it was an amazing feat of engineering that tempted people to use it just to see it. An average of six thousand vehicles a day poured onto the new highway which cut the trip from Pittsburgh to Harrisburg from five and a half down to two and a half hours. Then, one day an astounding twenty-seven thousand vehicles used the turnpike. Billy happened to be one of these. The tie-ups weren't untied until the following day. Billy sat for a long time in a line that was five miles long. Then, he pulled off to the side and slept in his car next to the highway. The following morning he got off as soon as possible and headed back to Reading.

The final of his trials and tribulations occurred as Billy was returning to Reading. There were two tunnels practically on top of one another with a narrow valley between. He went flying into the first one, the Kittatinny Mountain Tunnel, and two thirds of the way in, he had a blowout on a tire.

Good luck was on his side, as momentum carried him out into the notch or canyon between the Kittatinny Mountain and the Blue Mountain Tunnels, and he managed to get stopped off on the edge of the road, in the narrow canyon between the tunnels, rather than in the middle of one of them. With traffic screaming by him, he got the tire changed. He was shaking so badly he had to wait half an hour before resuming his travels. Anyway, he stayed near home after that.

Billy Kunkel's brother, Harvey, was sixty-four years old, clean-shaven and painfully fussy. He was shy until he got to know you. He was skinny when compared to Billy and hard of hearing, which he denied. Billy frequently tried to talk him into getting his hearing tested, so that he might be fitted with a hearing aid, but

Harvey didn't want to leave home to be examined. Chicken-Wing's father had a rare photo of him at a family picnic. He was sitting in a group, and if you looked close you could see that he had his right hand cupped behind his ear and was shouting something to the guy next to him, probably "Huh?" or "*What'cha say?*"

Harvey was a slow-thinker. This did not stem from low intelligence. He was very intelligent. His was the dedicated slowness of a person who identifies with slowness. He was proud of it. He saw it as careful and honest. It was just who he was. He was the more domestic of the two brothers. He kept house for the pair and cooked the meals and saw to it that the brothers always had immaculately clean bib overalls carefully patched whenever necessary.

Harvey's cooking was superb. The only problem for Billy was that Harvey had a tendency to shoot animals off the back porch and assimilate them into his dishes. He also prowled the banks of the stream behind the house with rod and gun looking for aquatic sources of food. Billy wasn't always certain what meat was in the evening's main dish. Billy said the components of Harvey's recipes were anonymous.

"*Vhere'd ya get seafood?*"

"*Oh, there and here.*"

The meals were really good, and so Billy said he "*tried not much to think on it.*"

Harvey had a habit of talking in clichés and peppering his speech with folksy sayings and proverbs. The problem was that he mixed his metaphors and used phrases out of context. Thus, he might say he had "too many cooks in the fire" instead of "too many irons in the fire."

He often tried to emphasize his planfulness and preparedness by quoting the German, *Ein Griff zur rechten Zeit spart viel Müh und Leid*, which essentially means, "A stitch in time saves nine." However, Harvey might translate it as, "A stitch in time is worth two in the bush."

Or he might try to quote the German, *Müssiggang ist aller*

Laster Anfang, which means, "An idle mind is the devil's workshop," but Harvey would end up saying something like, "The devil's mind is an idle workshop."

This sort of thing generally confused his listeners, who often tried to correct him. Since he was hard of hearing, the listener's comments typically muddied the waters even further, additionally confusing both Harvey and themselves.

Harvey was *hochmootich* where his flowers were concerned. He had a big garden and flower bed between the house and Billy's woodshop.

In most things, he was extremely attentive to detail, except in speech habits. Billy's father used a word to describe his son's attention to detail. Most Deitsch people in the area didn't use it anymore. The word was *umständlich*.

Proof the trait was part of Harvey's character resided in his use of whitewash. It is not so unusual that every spring, like clockwork, Harvey gave a bright new coat of whitewash to all the fences around the house and yard. But surprisingly, he also whitewashed the outhouse, the stepping stones of the walkways, and most surprisingly, the clay that filled the chinks between the dark brown, almost black, logs in all of the walls of the log house.

Passersby on the road in front of the house would sometimes stop their cars and photograph the idyllic setting featuring the big log house with whitewashed chinking and the swiss chalet workshop on the other side of the flower bed, with all the whitewashed fences, walkways, and lovely yard-art windmills, small playhouses, and such, installed by Billy.

Billy wasn't quite so meticulous as Harvey and a bit more creative. His woodworking crafts were really folk art. He designed his own articles, and his handicraft was known all around Reading. People from all over the area would come shopping on weekends.

Sometimes they'd supply a design for cabinetry or yard-art, but most times they'd simply select a finished item off the shelves in Billy's well-equipped woodshop which stood separate from the log house and was painted and trimmed just like a little Swiss chalet.

In wintertime, neighborhood men frequently gathered after lunch in front of the big iron wood stove in the center of Billy's woodshop to drink coffee and talk. Some of them also whittled little works of art during the meetings, using scrap from Billy's wood working and special pieces of wood saved just for carving. Harvey tended to avoid these gatherings.

Billy gave the visitors advice on how to whittle with a pocketknife, and this often led to a round of knife swapping. The favorites seemed to be Remington and Case whittlers and the old Russell barlow knife, either the small model or the big granddaddy barlow.

Billy kept a special supply of wood in his shop just for fancy carving. This was used when his friends wanted to do more than just whittle.

For fancy carving, Billy preferred the soft, creamy wood from the linden tree, called basswood. It was strong but light in weight and, according to Billy, as easy to carve as a piece of cheese. Some carvers prefer butternut or eastern white pine, but Billy liked basswood.

He noted that Native Americans carved it and also used the bark for cords, ropes, rugs, and bags. Also, it was used throughout history to make musical instruments, figureheads for the bows of ships, and cigar store Indians.

Billy sometimes found natural sources of basswood. If he found a linden tree, he left it intact but pruned some lower limbs or diseased limbs to dry at home before cutting them into small oblong blocks for sculpting.

He was good at finding the tree itself. He said the linden is straight, with smooth bark, and floppy heart-shaped dark green leaves having toothy edges. He said he identified the trees in spring by their red-tinted twigs that resembled coral and by their greenish sweet-smelling flowers that could be scented from a mile away. Billy said these flowers help bees make a high grade of honey. In the fall their leaves retain a distinctive golden yellow color long after most other trees are naked. He could give a long lecture on the linden tree.

Anyway, Billy liked basswood, and he taught some of the more advanced whittlers to carve it. He'd have them draw an outline of a figure on the side of a block, a figure they intended to carve. Then, he'd cut away, or "block out" as he called it, the unneeded wood, front and back, with a jigsaw. Sometimes he'd even ask for a profile on the front of the piece so that he could "block out" bits of the sides of the figure as well. This gave the carvers a big headstart and kept them from getting frustrated while they were learning. The carver had to add all the detail, and that was enough of a challenge in the early stages of learning.

Billy himself was so proficient at carving that he would go right at a block with a whittling knife and *aufdecken die statue* as he described it, uncovering the shape that he claimed to be already hiding inside the block of wood.

In time, the kids started stopping by Billy's workshop when they came over to fish. Ricky loved to watch the old men carve figurines in front of Billy's wood stove. After a few visits, he brought along his own whittler pocketknife that his Uncle Regan had bought for him, and he learned many sculpting tricks from the old men gathered around the stove.

Beaner was more interested in Billy's power tools. He helped her make a neat napkin holder to give her mother as a birthday present.

A freestone stream, Harvey called it a *sandstein fluss*, flowed right behind the Kunkel brothers' house and woodshop. It was clear, cold, spring-fed, and it was full of beautifully-colored descendants of the native Pennsylvania Brook Trout. These fish have roots in the long-ago time when glaciers came down from the north and invaded the eastern and western corners of the state.

The stream continued down to one of the reservoirs that supplied water to the city of Reading. The Brookies in that reservoir were huge. The ones behind the house were much smaller but much more colorful and lively. Their backs were dark green with bright yellow spots, and their bellies were bright orange, and they fought like they were from the netherworld. This is what motivated Chicken-Wing, Ricky, and Beaner to regularly visit the Kunkels, but it led to a whole host of other activities.

The first time the kids came over to the Kunkel's to fish, Harvey, who loved to catch fish himself for use in his cooking, warned them not to step on the *ausgräber wespennest*. He said it was next to the path down to the creek. When the kids asked him to translate, it turned out the Deitsch words meant "digger wasp nest." That required more discussion, and Beaner figured out he was talking about yellow jackets. They nest in burrows they dig in the ground.

Harvey said he warned Billy about the nest, but his brother stepped on it anyway, just a few days ago, and he got stung as a result. Harvey said Billy was distracted a lot. He had stepped on the nest because he was angry about the property tax bill they had just received. He wasn't paying attention to where he was stepping.

Harvey added, *"Vith Billy, if it ain't one thing, it's another. He's such a wino!"*

"Billy's a drunk?" Beaner asked with a surprised look on her face.

"Nah, nah, Billy ain't no drunk! Vhere'd ya get dat ideah?

"You just said he's a wino."

"Yah. He wines all'a time. 'Dis is wrong, an dat is wrong!' Like I sett, if it ain't one thing, it's another."

"You mean he whines a lot?"

"Yah. Dat's vott I sett. An ya can't tell him nothin. He knows

it all. Yah vell," he added. "*Ya can lead a horse ta water, but ya can't make him eat.*"

"You mean drink!" Beaner said.

"*Vott?*" Harvey asked.

"You can't make him drink!"

"*You schtill talkin bought Billy be'an a drunk?*"

"No! You were saying that . . . oh never mind."

"*Me an him nevah coult see toe to toe!*"

"Eye to eye," Beaner replied.

"*Vott?*"

"Nothing! Nevermind! Come on guys. Let's go fishing, before I go nuts."

As they turned to walk away, Harvey continued, "*Billy's such a slop. Messy, ya know vott I mean. Pappy sett Mum vass da same vay, an ya know vott dey say, da nut doan fall far from da tree!*"

Beaner looked over her shoulder and said, "That's the apple, not the nut."

"*Vott? Oh. Yah, da apple. Ya got bait?*" Harvey asked.

"Yep!" Ricky said as he stopped and turned to answer. "Beaner's got artificial flies."

Harvey kept talking as the kids started toward the creek. He was still thinking about the importance of being prepared to fish as he said, "*Ya got'ta cross yoah i's an dot yoah t's. Don't write before yoah pencil's sharpened!*"

"Now that I understood!" Beaner yelled back over her shoulder.

"*Vott?*"

"Never mind!"

On their way down to the stream they found the wasp nest, but it was dug up, and papery cellular structures were strewn all about.

Beaner pointed it out. "The yellow jacket nest! A raccoon must've dug it up. I've seen that before. A coon'll go after a yellow jacket nest like a bear digging into a honey tree."

Chicken-Wing said, "So he was after the honey."

"No," Beaner continued. "Harvey was right when he called them wasps. Bees make honey. Wasps don't. Wasps kill other insects to feed to their babies. I study insects."

Chicken-Wing protested, "You said those were honey combs."

And Ricky inserted, "She said LIKE a bear going after honey!"

"Yeah," Beaner continued. "Those are the little cells where the babies grow, but the grown-ups feed the babies insects that they catch and carry back to the nest. The raccoons go after the baby yellow jackets in those cells. There's no honey. I could never figure out how the coons can stand the stings of the grown-up wasps. I was out walking one day and accidently stepped on a yellow jacket nest. I ran like blazes cause the stings hurt like blazes."

Ricky added, "Beaner likes insects. That's why she wants to fish with artificial flies."

"Are we gonna fish or talk?" Chicken-Wing said.

They headed toward the creek, and Ricky was laughing as he added, "We can tell Harvey he doesn't have to worry about the *Ausgräber Wespen* anymore, or whatever he called them!"

As they were tying artificial flies on their lines, a butterfly flew up and sat on Chicken-Wing's rod for a second. He drew attention to it. Beaner said, "I was reading this story about a little girl who discovered that butterflies are really angels, the spirits of your friends and relatives that have died. They come back to visit you as butterflies."

Chicken Wing said, "I don't believe that."

"It was fiction," Beaner said.

"I still don't believe it."

"It was a novel. Fiction!"

"I don't care. I don't believe it!"

"You are definitely related to Harvey."

"What's that supposed to mean?"

"Never mind."

Ricky was laughing as he said, "Come on, let's fish."

On that first visit, as on virtually every one thereafter, they caught a creel full of trout. Actually, the kids didn't have a real creel. Ricky had made a substitute out of a big old wicker purse that his Gammy gave him before her death. For that matter, they didn't have real fly rods either. They fashioned usable substitutes out of light flexible pieces of bamboo. They taped on eyes made from bobby pins. They didn't have reels but just left the excess line coil up at their feet when they were pulling in a fish. They even made the artificial flies, with a hook and some thread and some chicken feathers. Of course, they had to buy hooks at the store, and also fly line. A good slippery, weighted piece of fly line can make even a simple bamboo branch into a usable fly rod, but you can't fabricate that homespun.

One day the kids walked a little way downstream and came onto the beginnings of a natural dam. A log had fallen across the creek and wedged between the shores, and leaf litter and mud built up under it, and now some of the water was flowing over top of the log, like a little waterfall. At present, it wasn't much more than a break, a little riffle, but the kids saw potential in it.

Chicken-Wing said, "Let's help it along." And with that they started to help mother nature build a dam. They hauled more sticks and leaf litter and mud over and tossed it on the upstream side. It washed into the breach and started to block the remaining gaps.

Later, Harvey walked down to see how the fishing was going. He got swept up into the dam-building project. He was stronger than the kids, in spite of his age, and he drug over some larger logs and even went back and got a shovel so he could toss more earth in. Then, he hauled a few large rocks over and tossed them on top of the earthwork to hold it solid.

Harvey urged them on to greater efforts, like a cheerleader. At one point, they were struggling to roll a big rock, and he shouted, "*Vee got'ta put more 'umpf' inta it!*"

As the backwater continued to build, the kids had the beginnings of a good fishing hole.

One time Chicken-Wing dared the others to jump in, and they all did. One, two, three. It became a swimming hole. The kids started wearing swimming suits under their clothes when they came to visit. Harvey swam with them one time, but he did it in his long underwear, and the kids laughed.

One day they all layed in the sun to dry off, and Chicken-Wing fell asleep. Ricky and Beaner stared at the clouds and daydreamed. Ricky imagined a story about dam building. Beaner imagined a watercolor with their little pond at the center. It was just daydreaming, but later both would have opportunities to put their fantasies down on paper and canvas. It would be part of their therapy.

In addition to their visits with the Kunkel brothers, Ricky, Beaner, and Chicken-Wing started to hang around with an older boy who had his driver's license and a car. His name was Johnny Lehmann.

The relationship started when Johnny discovered that Ricky was interested in wildlife and the outdoors. They discussed the subject at school and started to go fishing and hunting together. Since Ricky had lived in Indiana for several years, he didn't know where the good spots were in Pennsylvania. Also, Johnny's driver's license and car were definite perks.

Ricky and Beaner had become sort of an item in the junior high gossip mill, and so Beaner just naturally became friends with Johnny too. Beaner didn't hunt, but she loved to fish. Chicken-Wing went along sometimes, but mostly it was just Johnny, Ricky, and Beaner.

Johnny knew the location of an old open-pit mine abandoned since about 1910. Ricky's grandfather was born in 1913, so this was a very old mine. It was in the middle of a dense woodland. If you hiked through the woods and came upon it, all you would see is a big hill overgrown with trees. No matter what direction you came from, it just looked like a mound with a flat top, and chances were you'd walk around it rather than try to hike up the steep sides covered with brush. The only clue that something was up there was the absence of trees on top, not obvious from down at the base. You couldn't see the lake in the center unless you climbed up and looked over the lip of the embankment. Then, you'd see a big crater filled with water.

So the "mine hole," as the locals called it, was well camouflaged. There was a steep drop-off from the lip down to the edge of a body of water the size of a soccer field. It looked like the crater in a little volcano, but it was shaped more like a horseshoe.

The bank of the lake was an oblique angle straight down into the water. An abyss. A black hole. The mine hole.

No one seemed to know what they had mined down there, or how deep it was, or whether there were tunnels going off in different directions down in the blackness. It was generally a mystery, but those few who knew of its existence also knew that it was full of fish and frogs.

Johnny and Beaner did most of the fishing. Ricky generally brought along his expensive air rifle to shoot bullfrogs along the shores. Ricky took the bullfrogs home to eat. His Dad loved frog's legs and was happy to help clean them. He thought Ricky shot them down by the stream in the pasture in front of the barn. Ricky did shoot some down there from time to time, but his Dad didn't know anything about the mine hole and would have forbade him to go there if he'd known the layout. Ricky suspected this, and so he hadn't mentioned the place.

You couldn't walk along the shore. The banks were too steep. The only way to get down to the water's edge was by sliding the steep bank on your backside, and if you weren't careful, you could slip right down into the underworld. No one dared swim there for fear that they wouldn't be able to crawl back out of the water. Once you got to the edge to fish, you had to get a good purchase with your feet and stand still.

Shooting frogs was another matter. People think frogs are stupid, but they're not. You had to peek over the lip of the crater and shoot at them from way up around the edge. If you tried to get closer, they'd see you right off and dive into the depths. Sometimes you'd just peep over the fringe, and a frog would see you from fifty feet away. Then, he'd go "brrrrp," jump in, and spook the others in the area.

So anyway, you had to shoot from more than fifty feet, a long shot for an air rifle, but Ricky had a good air rifle. His Uncle Regan had given it to him as a Christmas gift. It even had a telescopic sight.

Ricky would leave the frogs he'd killed lie in place until he was ready to move to a new location. Then, he'd crawl down and gather them up. If he tried to go down and pick them up as he hit them, all the others in the area would jump in and disappear. He hit them in the head, and they died instantly and stayed lying until he crawled down to pick them up before moving on. Anyway, he had to really stalk them. Ricky's Pop Pop called such stalking pantherish, and Ricky could be really pantherish.

The kids would split up and each go their own way for awhile so that Ricky could hunt by himself. They'd meet toward lunchtime, start a little fire, and eat while they parleyed to tell stories of how many and how big and the ones that got away. Sometimes they took a sack lunch, and sometimes they'd cook up some of the fresh fish and frog legs.

While Ricky's and Beaner's relationship with Chicken-Wing and his *groszonkels*, Billy and Harvey Kunkel, were harmless fun, the one with the older boy, Johnny Lehmann, turned out to have a disastrous conclusion.

CHAPTER 8

Randy was up early in the morning, packing his truck and hooking up the horse trailer for a trip to Kentucky. He'd arranged a loan, with his Pop as cosigner, to purchase six American Quarter Horse colts to train on the farm. He was going to meet a friend named Pete Keggereis at the Reading Turnpike entrance. His friend also had a horse trailer, and if Randy hauled two horses and his friend hauled four, they could bring them all back to the farm in one caravanned trip. Pete's trailer didn't have sleeping accommodations, but Randy's did, and so they were going to double up and sleep in Randy's while in Kentucky.

As Randy was getting behind the wheel of the truck, Arsenic said, "*Ya be careful ought dere on dem bick roats. Doan go so fast vith dat trailer.*"

"I had the whole rig checked over at Kunkel's garage. It's in tip-top shape."

"*Schtill.*"

"I'll be careful." And after giving Ricky a hug, he started the truck and headed for the highway.

The trip out went smoothly except for two blowouts on Pete's trailer. They stopped for dinner in a little town in western Ohio, and Pete ran over some lumber that had fallen from another vehicle. Randy wasn't involved. Pete was leading off, and so Randy swerved when he saw what was happening ahead, and luckily, they were moving at only thirty-five miles per hour near the restaurant. A piece of two-by-four splintered as it was drawn up between the two in-line wheels on the right side of Pete's trailer. It blew out both tires. They spent the night in the parking area of a local garage, sleeping in Randy's trailer. When the mechanic opened in the morning, they had him replace the tires. This was an unexpected expense for Randy. Since Pete was just doing him a favor, Randy had made a commitment to pay all expenses.

Anyway, when they got to Kentucky, they lived out of Randy's trailer while negotiating with the horse trader. Then, had a safe return to Pennsylvania. Randy purchased five horses. Since he had room for six, he bought a mule from the trader's neighbor, a decision he would later come to regret. That mule would prove to be a big problem. In addition, Randy's son was going to head into a serious misadventure, and so Randy's life was about to become very complicated.

Two weeks after Randy's return from Indiana, Johnny, Ricky, and Beaner were on their way home from a Saturday at the minehole when they went to Pricetown for ice cream. There was an ice cream parlor in Pricetown right at the crossroads where the road from Fleetwood to Oley crossed the road from Reading to New Jerusalem. The Pricetown Road mostly ran along high ground from Reading to New Jerusalem. If you were headed toward New Jerusalem from Reading, and you turned left at the crossroads in Pricetown, where the ice cream parlor was located, you'd end up on a steep downgrade roller coaster ride into Fleetwood. If you turned right, you'd end up on a similar ride into Oley.

When Randy was a kid going on bicycle rides with his friends, Pricetown was a big decision point. You had a choice of two joy rides, one into Oley or one into Fleetwood, or a tame straightaway out-and-back ride toward New Jerusalem. If you took either joy ride, you had to pedal back up the mountain, or push back up is the more accurate description.

The ice cream parlor in Pricetown had curb service. The waitress came to your car on roller skates. It wouldn't be too long before the curb service stopped and cold weather began.

Johnny, Ricky, and Beaner were finishing up and the waitress handed the kids their change and was taking the tray off the window, when Johnny spotted his girlfriend riding as a passenger in a car owned by one of his old rivals, Bernie Hess, otherwise known as Slick. His girlfriend was sitting in the middle of the front seat with her arm around Slick when they pulled up to the stoplight, about to head down into Oley.

As the other car stopped at the crossroads, and then moved on, Johnny bristled. He backed his car out of the space so fast that tires squealed, gravel flew, and the waitress flailed wildly trying to keep her balance on her roller skates. She yelled a string of disparaging remarks.

Johnny intended to follow Slick and his heartthrob, for what purpose, he himself did not know. He was definitely angry. Slick was traveling fast, and by the time Johnny got his car facing in the right direction, on the road to Oley, Slick had a big headstart. Johnny roared up to the blinking red stoplight and then squealed away in the direction Slick and his girlfriend were headed, down the mountain toward Oley.

Johnny's partially rebuilt '53 Ford had a big V-8 engine substituted for the original six-cylinder, but it still had the original old suspension system. With a steep downhill grade aiding acceleration, Johnny, Ricky, and Beaner were soon traveling at sixty miles per hour. The car started to float a bit, rather than hugging the road.

The highway went downhill and then flattened out through a section of forest before it headed down another steeper and longer incline into the borough of Oley. On the flat space before the second downhill grade, the highway curved through the trees first to the left, then to the right, and then straightaway down the second grade into Oley. Water running downhill during rain storms had washed out the gravel at the right edge of the asphalt where the road curved left.

Momentum forced Johnny to take the curve a little wide, and his right front tire slipped off the edge of the pavement. The drop-off wasn't more than three inches, but when the tire slipped off, Johnny made the common mistake of trying to correct too quickly, especially with a car having soft suspension. He jerked the steering wheel to the left to get the car back on the pavement. It was already leaning to the right because of the curve, and the right front wheel popped too quickly back onto the pavement, at the same time the rear wheel fell off, and the car started turning sideways.

As the front-end of the Ford veered toward the center line, the whole car suddenly flipped over and slid along on its roof, staying nicely on the highway, upside down at close to sixty miles per hour. Gravel lying in the road was scooped into the openings left in the car when the windows shattered. It went flying through the car like bullets from a machine gun. For the rest of their lives, the survivors would remember the sound of that gravel and the scraping, scooping sound of the roof sliding on the road like a snow plow.

Ricky and Beaner were floating around inside like weightless astronauts. Johnny stayed pretty much in place, having slipped beneath the steering wheel.

On that short straightaway between where the road turned left and then right the car flew perfectly down the center of the road for seventy-five yards, but the trajectory carried it into the woods as the highway turned back to the right. The topside of the hood, now on the bottom, hit a stump, and the rear end of the car rose in the air and passed over the front, as it turned end over end into the trees.

Both Ricky and Beaner were knocked unconscious sometime after the initial flip of the car onto its roof, yet both would eventually remember the brief sensation of weightlessness, the grating sound of the roof on the pavement, and the gravel shooting through the car. They ended up in the trunk which remained intact like a little space capsule. When all motion stopped, it was quiet as a cave.

The two kids started moaning at about the same time, but they could move. As awareness returned, each inquired about the condition of the other. They would learn later that, in addition to extensive muscular bruising and skin abrasions, Ricky's left wrist was broken and Beaner had a broken collar bone. That was not bad considering the savagery of the crash. The psychological injuries would take longer to heal.

When they started calling to Johnny, the silence was deafening. Crawling out of their capsule, one at a time, each paused momentarily to stare at the form impossibly squeezed into the collapsed space between the dashboard and floor. Instinct told them Johnny was dead, but each shut off interpretation as the realization struck, and they continued crawling toward the only remaining exit, one of the side windows that hadn't totally collapsed. The image of Johnny's body squeezed beneath that steering wheel would remain with them the rest of their lives.

When they were back on firm ground and had regained their equilibrium, Ricky said in a subdued voice, "There's a house back there a couple hundred yards, in the woods. Let's call for help, get an ambulance."

Beaner nodded, and that was the only communication between them. They started walking, a bit bent over and wobbly due to injury. There were no other cars around. Silence. Not even a bird singing.

The residents of the house were home, but they hadn't heard the crash and were surprised by the two bruised and bloody kids at the door. They took care of the phone calls while Ricky and Beaner sat silently at the kitchen table, both near shock.

Two tastelessly conspicuous Cadillac ambulances arrived from two separate volunteer fire companies. The kids rode in one that left immediately for the hospital. The other waited while the EMTs and volunteer firemen worked on extracting Johnny's body from the wreckage.

The two kids were admitted to adjoining hospital rooms, but they never visited one another. They were covered with deep contusions and abrasions, and once they laid in bed, neither could move without extreme pain. The medical team kept them under observation in the hospital for three days while they were extensively examined and x-rayed. By the end of that time, the only confirmed physical injuries, other than the numerous ones to soft tissue, were Ricky's broken left wrist and Beaner's broken collar bone.

While Ricky was being admitted to the hospital, one of the EMTs, a friend of Randy, called the boy's father to tell him about the accident. Randy called Beaner's parents. Within an hour, family and friends were converging on the hospital.

From the waiting room, Randy telephoned his ex-wife, Ricky's mother, Stella. She was working as an accountant in Los Angeles. The news unhinged her for awhile, but Randy kept reassuring her that Ricky's injuries were relatively minor.

She hung up, called her travel agent, and then called Randy back on the phone at the nurses' station. Randy agreed to pick her up at the Reading airport.

The following day there were a few moments of tension when Sabrina and Stella entered Ricky's room at the same time. James and Rosa and Arsenic had come in while Randy was on the phone in the hall. Arsenic eased the tension by talking to both Stella and Sabrina as though their being there together was as natural as could be. Anyway, they were all focused on Ricky's injuries.

Ruby and Regan were there to help reduce the edginess. Ruby was pretty far along in her pregnancy, and Regan suggested she stay home, but Ruby said she'd be less stressed by the whole thing if she was able to talk to Ricky and try to be helpful. The pregnancy had been going smoothly and so Regan agreed.

Ricky didn't seem very responsive, but as he told them at a later time, their presence in the hospital reminded him that he was still alive, and that he had a past life to remember and a future one to anticipate.

The physician in charge was convinced both Ricky and Beaner had suffered mild concussions, but they seemed sufficiently recovered by the end of the three-day observation period and were released from the hospital. The psychological injuries were another matter, and that was how everyone came to appreciate the special skills of the woman who called herself "Mountain Mary."

⁀ ❄ ⁀

Ricky and Beaner were very quiet in the days following their return home. The parents of each kid suggested that it would be good to talk over the accident, but neither wanted to do so, and both remained in or near their beds much of the time. Neither wanted to return to school.

Stella had to return to Los Angeles, but before she left she was able to convince Ricky that it would be best to go back to school and try to resume a normal life. Since the accident had received considerable coverage in the local newspapers, Ricky was concerned about the perceptions and reactions of the teachers and other students. Randy and Stella dealt with that issue in their discussions with the boy, but Ricky was still embarrassed.

At first it was assumed that physical effects of concussion and shock were slow to heal, but as time passed, it became obvious that the lingering problems were more of the heart-searching variety. The families of the two kids put their heads together and discovered that neither youth had shed a tear as far as they could tell. That seemed unnatural. Both kids had missed Johnny's funeral.

One evening while Randy was out at the barn and Ricky was sitting in the front room by himself, Arsenic went in and sat with the boy. Ricky seemed to be in a daze. After sitting silently for awhile, Arsenic asked him whether he had anything he wanted to discuss.

At first, he thought Ricky hadn't heard him, but finally he got a response, "When Gammy died, you said you believe that when people die their spirits live on."

Arsenic said, "*Natürlich! You voult be thinkin bought dat, ain't?*

"*I can't say as anybotty got a right answer. If anybotty found ought vott happens venn ya die, dat person can't talk bought it no-moah, to tell us hauw it vent, ya know.*

"*I think vott answers vee got are like schtories, and some-*

times von's good as a'nutter. I like dat von bought da schpirit livin on cause I vonn'a talk ta Gammy. In my head, ya know?"

After waiting for a response from Ricky, but getting none, he continued, *"Dere's a'nutter vay a lookin at it. A'nutter schtory, ya might say. Schpendin life on a farm, an in da voots an fields, vatchin plants an animals grow, ya see dat venn dey die, dey become part off utter plants and animals. Like venn a hawk eats a rabbit. Or a momma horse has a colt an maybe da momma dies but da colt lives on. Da momma's part'a da colt, even though she ain't alife nomoah. Enerchy in von life goes on in a'nutter, ya know. Life goes on.*

"I think life's like a river oah a schtream, an vee're part off it, in da middle off it, an vee don't know vhere it comes from or vhere it goes. You an me an Peach an Chohnny alvays bin. Alvays vill be. You an me an Peach an Chohnny got a chance ta schtand up an look rount at da whole off da schtream an say, 'Huh! Dis is interestin!' But nauw Peach and Chohnny sat back dahn, dey're part'a da whole again, an vee're schtill schtandin. But someday vee'll sit dahn too, an be chust part off da schtream again. Vee din really begin, ya see, and vee din really ent. Vee chust schtood up an looked rount, but vee vass part off da schtream all along, an da schtream chust keeps on.

"An maybe if vee get ta schtand up again someday, vee'll do it better nex'time. Dat's vott yoah Aunt Rosa tolt me people from India belief. Dat ya get ta do it ovah. Do it bettah nex'time. She call't it ree-in-car-nation."

Ricky brought Arsenic out of his private reverie when he said he wasn't sure how that related to his question.

"Ach! I talk too much. Ya vasn't lookin foah somethin so complicated. Yah! Dat's my answer. I think da schpirit lives on. An I think ya can talk to it if yoah left behind."

Arsenic then hemmed and hawed a bit, and finally said, *"I guess venn I talk ta Gammy, it's like I'm talkin to da schtream off life, all life. Maybe. I doan know. I got myself a little confused."*

Then, to change the subject slightly, *"Is dere somethin ya voult like ta say ta Chohnny? Is dat vott yoah thinkin?"*

"I don't know. I'm just confused."

"Sorry I vasn't moah helpful."

"No. You were. You were helpful. I just need time to think."

Arsenic sat for awhile, but could think of nothing else to add and finally returned to the kitchen.

It was Ricky who suggested a cure that would help both he and Beaner.

Suddenly, one morning, seated at the kitchen table with a hangdog look on his face, Ricky said, "Dad! I wanna talk to Mountain Mary!"

Randy was at the stove cooking French toast. He stopped working and turned to look at his son, who seemed suddenly resolute. Randy was glad to hear the boy assert himself and glad to hear that he wanted to talk. After a pause, he said, "Well, I bet that can be arranged. Let me drive up to her place later and see if she'll ride down here with me, pay you a visit."

It was late in the afternoon when Mary followed Randy through the kitchen door. She was carrying a big basket filled with fresh herbs and vegetables. Ricky must have been awaiting their arrival. He appeared immediately from the walkway to the front room. He looked gloomy.

Mary said, *"Vhy yoah hairs are all strooply, Mr. Mauntin Climbah. Ya need ta fix yoah hairs."*

Without saying a word, Ricky dashed into her arms, almost hitting his cast on the kitchen table. They hugged, and Ricky started, finally, to cry. Mary was muttering. Ricky realized she was praying.

"Some bad schtuff dis fella's bin srough. Schtuff a kit his aych ain't rhetty foah. I know stronker it'll make'im, but he doan

know dat. Please help'im turn downside up. Vee know it doan rain all da time, an besights, rain brings flowers an all dat, but right nauw he doan know dat. Please help me get him ta see da best is yet! Amen."

Then, she loosened her hug, held Ricky at arm's length, stared straight into his eyes, and said *"Let's go talk in geheim?"*

"Where?"

"In priwate!" Then, looking at Randy, *"Dat o.k.? Vee go talk alone?"*

Randy smiled and nodded.

Ricky said, "We can go in the front room. Nobody's in there."

Thus began a series of educational experiences Ricky would never forget. Beaner's parents asked for Mary's help when it became apparent that Ricky was benefiting. Both families offered to pay, and both were dismissed with, *"All da money I need, I got. Pleasure off helpin's my reward! Thank's foah askin!"*

In gratitude, Ralph Deets started doing free repairs over at Mary's house, and Randy hauled extra manure for her garden and cut firewood for her stove. Also, as a group, the two families tore down her old shed and built a fine small barn to replace it.

In Mary's first session with Ricky, she focused on Johnnie's death. Later meetings would deal with philosophy. She began with a little lecture.

"Dere's a reason you an Beaner got saved an Chohnny didn't. Vee doan know dat reason. Chust be shuah ya don't shame yoahself. Ya din do nothin wrong.

"Vott's done is done. It von't chainch. Ya got'ta verk rount it. Ya got'ta always have still hope.

"Dis thing dat happen't ist part'a yoah memory, part'a who ya are nauw.

"Von life's lost. Doan make it two."

Ricky nodded agreement.

"Accept things first. IT is vott IT is. 'Näme es soo es komt!' Dat means take it as it comes. Ya may vish IT vass differ-

ent, but be shuah ya really know vott IT really is befoah ya do any vishin.

"Dis propply calls foah some weinen. Ya got'ta cry. Brüzhe my Mom call't it! Dat's hauw ya let go. Laytah vee talk bought gettin on vith life, but first brutz, cry yoah heart out! Den let it go."

Mary said she wanted to pray quickly before going to the kitchen to cook Ricky a special meal that would help him rebuild.

"I don't want it to be this way!" Ricky blurted out.

"IT doan care! Vott ya vish makes you no difference. IT ain't personal. Gott din pick ya ought ta schmack rount. Nor Beaner neither! Ya chust vass in dat place at dat time. Doan take it personal. It's all in vott'cha make off it.

"Same goes foah Chohnny. Gott din pick him ought neither. Some schtuff chust happens, ya know? Gott doan control it all like some schtring-puller in a puppet show.

"Mostly schtuff ain't happy oah sad by itself. People make it so. Sometimes, dey feel dey should'a kept a thing from happening. But vee doan control everything. Some schtuff chust is da vay it is. Ya got'ta verk arount factualness. Some things ya can fix an some ya can't. Dis von ya can't."

Mary conspicuously folded her hands before her and looked toward the floor. Ricky bowed his head as Mary said aloud, *"Gott. Help Ricky see vott's happened ain't his fault. It ain't ta his likin, but I expect it ain't ta yoah's neither. Chohnny's vith you nauw. Help Ricky see it ain't gonna help nothin if he throws his life aftah Chohnny's.*

"An help me not talk so much so's Ricky can talk about his own thaughts an feel his own feelins! But help me help him see he ain't alone. Amen.

"Nauw I got'ta get at cookin. I'll holler venn it's ready. Ya schtay here'n think bought vott I sett."

Ricky waited until Mary left for the kitchen. Then, he cried.

This pattern of visits was repeated two or three times a week, and the Deet's family, Beaner's parents and brother, seeing the results with Ricky, similarly subscribed to Mary's services.

On a regular basis, Mary walked the short distance over to the Deet's place and the longer one down to the Schlank's. She said the exercise was good for her. Once in awhile, she'd accept the offer of a ride, but mostly she walked. She pointed out that the walk down to Arsenic's was only a mile in length.

She fixed a meal everytime she visited the Schlank's because she suspected a house full of men didn't eat properly. No one complained, in spite of the fact that her cooking was mostly vegetarian. She always had plenty of cheese and butter, made from the milk obtained from her one very productive cow, and there were always "side dishes" with meat for those addicted to it. She insisted that it was the vegetables and herbs that contained the healing and rebuilding materials. Arsenic accepted the emphasis on vegetables, but always ate a lot of the "side dishes."

In subsequent meetings, Ricky seemed to grieve less and surrender more to acceptance of his circumstances. Mary focused her attention on the future, on appreciating the gift of life. She called it simply *freude*, literally "joy." This was her personal, short, way of saying, "joy of living," or *lebensfreude* in Pennsylvania Dutch.

She said, "*Life's a gift. Enchoy it! Freude! Freude!*

"*Let yoah own happiness help ya decide who ta be friends with and hauw ta be friends vith'em. An doan use people, an doan hurt people. Think bought deir happiness too. Freude ist best venn people're happy tagether!*

"*An doan be shamed off bee'in happy Some say life's chust pain, but I say even pain gift's choy if ya learn from it. Gott doan go round givin pain foah no reason. Schtuff happens, an learnin's vott Gott vonts. He vonts ya ta enchoy growin.*

"*Name somesin gift's ya freude. Vott makes ya happy, Ricky?*"

"I like to ride horses and go in the woods."

"*O.k. An vott abought venn ya sit alone. Vott ya think abought?*"

"Sometimes I make up stories."

"*Tell me von.*"

Ricky proceeded to tell her the fantasy he had when he was half asleep on the way home from the mountains. He told her about the fellow that got hit in the face when something fell from the underside of the car he was working on next to the highway. He told her about the explanation he invented. About the boy and his father and how much they loved one another.

"*Gute! Ya love yoah Pop, doan ya?*"

"Yes I do. And he loves me and his own Pop, too!"

"*Love's gute. Dat's some'a da fun in life.*

"*I vont ya ta write some schtories dahn! See if writin's fun. An tell me some off dem schtories venn vee meet.*"

Mary used the same tactic when next she met with Beaner. She discovered that Beaner liked to draw. And so she encouraged Ricky's writing and Beaner's drawing. And each discovered a new hobby and something therapeutic.

Ricky wrote down the story his Uncle Regan had told him about the hot air balloon that got hung up on the roof of the barn. He also made up a story centered on the building of the dam over behind the Kunkel brothers and also the horseback ride he and his dad and Sabrina and family had taken. Mary enjoyed the stories and always asked questions to see if Ricky was drawing any deeper meaning from them.

He seemed merely to think the balloon incident was funny, but a description of the ride he'd taken with his father and Sabrina and her kids led to more discussion, as he told about the mother raccoon and babies they'd seen on the way back to the barn, the ones hit by a car. This led to a discussion of both separation and death.

After Stella visited Ricky in the hospital and helped tend to him, Ricky and his Mom started to talk more frequently by phone. He confessed to Mary that he missed his mother.

"I wish she and my Pop were still married," Ricky said. "I never heard them fight much. I don't see what the problem was."

"Sometimes people rupp each utter da wrong vay. I never bin married, but I know bought ruppin people da wrong vay. How bought yoah Pop's girlfriend? How ya feel bought dat?"

"I like her well enough. And I like Michael and Michelle, her kids. I don't know. She's not my Mom."

"No. She ain't." Mary said this and then was silent.

After awhile Ricky said, "I was out of it in the hospital, but I remember well enough that it made me feel funny when they both came in to visit at the same time."

He was silent again, and so was Mary. Then he added, "They seemed to get along o.k., my mom and Sabrina, you know what I mean? With each other."

Beaner drew pictures of insects. They were so realistic that Mary asked about her technique.

"I find them out in the fields and woods," Beaner said. "Then take them home to draw the pictures. But I hate to let them go."

"Vhy?"

"They might get stepped on or something. They're so easy to kill, you know."

"Yah dat's true. Seems like dey're made foah a short life. Gott's 'least of these,' ya know, kind'a helpless. Ya feel dat vay sometimes, do ya?"

"No! Well, yeah. But I can take care of myself."

"Vott bought da accident?"

"Well, yeah. You're right there. I couldn't stop that, could I?"

"Like I bin sayin, ya can't control all'a'vit. Dis bug heah," Mary said, holding up one of Beaner's drawings, *"dat's a gottesanbeterin."*

"No. That's a praying mantis."

"*Yah. Dat's vott I sett. You got'im prayin too.*"

"You should've seen what he was doing when I found him. He had caught this grasshopper and . . ." Beaner paused.

"*Vott's wrong.*"

"I guess not all insects are harmless."

"*No. Life's complacated, ain't?*"

The two grinned at one another.

One day, walking past Maggie's on her way down to visit Ricky, Mary saw Maggie out with her cows. She entered the barn yard.

"*Hello, I'm Mountain Mary.*"

"*Yah, I know'd ya. Ya live schtill on da hill a little up?*"

"*Yah. I visit Ricky Schlank cross da roat on da Schlank Büararie. I thought I'd see if you'd gimme any service vith dat burden?*"

Ricky had returned to his job helping Maggie with the cows. Maggie said he seemed distant, less involved with his work. And that provided Mary with the substance for this day's discussion with Ricky. But Maggie seemed to want more talk.

"*Come on in an hav'a cup'a coffee once't.*"

"*Ya got any tea?*"

"*Yah. Shuah. Come in da kitchen.*"

They found common ground in a discussion of the Schlanks, and Ricky's accident, and gardening. Then, Maggie got personal.

"*I got'a eye problem. Can't see so gute nomore. I ain't told nobotty else. Any erps ya know bought dat might help.*"

"*Eat plenty eggs.*"

"*Eggs?*"

"*Yah. Specially yolks.*"

Mary finished her tea, started to stand up, and added that she'd like to visit again on the days when she walked down to see Ricky. She was running a little late on this trip but would stop by again.

"*Yah vell*," Maggie replied. And with that, she sealed an arrangement between the two of them.

Scientists knew egg yolks are rich in lutein, essential to eye health, but it seemed unlikely Mary knew anything about the science. Regardless, her visits seemed to help Maggie feel enabled and hopeful.

Mary left and traveled on to see Ricky. She would tell him Maggie felt he was preoccupied at work.

Mary said, "*Venn ya verk at da Büararie, schtay in da present. Jetzig! Da here an nauw! In da platz vhere Gott planted ya. Ya may vish ya vass somevheres else, but chust be shuah ya know vhere ya are nauw. Lot'a accidents happen cause people really ain't vhere dey are.*

"*People hurry up too much cause dey doan really vonn'a be dune vott dey're dune. Dey vonn'a get it ovah, but doan realize it's deir life dey're hurryin up. It's wrong ta be dune so many sings vee doan vonn'a be dune. Find a reason ta vonn'a be dune'em, dat's vott I say. Find some choy in dune vott ya got'ta be dune anyvays.*

"*Learn ta like vott'cha got'ta do, no mattah vott it is. Put yoahself inta yoah verk. An venn I say verk, it ain't chust money I talk bought. I'm talk'in bought anything ya choose ta put enerchy inta, vott'cha put life inta. Take it personal. It's yoah life yoah schpendin. Money'll take care off itself.*

"*Go back and schmeck dat vott ya done. Da verk ya finished, ya know vott I mean. Ya know dat vert 'schmecken?' It means take time ta enchoy da taste. Appreciate da results off yoah verk, yoah accomplishments.*

"*Dere's 'freude' again. Dat's vonn off da tricks ta likin verk. Even if it's chust burnin trash foah yoah Pop. Aftah ya finish, go back an look at vott ya done an say, 'Hey, dat's a gute chop I done!'*

"*If ya miss da freude, dat vay, ya know, if ya doan take time ta enchoy da finished chop, den shuah ya von't like verk. Besights, if ya schpent time dune verk an ya doan enchoy it, den it's part off yoah life you ain't enchoyin. Dere's a reason vee say 'schpent' time. Ya doan vaste money, so doan vaste yoah time neither! Learn ta vonn'a do vott ya got'ta do anyvays!*

"Alzo, let yoah friendships grow by dune deeds tagetter vith friends. Verkin tagetter. Enchoyin accomplishments tagetter. An give each a'nutter credit foah vott each von off ya done ta help get da chop done."

⇒ ✳ ⇐

Mary had a similar discussion with Beaner later that day, another discussion of *freude*. In Beaner's case, it included a discussion of *schadenfreude*, or taking joy in the failure of others, feeling superior when others fail.

Ricky had told Mary that Beaner had a tendency to do that.

Mary said, *"If somebotty's smaller, it doan make you bicker. Always take freude in your own accomplishments. A private joy. But doan brag an doan compare yoahself ta utters."*

Beaner was quiet. She didn't argue. Then, after awhile she said, "It isn't right."

"Vott ain't?'

"What happened to Johnny just isn't right! He was a good kid. You would have liked him."

"Ya vonn'a be 'right' oah ya vonn'a get better? Dat's da question, ain't it. Who's ta say vott's right anyvays?"

"It's hard, dealing with stuff like this!"

"Ya got sumpsin better ya ought'a be dune? Yoah schtill alife. Ya got'ta be dune sumpsin. Might as vell be dealin vith dis!

"Alzo, nevah let a day go by vithought learnin somethin. Dat's da fun in it. Learnin an growin. It's hard alright, but dat's da fun in it. An all dat schule learnin's fine, but if ya pay attention, ya can learn all ovah da place. Nature learn's ya plenty. Ain't it can?"

⚘

After one of Mary's visits to the Schlank's, Arsenic walked with her out to the end of his front yard under the guise of checking the self-serve roadside vegetable stand he maintained next to the main road. On the way, Mary once again talked as though she was the holy woman from the 1700's.

She said, "*Mauntain Mary's headed back up da mauntain!*"

Arsenic decided to test her sanity this time.

"*Ya got'ta be mighty olt ta be Mauntain Mary. She vass rount durin da Revolution, 1776, ya know vott I mean?*"

With irritation in her voice, Mary responded, "*I know I ain't really DAT Mauntain Mary!*

"*Durin da Dapression, venn lots vere schtarvin, I vassn't. Hatt plendy money. But I got sick anyvays. Vent to a powwower ovah by da Blue Mauntain, an he chainched my life.*

"*I got im ta pass on da gift' a healin ta me. I learn't from im. I vonn'a give back, ya know. My name vass already Mary, so I chust took on da nickname 'Mauntain.' Inchins chainched deir names all a time, ya know, an dey say Mauntain Mary learned from da Inchins. Besights, it's a nickname!*"

Arsenic said, "*Hey, dem Depression yeahs vass bad on all off us. Vee done vott vee hatt'a do.*"

"*Yah, an I done a lotta'vit!*"

Arsenic smiled and nodded. Mary smiled back and took her leave. She started to head toward the hill that led back up to her home.

Arsenic yelled for her to wait one more moment. "*Can ya talk to da dead, ya sink?*"

Mary thought for a minute and then said, "*Anybody in particular yoah talkin ta?*"

"*I din say I vass talkin ta anybody. But, Peach, dat's who.*"

"*Ah, shuah.*"

"*Any trick to it. Anysing I shoult know?*"

"*I belief already yoah dune it. Ya doan need my help. Alone's hauw people see olt folks like us dat's lost olt frients, an sorry's hauw dey feel foah us, but dey doan know its plenty frients vee got hidin in da back off ahvah heads! Vee got memories. Vee olt folks got ghosts ta keep us company. Vee doan got'ta chustify talkin ta dem ghosts, even if utters sink it's chust ahvah selfes vee're talkin to, ain't?*"

Arsenic nodded and smiled and said, "*I really set great store by vott ya done foah my granson.*"

"*Maybe I'm offsettin some'a da red ink on my balance sheet. Maybe it's me shoult be thankin you!*"

With that she turned and started walking home.

CHAPTER 9

Authorities from the Pennsylvania Department of Agriculture appeared at the farm with some very bad news. The man who sold Randy the mule was suspected of having glanders. Glanders is a highly infectious disease occurring mainly in horses, donkeys, and mules, but it can also be contracted by humans. The Dutch call it *de Rots*, which can also mean mucous or snot. The disease does typically cause chronic nasal discharge and ulcers on the mucosa of horses and mules. But the sores can also appear on the skin, in which case it would be called farcy. It's highly destructive. It was so dangerous and infectious that the Germans used it as a biological warfare agent during World War I. The prevailing way to control it is to destroy all animals in a herd when a confirmed infection is discovered.

The man with the disease, the fellow who sold the mule, was being treated with several antibiotics and showing signs of improvement. None of his animals had the disease, but the authorities were still concerned about possible spread.

Glanders was believed to have been irradicated in North America and Europe, but the man who owned the mule had been working with horses outside the U.S. That was how the authorities assumed he had contracted it, but if it involved his own herd here in this country, it could be disastrous. They were tracking down all the animals he might have had contact with in the United States.

The Pennsylvania authorities were placing a temporary quarantine on Arsenic's farm. The Schlanks were hopeful their animals would soon be released, since there were no visible symptoms in the horses or the mule, but the horses they boarded for outsiders would have to be quarantined along with their own. This might cause a big uproar and dent the reputation of the farm.

The Schlanks had to wear protective clothing when they worked with the animals and generally have minimal contact with them. They hired a veterinarian's assistant to help during the quarantine.

After the initial shock, the boarders proved to be loyal. They were tolerant and gave no sign they intended to move their horses when the quarantine was lifted. The Schlank farm had an excellent reputation to start with, and it was beginning to look like it would survive this embarrassment, assuming the animals were soon cleared and the quarantine lifted.

Arsenic and Randy worried most that they might have to destroy horses. They didn't speak to one another of these fears, but each told Mountain Mary about them. Arsenic and Randy kept reassuring one another that everything was going to be o.k. Mary started visiting the barn. She went alone, saying that she wanted to pray over the animals.

The Schlanks were relieved when the herd was cleared and the quarantine lifted. Damage control was easy since boarders themselves spread word that the whole thing was a silly misunderstanding. The fellow who sold Randy the mule in Kentucky recovered completely and his case was going to be reported at a national medical convention since successful treatment was rare.

The mule himself was doing well. Never did get sick. He was a whimsical addition to the farm. Quite a character! Fat called him *Bajazzo*, which means clown or buffoon.

Relief was sweet for Arsenic and Randy. As Arsenic pointed out, all had the heebie-jeebies what with Ricky's accident and the quarantine, now Ricky and Beaner were recovering and the quarantine lifted, and Mary seemed somehow dovetailed into the whole thing. Mary continued to mystify them all, and she was earning a special place in all their hearts.

Late one Saturday morning, Ricky'd gone out to the mailbox as soon as he saw the mailman's truck from the kitchen window. Arsenic and Randy looked at each other and raised their eyebrows as he went out the door. They had no idea why he was so interested in the mail, but he had been excited for a couple weeks now.

At Mary's insistence and without the family's awareness, Ricky had submitted a story to a monthly magazine, the *National 4-H News*. It was based on the incident that occurred when the milking machine salesman visited Maggie to sell her one of his company's milkers. Both Maggie and Arsenic had described the salesman's reaction when he thought he had run over Maggie's cat, and Ricky thought it was hilarious. He'd scratched out a draft that he read to Mary, and he revised it several times before Mary helped him get it typed by Beaner's mother and packaged and sent off without his own family's awareness. Beaner's family was sworn to secrecy. He wanted to surprise his own family if it was accepted for publication.

From the window, Arsenic watched Ricky tear open a big, brown envelope while standing by the mailbox. Then, he saw him jumping up and down and yelling.

"Come heah," Arsenic said to Randy, and he pointed out the window as he continued, *"vott'cha make'a dat?"*

Randy and his Pop were intrigued and waited expectantly near the kitchen door for Ricky to return to the house.

Arsenic and Randy didn't know that he had submitted anything to a magazine, but they did know that the local 4-H had given him recognition for one of his poems. One entitled, "The House on the Hill."

Ricky's Pop had the poem inscribed on a heavy piece of parchment by a calligrapher who made reproductions of classic Pennsylvania Dutch frakturs. It was done in elaborate script over a beautiful background image of ducks landing in a pond and *distlefinks* around the border of the document. It was framed and hanging on the wall next to the kitchen door. As they waited, Arsenic stood and absentmindedly read over the poem.

"From the house on the hill,
There came three men,
Three men from that house did come.
They all were dressed in hunting clothes,
And the cold breeze made them numb.

On a nearby bog,
There were three shots.
Three shots that bog did fill.
And that night a feast of ducks was held,
In the house upon the hill."

Arsenic finished reading and sat in a chair by the door to continue waiting. He said, "*Er hatt viele Verstanden sella kind*," which loosely translates as "That kid's got a lot of brains."

His mind drifted a lot these days. Even the chair he was seated in brought forth a memory. He started to chuckle as he recalled that this was the chair Peach used for "time-out" punishment for the kids. Peach would say, "*Dat's enough roughhousing. I vont ya IN DA CHAIR SITTING! Doan get up til I say's o.k.*" Randy always moaned when he heard the phrase "*in da chair sitting*." That was the signal that he'd just crossed a line and "time-out" was forthcoming. Peach didn't call it "time-out." "*In da chair sitting*" was just common sense.

Just then Ricky burst through the door.

"I got a surprise for you," he said handing Randy a letter with Arsenic looking over his shoulder.

"Wow!" the two exclaimed at about the same time. And Randy added, "When? When did you do this? Submit this?"

"About a month ago. I don't know what I would have done if they'd rejected it. I wanted so bad to surprise you all. Mary and Beaner's Mom helped me send it off."

"What is the story about?"

Ricky explained the whole thing and said he owed Arsenic and Maggie gratitude for giving him the idea. As he looked at the copy of the manuscript the magazine had returned to him, he said, "They only want a few changes. Small ones."

Two weeks after Mary declared Ricky and Beaner officially "healed," the Schlanks organized a family picnic to celebrate. They called it a *fersummling*, meaning a get-together. The kids thought it was just a baby shower to celebrate Ruby's pregnancy, but the families were also celebrating the return of the kids to the living. Since Ricky and Beaner didn't fully realize they'd been missing, the family just told them it was a baby shower for the Kutzs.

Arsenic and Fat Schmidt butchered a small pig. They cooked it in a pit dug the previous day with the front-end loader on the antique John Deere tractor. This was right near the butcher shed. Arsenic insisted on using the old tractor, though Fat pointed out they could easily do it with a shovel. Arsenic was always looking for an excuse to run the old John Deere. Chickit, chickit, boom, boom!

The pit was filled with a big hardwood fire early in the morning on the day of the picnic, and by nine o'clock the wood was spent and glowing coals remained. Half were raked out, pig layed in, hot coals raked on top. This was all covered with a layer of dirt and left to smoulder until late afternoon when it would be uncovered, washed with butter, and consumed by the guests.

The main staging area for the gathering was the patio between the back door and the platform where the outdoor hand pump was located. The men hauled down two big handmade oak picnic tables that usually stood outside the butcher shed. They also carried down a very heavy butcher block on which the pig would be placed.

By the time all the guests arrived, the centers of the tables would be filled with dishes. Each group brought a dish to share. The pregnant Ruby, who was getting big around the middle by this time, brought German potato salad. Rosa brought loaves of her homemade bread. Maggie prepared a huge pot of baked beans. Mary brought a salad of fresh organic garden vegetables and herbs.

Gifts for Ruby and Regan were displayed on a card table. Another card table was given over to drinks, including a tub filled with ice and bottles of Reading's Birch Beer, the old clear bottles with the painted labels. They also had a jug of elderberry wine that Peach made before her death. While Peach had reserved the wine for medicinal purposes, Arsenic said he wanted a dish of her's to be present at the picnic. They'd already eaten all of her chow-chow and other home-canned foods. Maggie had promised to cook up a big batch of chow-chow as soon as peak of the garden harvest arrived.

While they waited for the pork to finish cooking, some guests played croquet, while others sat around and schmoozed.

The evening before the party, Ricky and Arsenic set up a very novel croquet course. They put wickets in nearly hopeless places. Like on the sides of steep hills. A player had to take a long shot, because there was no way to inch close to the wicket without the ball rolling down the hill. When such a long shot missed, the ball seemed to roll a mile off course. The center wicket was set up in a section of the driveway parking lot between house and barn. Arsenic had used an auger to drill two holes in the crushed and packed limestone so Ricky could get it to stand up solidly. Loose rocks in the lot made the balls roll all over the place. Other wickets were set up with tree roots right in the arch so that the ball would tend to wobble right or left instead of through the center.

The picnic was scheduled to begin at one o'clock, and as guests started arriving, Arsenic jumped in his pickup truck and drove up to Mary's place to give her a ride. She needed help transporting the big salad of greens from her garden down to the Schlank's.

As they entered the driveway, Arsenic told Mary that Peach's brother Heinrich had arrived early. Heinrich had said he knew her from the old days, *de oolten tiet*. He wanted very much to see her again. Mary seemed surprised and a little nervous.

As they left the truck and started walking toward the house, Mary got close to Arsenic and said, *"Be sure I recognize him."*

"Who?" Arsenic replied.

"Heinrich. For I doan vonn'a embarass him. Not myself neither. Bin a lange time, an people chainch a lot. I vouldn't vonn'a not recognize'im, ya know vott I mean?"

"Doan verry. I'll valk ya right to'im."

And so he did. Heinrich was standing by himself, and no one else saw Mary coming, and so they walked right up to Heinrich. He seemed nervous.

"Heinie!" Arsenic yelled as they approached.

"Yah!"

"Ya rememper Mary?"

"Yah. Shuah. Hauw'd I foahget?"

Both Heinrich and Mary seemed a bit uncomfortable at first, and so Arsenic excused himself and went off to check on Fat and the roasting hog.

"Bin a lange time, Heinie!"

"Yah. Lange time. Arsenic tolt me bought yoah new profession. A doktor. Dat's real nice. I'm proud'a ya."

"Chust a powwow doktor, faith healer!"

"Yah vell. Dat's da best kind, ain't?"

"Sank you! Vott'chu bin dune?"

"A small farm I run. Keeps me busy an food on da table."

"Ya eber get yoahself married?"

"Nein. Nicht heiraten. I live vith myself alone. Like it dat vay. An you?"

"Nein. Ain't married neither. Pretty busy though. Vott kind'a schtuff ya race up on yoah farm?"

And as Mary and Heinrich got onto the neutral ground of gardening, their conversation flowed smoothly, and they were soon laughing loudly.

After checking on the progress of the roasting hog, Arsenic played croquet. In croquet, when your ball hits somebody else's ball, you can send theirs away. You do this by laying yours against theirs, holding yours down with your foot, and giving it a whack. The vibration sends the other ball flying off the court. In this manner, Regan sent Arsenic's ball down the hill into a patch of stinging nettle. The Dutch call this plant *brennartle* or *brennessel*, depending on who you ask about it. It has long blaze green leaves and long stinging hairs that instantly cause an extremely irritating rash when they touch the skin. A patch of this grew just above the springhouse, in the meadow down front of the farmhouse.

Arsenic waded in the middle and took four turns to smack his ball out. One of the plants sneaked under his trouser leg, and he was itching like crazy. The game was delayed while he rushed in the house to spread some menthol lotion on the itchy spot.

James had never before played croquet. While the group waited for Arsenic to return, he picked the instruction manual off the rack that held mallets, balls, and wickets and read the first paragraph.

"Hey," he yelled. "It says here the game of croquet evolved from a French game called *pell-mell*. That means helter-skelter, and I can see why they called it that!"

He was, of course, assuming the strange placement of wickets and resulting chaos were a normal part of the game.

Looking over his shoulder, Rosa said, "It says 'pall-mall' not 'pell-mell.' Anyway, you're right. This particular game we're playing should be called helter-skelter, not croquet."

Shortly after Arsenic returned from putting lotion on his leg, Heinrich joined the croquet game. Fat Schmidt then left the roasting hog in the hands of nature and went down to sit with Mountain Mary and talk philosophy. They cast an interesting image, broad and narrow, horizontal and vertical. Fat was serious about losing weight and very proud of the twenty pounds he lost thus far. Mary was his guru. He'd nearly become a vegetarian.

Arsenic had pointed out that vegetarianism seemed unbefitting for a butcher, and Fat had said, *"Yah! Ain't dat for true!"*

And so Fat still ate a little meat when he was butchering. His clients expected him to taste his concoctions although he really didn't need that kind of feedback anymore after butchering for so many years. Nevertheless, he did it for appearance, and Mary understood.

The croquet players resumed play, but then the game was again paused when someone drew attention to the fact that Fat and Mary had started to play badminton. Badminton can require a lot of running, but Fat and Mary simply stood right in front of the net and bopped the birdie, or shuttlecock, lightly over the net, placing it so that the other wouldn't have to move much. When Fat missed, he had trouble bending over to pick it up, so the tall, lithe Mary would reach under the net, pick it up, hand it back to Fat, and quickly get ready to receive his next shot.

Arsenic and Maggie were closest to the badminton court and they busted out laughing when they heard Fat blaming a missed shot on the size of the racquet, *"Deese dumb birdie-whackers! Dey ain't bick'enough!"*

Since the croquet game was again on pause, the combatants wanted to get a drink up by the back porch. During the delay, Ricky and Beaner challenged each other to a foot race. They ran up around the butcher shed then around the corn crib and back down to the porch.

Two scotty dogs leashed under a shade tree were watching the kids run. When the race was over, and the group was congratulating Beaner on her victory, and Ricky on a race well-run, the two dogs started straining at their leashes and yelling like banshees.

James and Rosa had adopted the dogs in the manner of newlyweds seeking a substitute for children. They were named Itty, a boy, and Bitty, a girl.

Rosa realized it was Ricky and Beaner's race that had set them off, and they were still straining toward the race course rather than toward the crowd. Intrigued, Rosa went over and let the dogs go. To everyone's amazement, they ran a race identical to the one the kids had run, up around the butcher shed, then around the corn crib, and back down to the porch. At the end of their race, they ran straight to the crowd and jumped up and down, seeking attention such as had been given to the kids.

"*Dat vass strainch!*" Heinrich said. "*Dem dauks think dey're people!*"

Heinrich then walked over to a patch of lawn to spit. He had the annoying habit of chewing tobacco. When he returned, he said to Arsenic, "*I need a spit pittoon.*"

Arsenic winced and said, "*Ya mean 'spittoon!' And yah, ya do!*"

Ricky's two pet beagles, Foxie and Moxie, were penned up near the butcher shed, and they had started yodeling when Itty and Bitty ran by. Ricky went up and opened their pen to see if they would do what the Scotties did. But Foxie and Moxie just ran off into the fields to hunt rabbits. They wouldn't return until nightfall.

"*Yah vell!*" Arsenic said when Ricky returned.

After dinner was eaten and gifts were opened, everyone joined in a game of hide-and-seek as the evening light was getting dim.

Beaner was "it."

Fat hid behind the big oak tree in front of the house, but Beaner saw his sides sticking out. Mary did the same behind a different tree, and Beaner never noticed her. Mary touched base and got home free.

First Rosa, and then James, had their hiding places revealed by their two scotty dogs. Rosa was in the wagon shed, and the dogs were outside whining at the door she had used. As soon as Beaner found Rosa, the dogs ran over to the pumphouse, where James was hiding, and thus James was caught in the same manner.

Ricky hid under a pile of cattail fluff in his clubhouse, or playhouse, formerly the shed Arsenic used to shelter turkeys. Arsenic had helped the kids clean out the shed when he gave up the turkey business. Up to that point, the kids had a habit of playing in the barn.

Arsenic had finally taken them aside and asserted, *"Ya kits got'ta schtop runnin da barn around. Ya'll get hurt. Da turkey pen vee'll clean ought, an dat yoah playhouse vill be. I ain't buyin no moah turkeys anyvays. So, no moah runnin da barn round. Da turkey pen vill be yoah new playhaus."*

Arsenic had decided to quit the turkey business after two decapitated turkeys flew away during butchering. Fat Schmidt was helping him get turkeys ready for sale at the holidays. The procedure was to chop off their heads, and then toss them a few yards away to flop around and bleed.

Arsenic always hated the process, but this time two of them actually took off and flew away, without heads. Two of them. And they flew in the same direction. They both landed in Maggie's front yard. They bled out, in flight, and dropped from the sky. Both plopped down right in front of Maggie's front porch. Plop! Plop! Maggie was walking back from the barn and saw it happen. She screamed, and Arsenic felt terrible about the whole thing.

"I qvit da turkey business!" he said.

Anyway, after the turkey shed was cleaned out, Ricky and Beaner and Chicken-Wing divided it up into little rooms so each could have a little private "office space" in the same building. They took canvas from an old wagon cover and cut it up and hung the pieces like curtains to form partitions.

Then the kids got into some kind of turf war. One or the other was using too much space. It was not a big shed. The argument escalated. Chicken-Wing went down to the swamp in a marshy area below the springhouse. He broke off a bunch of dead cattails. Each cattail had a big cottony head of dry fluff that would explode in a cloud of fuzz when hit against something solid. He launched a full-scale attack on Beaner while she was sitting on the floor of her little room. He pulled back her curtain and started smacking the cattails on the floor and walls so as to make the heads explode and thereby befog the room with seedy fuzz.

Beaner started coughing and spitting as little furry seeds flew all over her little den. It was filled right off with a cloud. Ricky, in his own curtained room next door, got drawn into the altercation when he heard Beaner shouting, "YOU BIG DUMB-HOLE. I'LL GET YOU FOR THAT!"

The action became what Arsenic called a *ding an sich*, or a thing-in-itself. The kids got carried away by the excitement. All three started attacking the space of the others, and pretty soon all were laughing and coughing and running back and forth from swamp to clubhouse, smacking cattail heads inside the playhouse. The result was a huge mess! The whole shed was filled with white fluff, loosely piled, six-inches deep, like snow. It started in anger but had quickly turned playful.

In the end, looking over the mess, Beaner said, "What did we do THAT for?"

The club broke up, because all knew it would take a while to get the place cleaned out, and no one had the energy to start the project.

Anyway, that's how the clubhouse got filled with enough cattail fluff to hide Ricky. He crawled into the middle of the pile and pulled some over himself. No one could find him. No one dared look in that mess. When all save Ricky were either caught or exempt, because they were able to touch base and get home free, Randy shouted loudly that the group declared Ricky the winner, and he should come out from his hiding place, wherever that might be. It was getting dark.

Beaner'd been hunting near the shed at the time Ricky heard his Dad's shouted concession. Sweat made the feathery cattail fluff cling as Ricky came out. He looked like the abominable snowman.

Beaner started screaming bloody murder and running back toward the gathered family. When Arsenic heard the scream, he grabbed a croquet mallet and ran past her toward the abomination that had emerged from the shed. He realized quickly it was Ricky in disguise.

Arsenic was laughing as he yelled, *"Vott in perdition? Ya look like a ball'a cotton!"*

Ricky and his Pop Pop walked arm in arm back toward the family, laughing at the expressions on the faces of the family members, and at Beaner who was hiding behind her father.

Ricky and Beaner seemed happy again, and the two families were very willing to cooperate when informed the pair wanted to attend a 4-H hoedown together, down in Oley.

The families had encouraged them to get involved in the 4-H as therapy during their recovery from the shock of the auto accident.

It kept them pleasantly distracted during recuperation. Each had to undertake and complete a project from a list of fifty handed out by their group leaders. Beaner chose home furnishing, because she could use her drawing skills in designing interior layouts. Ricky chose to care for a sow and her litter of pigs.

The families had listened dutifully as the kids practiced the pledge containing the four "H's." "I pledge: my Head to clearer thinking, my Heart to greater loyalty, my Hands to larger service, and my Health to better living, for my club, my community, and my country." They had also watched attentively as the kids practiced square dancing. It was no surprise when each asked if they could attend the hoedown together.

Beaner's father, Ralph, acted as chauffeur, and Beaner and Ricky rode together in the back seat of the car. He drove them to a restaurant after the dance so they could be with a large group of friends from the dance as they drank Cherry Cokes, ate cheeseburgers, and just generally amused themselves for a couple hours. To make himself scarce while the kids were at the restaurant, Ralph went to make an estimate on the cost of a repair job he'd been offered. He didn't want them to feel he was spying on them. He picked them up later and drove them home. They seemed happy.

Later, as Beaner's Mom and Pop lay in bed talking, her Mom said, "I hope they take it easy. No child marriages!"

"You mean like us," Ralph said, as he laughed and pinched his wife.

No one suspected that within a month there would indeed be a very unexpected wedding announcement within the community.

CHAPTER 10

As Indian summer temperatures warmed the fruits, the fruits began to ripen. Fruit trees were scattered everywhere in the Oley Hills, even in small clearings in the forest. Arsenic used to jokingly tell his kids that John Chapman, the famous Johnny Appleseed, had planted them. Then, he'd add that Polly Peachpit, and Pinky Pearseed, and Chimmy Cherrypit had planted the other fruit varieties.

Of course, Europeans had been tramping around the area for nearly three hundred years. So, anyone could have planted them. Some of the trees were in small abandoned orchards, but many were scattered about in unlikely places.

Arsenic and Maggie put a small stepladder in the back of the pickup truck and headed out to Pricetown and then down toward Oley to a spot where a fantastically productive apple tree was located on the edge of a swampy area about two hundred yards from the highway.

When Arsenic was a kid, he and his brothers hiked the area and discovered the tree, about this time of year. They had hiked through the woods at the bottom of the pasture down in front of the barn, the place where Ricky found his two pet beagles, Foxie and Moxie. The Schlanks called that woods the "lost forty," because no one seemed to know who owned it. It was on a big hill and had rocky cliffs, a bit smaller than those behind Maggie's farm. The trail to the swamp where the apple tree was located ran right along the base of the cliffs.

The mine hole that Ricky, Johnny, and Beaner visited to fish and hunt frogs was located back on the tableland on top of those cliffs. Arsenic and his brothers, Valentine and Washington, had visited that same mine hole and fished and shot frogs just like Ricky and his friends. He revealed this to Ricky in the past few weeks, when they finally discussed the events that led up to the terrible car crash. *"Ach, my brothers and me walk't dat voots all over."*

Anyway, the trail along the base of the cliffs led to the fantastic apple tree. But the hike was long, two miles from the farmhouse. So, Maggie and Arsenic rode the truck to Pricetown, then down toward Oley, and walked a short distance to the tree from the direction opposite. *"My shoes valk too heavy these days. Gettin too olt so far ta valk."*

This way they could bring the ladder. As Arsenic was climbing, one of the ladder's legs sunk a bit in the leaf litter, and the affair tilted slightly.

Arsenic said, *"Ya better schteady dis, huh?"*

"Yah vell," Maggie answered and grabbed hold of it.

In a little while, Arsenic carried down a bucket full to set on the ground, and Maggie said, *"Ya picked da basket full, but vee got a nutter, an dem on dat branch is low enough so's vee can get'em vithought da latter."*

While they were picking from the branch, Arsenic noticed Maggie tossing some green ones in the pail along with ripe ones, and so he said, *"Dem green apples'll give ya da howlin runnies yet."*

"Vott?"

"Dem green apples."

"Vott green apples?"

And so Arsenic first learned that Maggie was having trouble with her vision, and he insisted that she go see a doctor.

Fat was sitting with Mary in her kitchen. She'd been counseling him when suddenly she stood up and said, *"Dat's enough. I'm into the garden going. Got'ta pull veeds."*

Fat volunteered his help. He was jerking on the stalk of a weed that seemed to have roots of steel, when it finally pulled out, and he ended up on his backside. It was from this position that he noticed that

Mary had two old Schwinn bicycles in a shed behind her house, old ones with big round tires, big fenders, and heavy luggage racks.

Fat said, *"Dem bicycles. Dey verk schtill?"*

Mary was laughing at Fat's seated position as she replied, *"Yah. Shuah. Little air in da tires maybe, but dey verked last I knew. Vhy?"*

"Thought vee might ride."

Mary smiled and said, *"Yah. Yoah ready foah dat type'a thing, ain't? How much veight ya lose? Fifty pounds?"*

"Sixty! Ya vonn'a see me do a hand schtand?"

"Nah, nah! I belief ya!"

"I got'a air pump in my car. I'll air da tyahs up. We can ride the road a little down to where it gives a fork."

Half an hour later they were riding down the black top road in front of Beaner's house. The bikes were heavy and had no gears but one. Mary seemed to be straining, but Fat pedaled with ease. His great bulk dwarfed the bike. As a matter of fact, the bike was hardly visible.

Beaner came running out her front door, laughing, and yelling, "Well, look at you two!"

Fat lifted his arms straight up over his head and the bike wobbled but stayed on its wheels.

"You vatch it!" Mary yelled. *"I can't fix a busted head!"*

Fat yelled back, *"Now, admit it. I'm gettin hellsy."* And after grabbing the handle bars and circling Mary's bike, he added, *"Vith yoah help!"*

Beaner, from the top of the stone wall in front of her house, yelled, "Yeah, Mountain Mary. With your help, and thank you." Then, she added in a whisper, "God bless you!"

Fat yelled back, *"I hert dat!"*

"You didn't either. I whispered."

Fat replied, *"I got x-ray ears!"*

The pair rode on, but Fat soon said, *"I got'ta get down here off. Dis seat ain't big'nough. It don't ride so good."*

"Vell let's valk yet."

And so the couple pushed their bikes as they walked and talked.

"*I sink me an my Pop turned ought chust da same,*" Fat said.

"*Vass he a heavy man too?*"

"*Yah but it ain't chust dat I mean. Vee're da same in lot'a vays. Sings I use'ta criticize HIM foah nauw I'M dune, ya know.*

"*Venn he vass gettin olt an needed somevon ta take care'a him, I backed off. Figert vee'd not get along too good if vee lived tagetter. Pop alvays was of course dignified, but vee argued a lot. I feel real bad bought dat nauw. Bought backin off. He's long gone nauw. Can't tell'im I'm sorry, ya know.*"

Mary stopped walking and looked Fat directly in the eye. "*You can alvays do dat. Ya chust did. Ya said ya vass sorry! Vergebe die'selbst!*"

"*Forgive myself? Yah, I guess! Zo ist das leben, ain't! Such is life. I see hauw it come abought. If we'd'a both bin da same aich at dat same time, vee'da seen eye ta eye, but venn he vass olt, I vass young, an venn I vass olt, he vass gone. Dis olt me ist chust like da olt him. If vee coult'a bin olt at da same time, vee voult'a got along real fine, ain't?*"

"*Das ist halt zo, ya know, dat's da vay it alvays goes,*" Mary said smiling and shaking her head in agreement. "*Ya see alot lookin backwards, ain't? All ya can do ist learn! Besights, sounds like ya two're gettin along real fine right nauw!*"

Fat considered that and then said, "*Yah, I guess. Ain't?*"

On the way home, Mary said, "*It's real nice oughtsight. Vott season's best, ya think?*"

"*Me, I like harvest time venn da leaves turn. Venn dat fall foyledge takes on all dat color. Ich mag das am liebsten. Wie die Blätter schimmern.*"

"*Vell me, I like summer. Venn my garten grows.*"

Fat replied, "*Yah vell. All times're nice venn ya get ta be ahvah aiche, huh?*"

Then he looked toward the sky and added, "*Vott'cha think Pop?*"

⇒ ✳ ⇐

Chow-chow is complicated. It's a sweet and sour mixed vegetable pickle. At least a dozen different vegetables are used in a good chow-chow, and so it's generally made in the late summer when lots of fresh stuff is easily available. The many vegetables are chosen for flavorfulness and colorfulness. Flavor and color are about equal in importance as standards when judging the merits of a pint of chow-chow. But right below these two standards comes texture. You want the vegetables to crunch. If a diced vegetable gets a bit mushy after sitting in sweet and sour pickle juice, you don't want it in your chow-chow.

Maggie was making good on her promise of preparing a big batch to share with the Schlanks. They had eaten the last of the pint and quart jars bequeathed by Peach. Maggie and Arsenic's deceased wife Peach were always first and second in the chow-chow competition at the Oley Valley Community Fair, Department 15-2, Class 7-D. Check the records. Sometimes Maggie won, and sometimes it was Peach.

Maggie had promised to have a big supply all ready to be distributed prior to Thanksgiving and the rest of the roller coaster of holidays that occupy the early winter months.

Several people were seated at a picnic table between Arsenic's back door and the platform where the outdoor hand pump was located. Maggie and Beaner and Ricky carried containers of yellow and green stringbeans, red and green sweet peppers, celery, cauliflower, and carrots out to the picnic table. These all had to be washed and diced into pieces of precise size. Maggie was very particular about the size of those pieces. She was also very particular about the way the colors were arranged inside the canning jars, but that was a later stage of the process.

Maggie called Arsenic aside at one point and said, "*I'm gonna need moah sugar. Hauw bought runnin ought ta Windy Corners and get some?*"

"*Yah. I might could. Ya vonn'a go with?*"

"Naw. Got'ta keep at it. Use dis sale coupon. If I doan use it, it'll go bad. It's only good foah two veeks."

Arsenic got the coupon and headed for his truck. As he slid behind the wheel, he was laughing and muttering, *"Ha. 'It'll go bad.' Dat's funny."*

Then, he forgot why he was going to the store. As a matter of fact, he forgot that the store was his destination. He was just driving down the highway. He started to panic, but as he came over the hill and the store came in view, he grabbed the coupon off the seat and glanced at it, and remembered where he was going and why. He said, *"Yah. Sugar!"*

This sort of forgetting had occurred several times lately, and Arsenic was worried about it. He hadn't mentioned the problem to anyone. And he wouldn't mention it today.

Fat and Mary had gotten there early and went right to work on the vegetables. Others kept arriving throughout the morning and joined in. As one type of vegetable was diced, it was placed in its own separate pot and taken right to the kitchen to be briefly scalded. Maggie called this scalding *bräje* and said it improved the color and integrity of the cut vegetables. Maggie had already soaked all the dried beans during the night, and she was slowly warming them on the stove while the other vegetables were scalded.

Vinegar and sugar, along with a little salt, garlic, mustard, cinnamon, tumeric, and celery-seed were heating in a big stainless steel pot on the fireplace out in the butcher shed. There wasn't room for this big pot on the kitchen stove. When the vegetables were all cut and scalded, they were carried to this second kettle, along with all the beans, onions, and such, and the mixture was brought back to a boil and then simmered. While this was simmering in the butcher shed, most of the helpers were busy in the kitchen, sterilizing canning jars and getting lids and rings lined up close to the big boiling-water-bath canner.

When the time was right, everyone started ladeling chow-chow into jars with Maggie carefully supervising and making frequent rearrangements in each jar so that the color would have maximum impact. Several times she ordered a total repacking of a jar because the color arrangement wasn't quite right. That's one of the details that had gotten first or second for Maggie or Peach at the fair every year. After a quick bath in the canner, *da char lits* were laid on to form a vacuum as the jars cooled.

The group sat around the fireplace after work was complete, roasting bratwurst on sticks and eating baked beans, or *bohna*.

One day, Fat and Mary were up at Mary's place hauling manure from a neighbor's barn over to her famous garden.

Mary started to say Fat's name but paused when she realized she didn't even know his first name. So, she said, "*Ich weisz nicht dien nahma. Dien vor-namen. Vott yoah parents call ya? I know it ain't 'Fat.' Vott's yoah real vor-namen.*"

Fat smiled shyly and said, "*Anton.*"

"*Vell, nauw, das ist shae! Dat's a real pretty name!*"

Fat said, "*O.K. nauw, what's yoah real name?*"

"*Mary!*"

"*I know dat much!*"

"*Wass ich nicht weiss macht mich nicht heiss!*"

"*Vhy voult it bother me ta know yoah full name?*"

"*Vee'll talk bought it some utter time.*"

Fat made it clear that he didn't care about her past by saying, "*Macht nix aus zu mir!*"

One early dry fall morning before the leaves changed color, Ricky and Beaner set off from the shore of a nearby lake. They were paddling a canoe. There was a dustiness in the air. Beaner's uncle had a cabin on a big lake near Reading. Her father took them over to the cabin to spend the day paddling around in one of the canoes his brother stored in his boathouse.

Ralph had been skeptical.

"The paper wants rain," he said.

"Only a small chance," Beaner argued. And they went, and it did not rain.

Although the kids seemed to be their old playful selves, they were more mature and insightful since the accident. They were pretty deep for their age. It wasn't obvious at first, but showed up when a problem called for quiet thought, and a little sadness. They had more tolerance for all those feelings that fall short of jolly, the ones that often reveal a compromise solution.

They brought along a lunch and picnicked on a spit of land where little ledges stuck out all along one side and where waves slapped the undersides sounding like metronomes in their regularity. Ricky talked about the fish kill on Regan's pond and about the environmental implications of overcrowding and water pollution and such. Before she told Ricky her reaction, Beaner started laughing, and said she had what Mary called a big flash of understanding, a *Gedanken-blitz*, which means a "thought-explosion!"

"I'm interested in what my Gram-paw called *'Wassers-cheide.'* In school they called it a watershed. It's a point where water divides and, for example, half runs east and half runs west. Maybe it would be possible to protect one half of a watershed, like the part that's flowing east, even when it's too late to protect the part flowing west, like when there's too many factories and cities to the west." She added that she wanted to do volunteer work with the National Park Service when she graduated from high school.

Before returning to the boathouse to meet Ralph for the return home, they took a long, slow ride along the southern shore. Cicadas sounded like tiny Harley Davidson motorcycles, revving their engines. They surprised a great blue heron that took to the air shouting a deep guttural "bawwk, bawwk, bawwk."

In due course, they came onto an inlet that looked like a

creek emptying into the lake. Overgrown with a leafy emerald frame it was a tunnel into the depth of the old forest. A shadowy strap of water snaking its way through big trees. It was too mysterious to pass up.

There were surprises of birds, beavers, muskrats, and dragonflies around every bend. One beaver, gnawing a tree, watched them over its shoulder. It suddenly realized that the canoe was not a floating log, and it dove on its belly down a steep, inclined water slide. The splash alerted a dragonfly perched on the tip of an unstrung fishing rod the kids had brought "just in case." As they watched the dragonfly take to the air, a desperate buzzing echoed through the aluminum canoe.

A large horsefly, sitting just above waterline on the side of the hull, got caught up and pulled under as the canoe was rocked by the splash of the beaver. Caught between air and water, between life and death, the fly was frantic. The rocking motion continued, and a rebound wave from the shore rocked it enough to release the fly. It floated and buzzed but was too waterlogged to take to the air. It floated by Beaner's end of the canoe. She reached over, grabbed it, and laid it on the floor of the boat. Both kids watched with deep interest. It preened then flew away, as both kids whispered a laugh.

"I thought he was a goner," Beaner said softly.

"Yeah. Me too," Ricky replied, and both seemed relieved to see the fly fly off in spite of the fact that it might return later and give either of them a nasty bite.

In places the banks along the inlet were ten-feet high, little earthen cliffs. One of these eroded banks exposed half the roots of an old oak tree leaning over the water. It looked like it could topple at any minute. Ironically, enormous grape vines had grown up with the tree and seemed to be holding it up. They were stretched from far back on the bank up to the treetop like guy wires, keeping the tree upright in spite of the tumbling forces of nature. Those same grape vines probably threatened to strangle this tree in its early years, but now they were holding it up. Now, they were partners. Ricky and

Beaner recognized the irony. They looked at each other and smiled. Irony wasn't lost on them these days.

As they got close to the back of the inlet, the surface was covered with algae and scum. The movement of the paddles made little windows in the water. The tea from rotting leaves stained the water golden yellow, but they could clearly see into the depths. A couple times, they saw turtles walking on the bottom. Once, Ricky reached over and picked up a little one no bigger than a quarter and it bit onto his finger just as he lifted it above the surface. He shook his hand and the turtle flew back in the water. They both laughed.

Now, this "stream" was looking more and more stagnant. Turning the last bend, they realized it wasn't a stream at all but a long, thin finger of the lake. A dead-end.

Ricky was wondering if life's choices sometimes were like this. Maybe sometimes you travel "streams" that bend and tempt you along, but wind up as dead-ends. This abstract thought got interrupted when Beaner whispered a very concrete "Pssst," and pointed up to the branches of a tree extended over their heads.

There were three baby racoons. They'd been climbing single file out the length of a branch, and the lead one had reached the end but had no way of telling the others that there was no place to go. The two behind were pushing for it to continue, not knowing it was the end of the line. As Ricky and Beaner watched, the one in the lead fell, pushed off by the two behind. It landed with a splash right next to the canoe. Ricky grabbed his jacket and tossed it over the youngster, wrapping it so as to pick it up without being bitten. He scooped it into the canoe and said, "Let's take it home. As a pet."

Beaner first looked dubious but then asked, "Do you think we should?"

Ricky said, "Sure!"

Thus, the kids acquired a new and temporary pet and some new responsibility. They housed it in the turkey house which had become a playhouse, that building abandoned after the incident with the cattail fluff and later involved in the hide-and-seek game at the family picnic. This new pet gave them reason to finally clean it out. Now, they built a big cage on one side and used the rest as a clubhouse again. The kids were keeping the raccoon sort of as a mascot for their club.

They tried feeding it canned dog food, but the little guy kept trying to wash it in a big water container in the corner. Of course, the canned food just fell apart in the water, and the raccoon would stare like he was thinking, "What happened to that delicious looking chunk of meat?" He didn't understand canned food.

So, they started feeding him fresh road kill. He could wash that without it falling apart. The problem was it started to stink if he didn't eat all of it. They had to clean out the cage pretty often.

The issue of cleanliness in the clubhouse, combined with remorse of confining a cute little wild animal, and combined with the raccoon reaching an age where it could probably fend for itself, thereby led the kids to release it. They just left the cage door open, as well as the main door to the clubhouse.

For two weeks Rocky, they called the raccoon Rocky, would go out at night and then come back to sleep in the clubhouse during the day. Apparently, the shed just felt like home. Ricky and Beaner were starting to think they'd never get their playhouse back, but he finally didn't return.

Ricky said, "He probably found a girlfriend."

Ricky still frequented the rocks above Maggie Stoltzfusz's place. He'd go up there alone on occasion to meditate, or *Nachdenken* as Mountain Mary called it.

Ricky would bushwhack straight through parts of the woods that had no paths and then sit and think in some patch of sunlight. One day he found a very old bicycle in the middle of a dense section of thicket above the cliffs. He sat with his back against a tree and stared at it.

The bicycle was laying on its side facing downhill. The handlebar and pedal on the underside of the bike as well as the bottom of the front wheel were sinking into the forest floor as though the bike was slowly being swallowed by the earth. The rubber grip on the exposed handlebar had rotted away and the end of the handlebar itself was half rusted off with a few rust flakes dangling and pointing toward where the grip had disappeared. Likewise, the seat was totally gone, just two springs and a brace remaining. The spokes on both wheels had rusted off where they connected to the axle, and the wheel rims with spokes attached had fallen straight down. Landing on the ground in precisely the configuration they'd been in when connected to the axle.

Ricky stood and looked from directly above, at each wheel, and ignored differences in distance between axles, wheel rims and spokes, and it looked like the bike was still perfectly assembled. How could the configuration fall so perfectly straight down like that, all at once? How long does it take for something to rust off like that?

The chain was still on the sprockets, but the pedal that was on top had lost both rubber pad and peg and gone the way of the hand grip and seat. One tire was still on its rim. The other had fallen partly off. Ricky wondered if the rubber used in tires was stronger than that used in hand grips and pedals.

The most striking thing about the scene, the feature Ricky was fixated on as he sat there staring, was the trees that had grown up through the frame and between the chain and sprockets and even through a basket that was still fastened to the front handlebars. The largest tree was the one growing through the basket. It was at least seven feet tall and approaching two inches in thickness. It had grown as a seedling through the cross hatching of wires that formed the basket, and its thickness now forced the wires apart as it grew.

How long would it take for something like that to happen? It occurred to Ricky that he could cut the tree and count the growth rings, but he couldn't bring himself to disturb nature that way.

There were two unbroken bottles lying on their sides near the bike. Each filled with plants that apparently grew from seeds that found their way inside over the years. Two little terrariums. Jungles in a bottle.

Ricky sat back again against the big oak tree, closed his eyes, and left his mind wander a sleepy visionary path.

He imagined the boy they'd been told about to scare them away from the rocks, the one who fell from the rocks and was killed, and was partially eaten by animals. This had been his bike. He had sneaked two bottles of whiskey out of the house and put them in the basket on front of the bike, and he'd ridden down that road up on top of the mountain, and drank one bottle, and then he'd gotten the silly idea of riding this bike straight down through the woods, and he'd gotten this far when he stopped and drank the rest of the whiskey, and he had left the bike, stumbled downhill, and fallen from the top of the cliffs. Ricky knew how easy it was to fall off those big rocks.

Ricky opened his eyes, shook wakefulness back into his head, and said to himself, "Ah, the bike's probably just a piece of junk, and probably the bottles have no connection. Good story though! How long would it take for a bike to start to sink into the forest like that? Time is strange. Nothing stays the same. Nature's big and complicated! Nothing stays the same. Sometimes things just happen!"

Ricky stood and started walking between, and around, the rocks that formed the cliffs above Maggie's. He was generally heading down toward his Pop Pop's farm.

There was a very old tree at the foot of one of the biggest rocks, and it reached well above it. Ricky went back up on top and crawled from the rock out onto one of the tree's gigantic branches. He sat up there for awhile and thought and felt.

He carried a little notebook in his pocket, and a pencil, and he wrote a poem:

there's this huge tree
in a patch of woods

where no one seems to go
and I hugged her
and I kissed her
and I told her I loved her

when I get to feelin low
I think about lyin up
in one of them branches
wide as a hammock
lookin up at the sky
and feelin in perspective

He was thinking about Beaner. He read over the poem a few times, smiled, folded and refolded the page into a little bundle, and tucked it in a knothole in the tree. Then, he climbed back over onto the cliff, and walked around the rock and down toward Pop Pop's house. It was getting late. The sun was just whispering out of sight behind the trees.

One Saturday morning, Fat went down to Fleetwood to the feed store. Mary needed some ointment for her cow. She said she never could make anything herself that worked as good as this balm she wanted Fat to pick up for her.

Fat walked into the feedstore and was immediately struck by the fact that no one was around. In a little voice so as not to scare the owner, he said, "*Halloo.*"

No answer. He started wandering around the piles of feed bags. He heard a man blowing his nose out on the back loading dock. The Reading Railroad had a line that could stop right by the back of the Fleetwood feed store, at a loading dock.

The owner was sitting on a bench back there, and it looked like he'd been crying. He told Fat that he had just dealt with a customer who told him of the death of an old friend of his. Told him, in fact, that the guy had died seven years ago.

"I don't know why that should bother me so much," the feed store owner said. "I mean finding out he's long dead. Been dead for seven years, the guy said. Seven years already. Grieving don't seem natural now." He said this and then blew his nose again.

"*Well, it was news to you,*" Fat said.

"It just never occurred to me, I guess. That he could be dead. And then to feel it so deep now. I mean he's been dead seven years already. Seven years."

"*Well, like I said, it was news to you.*"

"I guess I just never realized how much he meant to me. How much he did for me. Until I heard he was dead and realized it was too late to tell him anything at all. It just never occurred to me."

He paused, and stared at the railroad tracks, and then he said, "I never thought about him much. Never missed him, ya know. Now, I miss him like Hades and he's already been dead seven years! Caught me by surprise. Always figured there was time, I guess. Time to deal with old stuff."

The man wiped his face and blew his nose again with his big red handkerchief and then stuck it in the back pocket of his bib overalls such that half of it was hanging out.

"What do you make of all that?" he asked, as he looked up at Fat who had remained standing while the old man talked.

Fat was obviously moved by the owner's soliloquy, but he seemed to have trouble expressing an opinion.

Finally, he shook his head and said, "*Time's funny.*"

The feed store owner seemed to know exactly what he meant, and he shook his own head yes, and he repeated, "Funny."

They stared at each other for awhile, and then the owner said, "What can I do for you?"

Fat couldn't remember why he'd come in, but they worked it out while discussing the weather, and then Fat headed back toward Mary's. He took the long way.

Later, Fat and Mary were seated at Mary's kitchen table. They'd just finished a vegetarian lunch.

Fat had been thinking a lot about his encounter with the feed store owner, about his saying he always figured there was time.

Over a cup of coffee Fat said, "*Ya evah bin married?*"

Mary was surprised. "*Nah! Nevah bin.*"

"*Me neither.*"

"*I nevah bin ast even.*" Then, Mary added, "*Vhy?*"

"*Vell, vee both live vith ahvah selfs alone, ya know. Maybe vee could live tagetter, zusammenleben, ya know. Heiraten, ya know.*" And with that, Fat proposed marriage.

He added, "*Da leading is taking me in dat direction.*"

Mary simply responded, "*Let me think on it.*"

Fat added, "*Ich gleiche dich viele.*"

This was his way of expressing affection. Telling Mary he liked her. Avoiding the word love, as is the tendency among many of the old Dutch. They seemed to reserve the L-word for church services. But after a moment of red-faced thought, he strengthened his statement to a pure declaration of love, "*Ich liewe dich!*"

Mary then also became a bit red in the face and responded, "*Ich du dich, aw.*" Which was the equivalent of saying, "Yeah, me too." She was also hesitant to use the L-word.

Fat was embarrassed and wanted to lighten the moment, and so he waxed poetic as he added, "*I hope ya know hauw much ya mean ta me. It's a pleasure to breath the air you breath, an honor to breath your exhaust!*"

Mary busted out laughing which clearly embarassed Fat even more.

She quickly added, "*I nevah knew a guy like you, an I think I done enough thinking. Yah! I'll marry ya.*" And with so few words, the betrothal was sealed.

⌐ ❋ ⌐

The announcement of the espousal of Fat and Mary surprised and delighted the community. They were married quietly in a small civil ceremony.

The wedding was held on a sunny Saturday with a unanimous blue sky. There were ten people in attendance. That's all that could fit in the judge's living room. As the service began, all stopped talking, and the only sound was a "bing, bing, bing, bing" coming from the flapping rope on a big flag pole out front of the judge's office.

Fat actually bought a suit to wear. It was of large size but smaller than it would have been had he been fitted before working with Mary. Mary wore an elaborate antique dress and wooden shoes.

The proceedings were short, but dignified. A train passed during the ceremony and some of the script was hard to hear. "Do you take this man . . . Do you take this woman . . . You may kiss the bride."

As Fat leaned over to kiss Mary, he whispered, "*I vill not leave you forever.*"

"*Me neither,*" Mary whispered back.

Most in attendence went directly to meet a larger group already gathering at the *bierstube*, the beer hall, of a local fire company for a wedding reception, *die hochzeit*, they called it. The high time.

Fat and Mary were made to ride in a noisy caravan that wound its way around the township before heading to the reception. It was a string of decorated cars with horns blaring and tin cans rattling along on strings dragged behind bumpers.

Mary's neighbors, the Burnables, volunteered the use of their Model T Ford truck to lead off the traditional noisy procession of vehicles. He was the man who, with his wife's help, delivered fresh produce in the area. They took the shelving out of the back of the truck, rolled up the canvas sides on the bed, and set up a wicker couch behind the cab. Fat and Mary rode back there on the couch.

Billy Kunkel volunteered his black 1942 Ford coupe to follow behind the lead vehicle, but he demanded that he be the driver. This was no small commitment since Billy rarely drove outside his own neighborhood. To everyone's surprise, his reclusive brother Harvey accompanied him on the drive and even went into the reception. The remainder of the procession was a string of pickup trucks with horns blaring.

The vehicles and the beer hall were decorated by Ricky and Beaner and some of their friends. They made hundreds of imitation carnations out of tissue paper and plastered them all over cars, trucks, and the *bierstube*. Crepe paper, hand drawn signs, and tin cans rounded out the decorations.

Not a single relative of Mary's attended the wedding or the reception. She had once mentioned a brother in one of her conversations with Fat, but when he suggested they invite him to the reception, Mary refused, saying he was a drunk. "*Er trinkt zu viel.*"

Arsenic wanted to be certain all was ready for the reception, and so he skipped the noisy caravan and went straight to the *bierstube* at the fire company. He seemed to worry a lot lately about being forgetful and double-checked everything. He was watching out the window for the convoy, and he announced the arrival with a shout of, "*Sie sind angekommen.*"

Everyone ate, laughed, drank, and danced. Oh, did they dance! Even those that said, "I don't dance." One time the music stopped while Fat and Mary were still dancing, and you could hear the "clop, clop, clop, clop" of Mary's wooden shoes on the *bierstube* floor.

CHAPTER 11

It was Saturday, seven o'clock in the morning, and pretty blasted chilly for this early in the fall. Ricky and Beaner were working for Maggie over on the dairy farm. They were hired to help make apple butter.

Several volunteers were scheduled to drop in and help as the day progressed, but Maggie needed a few helpers to start early and stay late. Along with the two kids, Maggie hired Amos Zimmerman. Everyone else was a volunteer.

Amos was the man Maggie got to run her two new milking machines. He lived up on the hill behind Maggie's. He was an enigma. The inside of his house was a mess, and the outside always looked like he was having a yard sale, and yet he was a good, tidy, and trustworthy worker when someone was telling him what to do.

When he finished milking, Amos came over in front of the barn to build a fire in the big outdoor firepit with tripod and cauldron that Maggie used for canning jobs and for butchering. Maggie was in the house starting to get the materials lined up.

Amos talked to the kids as they helped carry wood over from the wood pile. *"It chust seems cold,"* he said. *"Ya ain't use'ta it yet."*

The kids wanted to discuss cataracts. Arsenic had gotten Maggie to go see an ophthalmologist who diagnosed cataracts and referred her to a colleague who specialized in cataract surgery.

The kids were trying to figure out what cataracts were. They knew it involved a clouding of the eye's lens and prolonged exposure to sunlight was involved. They learned that much from listening to their parents, and Maggie was out in the sunlight most of her life.

However, the kids also heard adults say that artificial lenses would be inserted in place of the natural ones. The idea of cutting on someone's eyes scared the heck out of them. What if something went wrong, might Maggie end up blind?

Amos assured them he had known lots of people who successfully underwent the surgery. He pointed out they only do one eye at a time in case some complication develops. But then he got to talking about an acquaintence who had problems with both surgeries and did end up partially blind.

"Bought blind he vass, ya know, couldn't see hardly t'all. He needed a sight-seeing dog."

Beaner said, "You mean Seeing Eye Dog, a guide dog. And nothing's going to go wrong. Maggie'll be fine!"

"Yeah!" Ricky added.

And Amos said, *"I vassn't predictin no bad luck, ya know. I vass chust talkin."*

About that time, Amos uncovered a black rat snake or racer in the woodpile, and it shot out toward the barn.

Amos shouted its *Deitsch* name, *"Ein schlange!"*

Beaner raised a piece of wood in reflex as though to strike it. No one expected a snake in this cool weather.

"Whoa!" Amos yelled. *"Loes ihm gehe!"*

Beaner lowered the stick and said, "No need to yell. I wasn't going to hurt him. It just scared me."

"Dey keep rats ought'a da barn."

"I know," Beaner said.

"Hey!" Amos changed the subject to relieve the tension. *"Vott's yoah real name? It ain't Beaner. I know dat much."*

"I like being called Beaner."

Ricky chimed in, "Hey, you know, I don't even know your real name. Come on. We won't tell anyone!"

Beaner hesitated for a long time, and Ricky started to repeat himself.

"I heard you!" she said. "You promise not to tell?"

"Sure!"

"I'm not telling Amos though. I'll whisper it in your ear."

"*Hey*," Amos said, "*me ya can trust.*"

"Maybe so, but I don't know you well enough yet."

She whispered the name in Ricky's ear.

"I like it! It's beautiful."

Beaner blushed. The name she whispered was "Sisley."

Partly to change the subject again, Beaner asked, "What's Fat Schmidt's real name?"

Amos said, "*I nevah heard his real name. Niemols! Never!*"

Amos and Ricky shook their heads in bewilderment. It hadn't occurred to them that Fat could have any name other than "Fat."

They dropped the topic, and since the fire was still roaring, and they needed to wait for it to burn down a bit, they started washing out the big forty-gallon copper kettle.

Arsenic arrived after he'd finished his own chores. Randy, Sabrina, James, and Rosa were coming over midmorning. Regan and Ruby in the early afternoon. Arsenic went straight in the house to help carry apples out to the big picnic table for slicing.

This slicing of apples into small pieces was called *da schnittin* in Berks County, or *die schneiden* over in Lancaster county. The little apple slices were called *schnitz*, and they were usually dried to preserve them. Dried *schnitz* were used in a popular local dish called *schnitz und knepp*. *Knepp* were little dumplings. They were added after the *schnitz* were boiled with *schinka-fleisch*, the Dutch word for ham. They could also be baked into a *schnitz* pie.

Maggie was going to parboil raw *schnitz* and then shove them through a sieve. This was her unique way of avoiding having to peel and core the apples for apple butter. Pressing them through a big sieve or colander removed the skin and seeds and produced a pulp which was then cooked in apple cider to make apple butter.

While the *schnittin* was going on, the apple cider had to be heated in the big copper kettle. Arsenic poured ten gallons of apple cider into the kettle. Maggie called Beaner over and asked her to stir it while it was heating. Maggie added dark brown sugar, salt, cinnamon, cloves, and ginger while Beaner stirred.

The rest of the helpers were now working on the apples. Ten bushels of apples, five macintosh and five red delicious, were lined up. One pair of helpers was slicing them, another was quickly parboiling small quantities in smaller pots in the summer kitchen. The rest of the workers were pushing the cooked apples through the colander and dumping the apple pulp into the cider. Water was added as needed throughout the process to keep the mixture loose. The apple pulp and cider had to be stirred continuously for five or six hours. Everybody took turns stirring. The paddle had a right angle in the handle so you wouldn't have to hold your hands right over the hot kettle.

When all the pulp, cider, and spices were finally combined, and someone was stirring it, the rest of the helpers sat around the fire pit in little groups, talking and snacking, as though they were out on a camping trip. Arsenic took the opportunity to ask Maggie about her upcoming surgery.

"*Ya positive ya doan vonn'a schtay ovah at my farm vhile ya get ovah dis searchry?*"

"*Nah. I belief I'll be fine, an da healin be faster if it's myself I haf'ta depend on. I'll call ya on da phone if I got problems. I'm chust glad ya'll drive me to and from. Dat by myself I can't do.*"

"*I'll drive ya, cook foah ya, an vatch yoah farm.*"

"*I'd rather ya din cook foah me, but da utter schtuff vill help lots.*"

"*Vott's wrong vith my cookin?*"

"*Yoah pretty vergesslich lately. Who knows vott ya might put in da food.*"

Then, she laughed, but Arsenic didn't, and so she added, "*It ain't dat. It's chust dat cookin is von'a dem things I alvays done myself. Like I sett, it'll make me heal quicker if I do foah myself. Besights, I think Mary's helpin me too. Vee'll see.*"

Ruby took a break at one point to go in the house and prop up her feet for awhile. She was getting a bit front-heavy these days, and her doctor told her to take lots of breaks and raise her feet higher than her head while she rested.

Her obstetrician was Jean Himmelreich, Florence Himmelreich's daughter. Florence was the old woman who had been under the hairdryer over at Ruby's beauty shop when Ruby first revealed she was pregnant.

At her shop, Ruby had been plopping down in one of the hairdryer chairs periodically between clients to rest her legs. She'd announced to her customers that she would be taking two months off to have the baby and get things stablized at home. She arranged for a friend, a retired beautician, to cover for her while she was gone, but most of her customers arranged their appointments and expectations to try to fit in with Ruby's scheduled return. Of course, since the shop was in her house, Ruby expected she'd have to pop in now and then even when she wasn't officially "on duty," in order to show the new baby to some of her old customers.

As the apple butter started showing signs of carmelizing everyone busied themselves washing and preparing quart jars, lids, and such. It was dark by the time the apple butter had been ladled into jars and capped.

Since Maggie had pizza pies delivered in the middle of the afternoon, most helpers declined when she offered to make dinner. However, they were enthusiastic when she offered to bring out loaves of homemade dark rye bread, *schwarzbrot*, and a big tub of cottage cheese, *schmiere-käse* or literally "smear cheese," in *Deitsch*. Everyone in this group knew that you eat apple butter either on a piece of scrapple or on a piece of *schwarzbrot*, *schmiered with schmierkase* and apple butter.

The most amazing thing happened when Maggie went for cataract surgery. Arsenic drove her to the clinic and waited in the waiting room while the nurse took her into the room where the surgery would be carried out.

In only half an hour, Maggie came walking back out with a

big smile on her face. The surgeon had gotten ready to start and then said, "You don't have cataracts!"

Maggie said he concluded that her problem had been mis-diagnosed by the other optometrist, but that sounded dubious since the surgeon himself examined her eyes a couple weeks ago, during a pre-op exam.

Maggie said to Arsenic, "*Ain't it funny hauw it goes some-times?*" She added that she'd been seeing better lately. She also made a mental note to buy Mary a present.

Three days after the miraculus improvement in Maggie's vi-sion, James got home from college mid-afternoon. Arsenic walked up to the trailer his son-in-law and daughter had set up behind the barn. He wanted to tell his son-in-law someone had come by to look at the trailer. Recently, the couple put it up for sale. They were preparing for their move to State College to attend Spring Term classes at Penn State. The university had accepted James into its graduate program in Psychology and agreed to let him start some classes in the middle of the traditional academic year.

James had been his hospice volunteer while he was fighting cancer, and during that time Arsenic came to appreciate and look forward to their conversations. James married his daughter right after Arsenic's cancer abated, and so their relationship became permanent. Arsenic knew he would miss James and Rosa when they moved to Penn State University. Anyway, as he walked up the stairs to the trailer, Arsenic promptly forgot what it was he wanted to tell him.

After Arsenic rapped on the door, James stepped out on the wooden porch attached to the front, and Arsenic hemmed and hawed and then said, "*Hey! Taday is December the seventh!*"

"O.k.," James said slowly, and then after a pause, "what happened on December the seventh?"

"*Pearl Harbor!*"

"Oh, yeah. The Japanese bombed Pearl Harbor!"

Arsenic said nothing else. So, James said, "Hey! Have a seat."

The two sat on a pair of lawn chairs and looked over across the fields toward Regan's place. A cock pheasant flushed from the top of the hill and sailed toward Regan's place, cackling as it flew. This prompted Arsenic to comment that there are fewer pheasants nowadays, and James replied that there are also fewer farms.

"It's some warm out taday, ain't?"

James agreed then chuckled and proceeded to tell a joke he heard on the radio on his way home. "During a discussion with his wife, an old gentleman with Alzheimer's disease was trying to remember a detail when he had an attack of déjà vu. He exclaimed to his wife, 'I do believe I have forgotten this once before!'"

Arsenic didn't laugh. He said the thought of Alzheimer's scared him.

James had started to laugh but quickly changed the subject, "It seemed funny at the time. What did you do today?"

Arsenic replied, with a touch of angst in his voice, *"I got'ta tell ya sumpthin. I can't find the title ta yoah trailer. I fond it missing! I know ya need it ta sell it venn ya move ta Penn State. I looked the house all over, but cannot find it!"*

James looked a bit perplexed as he said, "You gave it to us already, Arsenic. We have it in our safety deposit box."

Arsenic said, *"Oh. I did?"*

Then he changed the subject, *"Somebody run inta a hay vagon over front'a Maggie's taday. Did more damage ta da car den da vagon. Nobody hurt. Too many cars on dis roat! Din use'ta be dis vay!"*

James agreed, shook his head, and added that traffic seemed particularly bad that afternoon. He started to tell Arsenic about a college course in which the instructor discussed urban sprawl, but Arsenic seemed in a deep study, and so James entered one of his own.

Silence didn't bother them. They sat there enjoying their own thoughts, each other's company, and the afternoon breeze.

The Pricetown Road certainly had changed since Arsenic's birth. He was born in 1913. Although the road already existed at that time, Arsenic recently mentioned to his son Randy that he remembered men building it with huge steam-powered road graders. When he said that, Randy pointed out it was impossible he had witnessed it.

Arsenic realized then that his own father's stories had taken on a reality of their own over the years. Older people sometimes get confused and think they actually experienced things told to them as children. His father, Benjamin, talked frequently of the old days, and Arsenic was a good listener with a rich imagination. Benjamin said the graders looked like steam-driven locomotives, and they scraped and pressed stone and clay into a roadbed that would rival modern concrete.

The Pricetown Road followed an old game trail that had become a wagon path before it became a highway. It ran about twelve or fifteen miles from Reading to New Jerusalem, through Pricetown, from whence it eventually got its name.

The Church of the Brethren have a meetinghouse in Pricetown. It was built in 1777 and is used periodically for services to this day. The town was named after a man named Price who was one of the original twelve Brethren pioneers who settled the area in 1754. Pricetown was a major outpost, and people bought supplies there or passed through on their way to sell produce in Reading. It once had three taverns and adjacent general stores.

Arsenic's dad told him all this for he loved his people and their history. He said it took months for the steam engined road graders to complete the highway, and the noise and commotion kept kids along the right-of-way fully entertained. It wasn't everyday locomotives passed through the farm fields.

Arsenic had been pretty retrospective lately, and sometimes he felt like he'd been one of those kids sitting on the hillsides and dirt banks watching the road construction. But, it was his father who watched and heard the huge chuffing machines and then told vivid stories to young Arsenic. Memory's a funny thing.

One exceedingly vivid detail he was certain had come from his father. A man's shirtsleeve had gotten caught in the rock-crusher and he was being pulled into the teeth of the grinder. He was a big man, Benjamin said, and driven by fear and pain, he placed one foot on the frame of the crusher and literally tore off his own arm at the shoulder.

Arsenic knew he had not seen that happen, but his Pop's description made him wince to this day. Arsenic had actually once seen this fellow, a big old man living in Pricetown. Indeed he had only one arm. Lots of men in Arsenic's generation had lost arms, fingers, and legs to those big old contraptions used on farms and roads, but they'd been cut off, or crushed, or blown off. They hadn't actually torn off their own limbs with brute force. That was a god-awful thing to think about, and your feelings won't let you forget a description like that.

Anyway, Arsenic did for sure remember when his father would grade their own driveway each spring, and he told James about that now.

He cleared his throat to break the reverie and get James' attention. Then, he pointed down at the driveway and said that after the winter thaw, it would be deeply rutted. His father would smooth it out with a weird horse-drawn contraption he borrowed from the county. Arsenic said that the county didn't use it anymore, because they were switching over to gasoline engines. They kept the horses for old times' sake. The grader was a great iron affair with a typical wagon seat on top and a heavy blade down under the seat, between the four sizable iron wheels.

Arsenic said his father had to stop periodically to adjust the height and tilt of the blade. He did this by turning cranks on the back end of the device to move chains which raised and lowered and tilted the blade. There was a seat on the back end for an assistant to do this cranking while the grader was moving, but Benjamin had no assistant. Arsenic said he was too young to be of much help, and so his Pop would stop periodically and fiddle with the cranks.

He said he did get to sit up on the wagon seat next to his Pop, and he had vivid memories of the horses. Of course Benjamin had work horses on the farm, but these that pulled the county's road grader seemed big as elephants. He remembered their muscles bunching and rippling as they pulled the contraption to scrape off high spots and flatten the road surface. He said he could still picture those huge horses.

"*Ein lange tziet*," he concluded, referring to all the water that passed under his life's bridge since his father's death. The long-ago. He grew quiet again and stared across the fields. An empty dump truck bounced as it hit a bump on the road out front of the house and made a big "kerthump, kerthump" sound.

When Arsenic was a boy of seven, there were thirteen people to every car in the United States. By the time he reached thirty-seven, there were four people to every car. By the time he reached sixty-seven, the ratio was approaching two to every car.

When he was seven, it was a big all-day project taking excess produce to market in Reading and picking up store-bought supplies. In wintertime, it involved the heating of bricks to lay on floorboards of the wagon or the Model T Ford just to keep your feet from freezing. Now, it was a big project just pulling out of the driveway to merge with the traffic.

Arsenic blurted out, "*Sometimes feels like I'm gonna have a nervous wreck drivin on dese roats. Gets me fershimmled. Can't think so quick nomoah.*"

James assumed he was again thinking about the crowding issue, so he just nodded and maintained his silence.

When Arsenic was seven, German farmers were always trying to add acres to their farms. Land was like money in the bank. Better. But lately there were signs of sell-outs. Self-reliance and sustainability were being replaced in the Fancy Dutch culture by the need for the Almighty Dollar. Kids who inherited the farm were tempted to sell out to realtors who wanted to build Reading's bedroom communities. Some of the homeowners even commuted to work in Philadelphia, sixty miles away. That was an unthinkable thing in Arsenic's day.

The trend started right after the Second World War. During the interval since Arsenic's thirty-seventh birthday, the number of farms and the total farm acreage in Berks County had been cut in half.

Ironically, James had been silently musing the same general topic, and now he told Arsenic about the class he had in college, the one he tried to discuss earlier when Arsenic was meditating. He said that when he studied urban sprawl, they covered the crowding issue thoroughly. He told Arsenic some of the things he learned using words like "bedroom community boomtowns with affordable all-in-a-row sameness." He also spoke of "high achieving superstar castles" and "the sparkling jewelry of a valueless culture." He called the manicured lawns "shrub-burbia!"

James asked him what he thought of all that. Arsenic seemed confused. Then, he shrugged and said he just knew it was taking longer and longer to pull out of the driveway. He also complained that his reflexes were slowing, and he was getting distractible.

He said, *"People got too many shoes on deir feet dese days. They're too busified. I can't keep up nomoah."*

James called the huge fancy castles *"bedizened,"* explaining that the meaning was exactly the opposite of what the Amish meant when they used the word "plain."

Suddenly, Arsenic found a word he could relate to, *"Ach, ya mean . . ."* Then, he seemed confused again, but he finally blurted, *"Hochmüt! Dat's vott ya mean. Dose bick hauses are hochmütich! An dey seem ta be poppin up everyvheres."*

James commented that this sort of growth is not sustainable, and he said the government hierarchy should recognize this fact, and Arsenic started laughing at the word "hierarchy" and said he would call it a *"lowarchy!"*

At this point they both noticed Regan's truck coming from his place toward Arsenic's. It was traveling slowly on the wagon path avoiding the bumps. As it neared, they noticed Ruby next to Regan on the seat.

Regan stopped in front of James' trailer and yelled, "Ruby's water broke. We're headed for the hospital."

Ruby, on the passenger side, held up both hands and shrugged. "When it's time, it's time!" she yelled.

"*O.k.*," Arsenic replied, suddenly alert. "*Go'head. Vee'll come soon's I lock up a few things!*"

Ricky was at a 4-H meeting and Randy was off somewhere trying to find a used part for one of the tractors, and so Arsenic wrote a note explaining where he and James had gone. By the time he finished the note, Beaner's dad dropped Ricky off, and Ricky wanted to go along to the hospital. So, Arsenic crossed Ricky's name off the note, drew an arrow to the margin, and added more explanation, "Ricky's here now. He'll go with us. Come to hospital if you got a chance."

Up at the trailer, James left a note for Rosa. Then, he pulled his car down next to the farmhouse, picked up Arsenic and Ricky, and the three of them went to the hospital.

When they got to the maternity ward, a nurse showed them where they could wait. Regan was in the delivery room with Ruby. James got two cups of coffee from an urn in the waiting room, and he got a Coke for Ricky, and the three parked in the corner. To pass the time, they told Ricky what they'd been discussing before Regan showed up with Ruby in the truck. Ricky said his teacher had taught them that there is a population explosion. He glanced around the room, remembering that they were in a maternity ward right now.

Suddenly, Regan came out. He looked hollow-eyed. He sat down, stared at the floor for a moment, and then told them Dr. Himmelreich had informed him that it was going to be a difficult delivery. Then, he pulled a piece of paper from his pocket and read something to refresh his memory.

"She referred to the situation as 'a posterior position of the occiput.' It has something to do with the position of the baby's head with reference to Ruby's pelvis. Its head is down, but it's facing Ruby's abdomen. It's supposed to face the other way. Anyway, she says it's going to be difficult. Boy, would I like a cigarette."

"Get a cup of coffee," James suggested.

"Yeah, good idea."

When he returned to sit next to them, he tried to analyze the situation. Dr. Himmelreich said the baby would probably turn, but it might take a long time. While James and Regan were discussing what the word "occiput" meant, Randy and Rosa came into the waiting room along with Mountain Mary and Fat Schmidt. They had all met by chance at the farm, and Mary and Fat wanted to come along into the hospital.

Regan greeted everyone and then headed back into the delivery room, saying that James and Arsenic would explain Ruby's condition to them.

Arsenic looked at Rosa, and then at James, and then back at Rosa, and finally said it had something to do with the the baby's head. He said he didn't really understand. James came to his assistance. Arsenic was obviously perplexed. They all assumed he was just worried about Ruby and the baby.

James explained what Regan said, and Ricky added that it sounded like everything would be o.k.

Within forty-five minutes, Regan was ushered out by a pair of nurses. He had complained of dizziness, and the nurses wanted him to take a break.

Fat said, "*Hey, lots'a guys pass out. I pass out all'a time.*"

Mary looked at him.

"*Yah vell. Sometimes I do. I get dizzy anyvays.*"

They sat for another ten minutes. No one saying anything.

Then, Mary announced that she wanted to see Ruby. Regan looked at her, then at the nurses' station, then got up and walked over to talk to the nurses. He was over there talking awhile. He was a good talker, and he was able to finagle a visit for Mary.

Finally, he came back to the group and said the nurse in charge had agreed to let Mary go in, if she didn't stay too long. The nurse had called Ruby's doctor, who was off in a different part of the hospital. The nurse knew that Dr. Himmelreich was a friend of the family and wasn't too surprised when she said, "O.k. Maybe it'll calm Ruby down."

Ruby had been fixing June Himmelreich's hair lately, and they developed a close relationship. June knew a lot about Mountain Mary, mostly through her hair-dressing conversations with Ruby. Anyway, Ruby was still in one of the little satellite rooms attached to the delivery room, waiting for contractions to speed up. A nurse could take Mary through a door directly from the hallway, around the corner from the waiting room. A quick visit from a non-family member wouldn't even be noticed.

Mary went in and came out about twenty minutes later. She took her seat.

Regan went back in.

An hour later, Regan surprised everyone by coming out and announcing that he was a father. He started dancing around, pulling people out of their chairs, waltzing with them.

Dr. Himmelreich came out later and seemed a bit bewildered. Ruby's baby was a perfectly healthy boy weighing seven and three-quarter pounds. She said the delivery went quicker than expected. She was sorry if the early assessment of the situation upset the family, but at that time it looked more complicated then it turned out to be in the end. As though imitating Ruby's sentiments just before Regan brought her to the hospital, June held up both hands, shrugged, and said, "Anyway, when it's time, it's time!"

Fat glanced at Mary who was looking toward the ceiling, muttering and smiling. She nodded her head when she saw Fat looking, and she whispered, *"Eversing's o.k. nauw."*

Regan and Ruby's baby was born on Pearl Harbor Day. They named him Jeremiah Arsenic Kutz.

A week after Ruby came home from the hospital, Maggie and Arsenic took a free bus ride from Reading to Atlantic City. The casinos offered free trips to senior citizens on weekdays. It was a way of increasing business. With the holidays coming, Arsenic joked that he might be able to win enough to pay for Christmas presents. The truth was that Maggie and Arsenic intended to spend much of their time just walking on the beach.

Arsenic did like to play Blackjack, but most of his experience with the game involved play with Randy and his friends many years ago. He never expected to win much money. His goal was to break even. Also, when he went to the casinos, he carried a separate sum of money earmarked for gambling, and he quit if he lost it all.

Maggie agreed to drive them into Reading to meet the bus. She was happy about her new visual acuity, and wanted to show off. Anyway, Arsenic's driving was very slippery these days. Ricky was with him recently when he sat through a green light. Ricky wasn't paying close attention, and when he realized they were looking at their second red light, he pointed it out, and Arsenic seemed excessively embarrassed. He kept mentioning the mistake throughout the afternoon.

Today, as Maggie picked him up to go meet the bus, she was about to pull out on the highway when he announced that he forgot his wallet and needed to run back inside to get it.

As they finally got underway, Maggie teased him about being forgetful, *vergesslich* she termed it. She kidded him often on this subject, but Arsenic seemed to be irritated by the comment, and so she dropped it.

A little later, after the bus got underway, Arsenic confessed that he did seem to be increasingly forgetful, and it worried him. He said, "*Alzheimer krankheit gifts me angst!*"

He said he read in a magazine article recently that the disease appeared in 1906, and was once rare, but now it's much more common. He said Ricky jokingly called it "old-timer's" disease, but Arsenic emphasized that he didn't think it was anything to joke about.

He mentioned that he'd been a bit confused lately, *verwirrt*, he said, or what Ricky called "wierded out." He added that his father called it *fershimmled*. When Maggie asked for more detail, he changed the subject, referring to the snowflakes flying by the bus window. "*Hauw much snow dey predictin?*"

"*Chust a little. It's warmin' up.*"

Then, to seal the change of conversation topics, he referred to the Philadelphia scenery passing by the bus window. Pointing to the resting place of the Liberty Bell, Arsenic said, "*Did ya know dat venn da English took Philadelphia in 1777, vee sneaked the Liberty Bell ought'a here and hid it in Zion Church in Allentown?*"

Soon they were in Atlantic City.

After Maggie memorized the time and place to meet the bus for the return trip, the pair headed across the boardwalk to get something to eat. The boardwalk, casinos, and storefronts all had elaborate Christmas decorations. Most waiters and waitresses were dressed like elves, and santas, and reindeer and such.

They went down on the beach then, but the air was mighty cold. Walking the sand at the edge of the ocean, Arsenic remarked that the sound of the surf reminded him of wind blowing through pine trees. Maggie laughed and Arsenic said defensively, "*Did I say sumpthin schtupid again?*"

"*Naw, naw! I vass chust thinkin people say it da utter vay rount. Da vind in da pines reminds dem off da ocean. Dat's all.*"

"*Oh. Yah, dat's true, ain't?*"

They went back up on the boardwalk, and Arsenic said, "*Let's go play flapjack.*"

"Ya mean Blackjack," Maggie said.

"No. Dat game I play."

"Yah, Blackjack."

"I thought . . . Dat's right. It's Blackjack. Flapjacks is pancakes. Ain't?"

In short time Arsenic lost the money he'd brought for gambling. He wasn't playing well at all. He seemed tired, or depressed.

They took a ride in a "rolling chair," a sort of rickshaw. The driver layed blankets on their laps against the cold, and it was fun. Then, another walk on the beach and some dinner, and then Arsenic fell asleep on the bus ride home.

The morning of the day following their return from Atlantic City, Randy found Arsenic out at the barn sitting on the step of the concrete under the *vorbau* and staring out across the pasture.

At first Randy thought he was asleep and said quietly, "Pop. Are you o.k.?"

Not asleep. Arsenic looked up.

"I come ought foah sumpthin. Can't remember," his voice trailed off, and he made a little plaintive sound.

Randy said, "Maybe we should go see Doc Klein."

An anonymous sound came from the top floor of the barn.

Arsenic looked toward the barn and muttered, *"Ratz!"* Then he took a deep breath, got up, and said, *"Doan need no doctor. I'm o.k."*

He didn't visit a physician, but he did disclose his fears to Mountain Mary. After some discussion and a prayer, she suggested turmeric, the main ingredient in curry, as a remedy. She said James could visit a health food store on his way home from college in Reading. He was to obtain essential oil of turmeric, a distilled, concentrated form. The active ingredient in turmeric was curcumin. Mary called it *die Kurkuma*. As a reminder, she fixed Arsenic a curried dish for dinner and had Fat deliver it.

After a week of turmeric and some herbal acid indigestion, Arsenic claimed to be feeling better. He said he was more alert, less forgetful. Ricky supported him in this claim, but Randy and James feared he was just trying harder. Nevertheless, they hoped for the best and took a wait and see attitude.

A week after that, Arsenic about passed out. It was in the evening. He was walking into the front room to watch Randy and Ricky put the Christmas decorations up. Arsenic wasn't too gung-ho this year. This was only his second Christmas without Peach. Last year he was just numb, but this year he was sad.

"*Yah vell*," he said to Randy. "*You know vhere da decorations are. You and Ricky do it.*"

Anyway, he was walking in to watch them decorate when he just slid down the doorjamb by the front room, pulling down Christmas cards Randy had taped to the wood door frame.

He sat on the floor for a second, then started to get up as he said, "*Told ya not ta hang them cards there.*"

Arsenic claimed to be feeling fine, but Randy got on the phone to the family doctor, Doc Klein. After asking a lot of questions, Doc decided they could wait til morning and then bring Arsenic over to the office.

Doc's office was located on one end of his home, and his wife Pearl was receptionist, nurse, and homemaker. Pearl took Arsenic into an examining room the size of a big closet, and the doctor came in shortly thereafter.

Randy got comfortable out in the combination reception area and waiting room and talked to Pearl after she returned.

Doc Klein was an old-fashioned diagnostician who listened to his patients' stories. He also listened to, looked at, and probed their bodies. He even used his sense of smell.

He listened carefully to Arsenic's descriptions of memory failure and confusion, but when Arsenic verbalized his fear of Alzheimer's, Doc Klein said, "Let's not jump to conclusions. Take your shirt off."

It seemed to Arsenic that Doc was spending an awful lot of time listening to his chest and heart when it was his head he'd complained about. Finally, Doc worked his stethoscope up to Arsenic's neck, and Arsenic expected him to continue on up to his head, although he couldn't for the life of him imagine how you could learn anything by listening to someone's head.

Doc never got beyond Arsenic's neck and he kept saying, "Ah. Yes. Uh huh." Arsenic finally asked what his neck had to do with the problem.

Doc didn't say a word but took the stethoscope's ear pieces out of his own ears and put them in Arsenic's. Then, he held the other end against his own neck, and then Arsenic's neck, and then his own neck. He repeated this a few times then took the stethoscope back and said, "You hear any difference."

"*Yah. Yoah's goes 'rump-rump' and mine goes 'roomp-roomp.' Vott's dat mean?*"

"Carotid artery stenosis. In my opinion. Your heart's not getting enough blood to your head. We need to run a drain opener up there. Just kidding!"

Arsenic was wide-eyed as he said, "*Vott part is it vee are kidding bought?*"

"Well, this is just my opinion. We'll schedule you for an ultrasound, but I think the big arteries in your neck, my Amish patient calls'em *blootoders*, well, they're getting clogged. That's why you're confused. It's like somebody's strangling you."

The *Deitsch* word Doc used for artery comes from *bloot toote*, or "blood bag." Doc laughed as he thought of this, and that upset Arsenic even more, and his eyes got even wider.

"They can fix this. It's not uncommon. You'll be o.k. If they fix it, your intelligence will jump up about twenty points. You'll be amazed. The procedure's called carotid endarterectomy. They open those *blootoders* and clean out . . ."

"*Vell now,*" Arsenic blurted, "*I'm not sure I . . . Vott happens if I chust leave it alone?*"

Doc didn't like that idea, and his voice got firm as he said, "You'll have a stroke. You're probably close to having one right now. You might have already had some small ones."

"*O.k. O.k. Ich verstehen. I got da ideah!*"

"I'll set up an appointment at the hospital for the ultrasound. They just hold a mike against the side of your neck. If I'm right, they'll schedule you for surgery by the end of the week. Within a few days, you'll feel better than you have in years."

The ultrasound supported Doc Klein's diagnosis. A surgeon who specialized in carotid endarterectomy met with Arsenic and explained the procedure. Incisions would be made in the neck, and the plaque would be removed from the arteries while a temporary bypass insured that blood was supplied to the brain during the procedure.

Arsenic asked if the rattlesnake bite he'd received in the spring might have contributed to this problem. The surgeon laughed and said it had not, but then he laughed again and said it might actually have made it better for awhile.

Arsenic was about to ask for some elaboration on that surprising statement, when a nurse poked her head in the door and said the doctor had a phone call. While he was out of the room, Arsenic plumb forgot what he was going to ask about the snake bite.

When the surgeon returned and asked if there were further questions, Arsenic just said he hoped he could go home right after the surgery. The surgeon smiled, shook his head no, and said Arsenic would have to be asleep for the operation, and stay in the hospital, but he could go home in a couple of days.

At a later time in history, they would indeed start doing this procedure as they did many others, with a local anesthetic, and when finished, wheeling patients to the door of same-day surgery so that they might stagger to the family car and go home, and hope for the best. Fortunately, at this point in time, patients received complete overnight care in a hospital room.

Actually, there would come a time when a long hollow tube could be inserted in an artery in the groin and run all the way up to the carotid artery, in a procedure called carotid angioplasty. A little balloon would be inflated to open the artery, and a metal mesh tube, a stent, inserted to keep the artery open. Then, the patient would be wheeled to the door of same-day surgery, as already described.

The specialist said Arsenic might experience a little neck pain after his hospital stay, but he should recover fairly quickly and notice great mental improvement even while he was still in the hospital, as soon as the anesthetic wore off.

The surgeon said, "Keep you in the hospital a couple days just as a precaution." He added that there was some risk of stroke from the loosening of plaque during the repair. He added that Arsenic would definitely have a stroke if he didn't have the repair done.

"*Yah vell,*" Arsenic said. "*Vee alvays have still hope.*"

"You're lucky," the surgeon said, "I think we caught it in time.

Arsenic checked into the hospital later in the week. Strangely, the stack of forms he was asked to complete had a page with a box labled, "time and place of death." Arsenic drew a big X through this section and wrote in capital letters, "NOT RELEVANT!!"

The surgery went smoothly, and Arsenic spent two days in the hospital. Maggie visited him in the evening of the first day, but he was still very drowsy. He didn't even notice when she left to go home. On the way toward the door, she asked Randy if he'd like to go for a little walk. She wanted to talk. They headed down the hall toward a sun room.

Maggie was concerned about Arsenic's drowsiness. Randy assured her the doctor was very pleased by the outcome of the procedure, and he was certain recovery would be quick and smooth.

Then Randy laughed softly, and said, "Pop was trying to get out of bed when he first came down from surgery. He wanted to go home. Said he'd rather die in the woods than in front of a television set." As he said this, Randy nodded toward the T.V. playing in the corner of the sunroom as seemed to be the case in every other room in the entire hospital.

When Maggie returned the following day, she poked her head in Arsenic's door and asked after his condition. He said he had a little neck pain but felt pretty good. Then, he laughed and said, "*Kommen sie heah. I got'a goot choke ta tell ya. It's bought dis ulte man vith Alzheimer's.*"

Maggie was surprised he'd bring this subject up.

"*Dis ulte guy vass tryin ta tell his vife sumpthin but couldn't rememper vott it vass. After be'in confused foah avhile he says, 'Ya know. I sink I foahgot dis vontz befoah, ain't?'*"

Arsenic busted out laughing and then held his hand to his neck and said, "*Ahhch!*"

Maggie didn't see what was funny about the joke but laughed to be polite. She made a few comments about how cold it was outside and how lucky Arsenic was to be in bed, and then she headed toward the door and said, "*Vell, see ya tomarra.*"

Arsenic said, "*Not if I see you first!*" Then, he laughed and grabbed his neck again.

Out in the hall Maggie met Randy again, on his way in for his first visit of the day.

"How's he doing?"

"*Er ist schwindlig!*"

"Yeah, I think the anesthetic is still affecting him, but his memory seems sharp as a razor."

"*I guess! He tole me a choke dat made no sense, but he laughed plenty, so I guess he's feelin goot.*"

Maggie's word *schwindelig* was funny. *Schwind* meant fast, but by adding the -elig, it became something like "so fast his head's swimming." Randy was smiling at that but took on a serious expression as Arsenic's specialist came down the hall. The surgeon stopped and told Randy and Maggie that everything was going well. He mentioned that Mary's recommendation of turmeric, and its curcumin ingredient, seemed reasonable and at least harmless. A physician from India had recommended it to him for treatment of inflamation. It was used in India for centuries. He added that inflamation was related to coronary problems, so reducing it seemed good. Anyway, he laughed as he said he knew it tasted good.

Arsenic retained the habit of eating curry when he returned home. He also remained sharp as a razor, or *messerscharf* as Arsenic called it.

Three weeks later, it was moving day for James and Rosa. They wanted to get to State College a couple weeks before the Spring Term started. You would think it would be less hectic if you started in the middle of the school year, but the fact is it was hard to get stuff done during the holidays, like get your electricity, gas, and phone hooked up. It was also hard to get scheduled for classes, because the typical student starts in September, not January.

Arsenic walked out in the parking area just as James pulled in with a big rental truck to be used to haul furniture to State College. James stopped, reached across the seat to swing open the passenger-side door, and shouted down to Arsenic.

"What do you think?"

At that moment Randy pulled in behind him with a big rental trailer attached to the back of his pickup truck.

James' truck was twenty-six feet long, the biggest they had to rent. It had over fifteen-hundred cubic feet of space. Randy's trailer provided an additional four-hundred cubic feet plus the space in the bed of the pickup.

Arsenic looked from one vehicle to the other, then laughed and shouted, "*Zu viel grosse!*"

Rosa had been teaching James to speak *Deitsch*, but Arsenic's reaction was a bit confusing. It meant literally, "Too much bigness!" Finally, James understood, and argued, "We have a lot of stuff.

Between the two of us! We need all the trucks and trailers we can get!"

Arsenic laughed again and said, *"Maybe vee need a fendu. Ya know dat vert?"*

"Yeah, it means 'auction,' and no we don't need one. We're going to take all our stuff along with us to State College!"

Arsenic laughed again.

James and Rosa were hoping to leave the following day to move into a house they rented in State College, the hometown of Penn State University. Rosa'd gone out to the town by herself in the autumn and reserved the place. She'd visited Randy, Stella, and Ricky several times while Randy was still a graduate student. Randy earned his Ph.D. from Penn State when he quit practicing law and decided to become a sociologist. Rosa had become familiar with the layout of the town when she visited Randy. She had a rough idea regarding which places were close to campus, the price ranges for rents, and so on. James was currently very busy finishing his senior thesis. He would graduate from his undergraduate program in Reading just before the Christmas break.

For the move, James was going to drive the big truck. Rosa would follow in her car with the two scotty dogs, Itty and Bitty, riding in the back seat. They had sold James' car for extra cash.

Randy and Regan would bring up the rear of the caravan in Randy's pickup with the trailer attached. They'd help them move in and then leave the rental equipment in State College before returning to Reading the following day.

The whole process went smooth as silk.

Since he was near the University, after helping with the move, Randy visited his old dissertation advisor to explain why he left his university job in Indiana and started training horses. The old professor confessed to Randy that he wanted to be a forest ranger before becoming a college professor, and there had been many times he wished he'd followed his dream. "You're young," he said, "follow your own vision."

The visit was brief, since the professor had to put the finishing touches to a lecture scheduled within the hour. And so Randy and Regan headed for an early dinner or late lunch in a restaurant where Randy and his ex-wife, Stella, enjoyed happy times while living in State College. It was called the Monastery Speakeasy.

The little town of State College was organized in 1859 as a borough. It was situated in the Nittany Valley between Tussey Mountain and Bald Eagle Mountain right near the state's geographic center. Since it grew up around Penn State College, the town chose to call itself by the unoriginal name of State College. Only four years prior to that, the school had been called Farmers' High School of Pennsylvania. Luckily, the town didn't choose to call itself by that name.

The restaurant Randy picked had indeed been a speakeasy during the Roaring Twenties. Many of the tables were located in little intimate lacy-curtained cubicles. Hidden from the view of fellow diners and drinkers! The heading on the cover of the menu was, "Speak Easy, Friend!" Below that it stated that the word "speakeasy" was used in the years of prohibition to emphasize a need for secrecy when consuming or ordering alcohol, which was illegal at the time. In those days, a bartender might tap a loud customer on the shoulder and say "speak easy, friend."

Back in Reading, Arsenic was still recovering, but he watched as Ricky helped Fat move some stuff into James and Rosa's old trailer. Fat was going to move in with Mary, but he had to store some stuff, so Arsenic told him to put it in the trailer, since it hadn't sold. Mary eagerly sent a rent check to James and Rosa. She wanted to help them out with their finances. As it turned out, the trailer sat where it was for years, and it became a playhouse of sorts for both children and adults.

Fat had sold his house and was moving in with Mary so she could keep her beloved garden, but he couldn't fit all his stuff in

Mary's place. Arsenic offered to let the couple use the trailer anytime, free of charge, but Mary seemed to feel that James and Rosa needed money, and she said she and Fat had more than they needed, and so the couple paid rent and hung around the farm a lot. There would be times when Fat and Mary would use it like an extra residence while Mary helped care for Jeremiah. In spite of her initial lack of experience, Mary developed a genuine fondness for the child and was very good with him.

Postlude

Nine months had past since Arsenic's surgery. Arsenic was definitely a changed man. He did a heap of working and a heap of playing around the farm. He enjoyed the new grand baby, and he enjoyed the company of Fat and Mary, who hung around the farm quite a bit.

What with visits to and from James and Rosa in State College, and with Ricky and Beaner becoming more full-fledged teenagers, and Maggie and Arsenic's companionship deepening, and the new baby growing like a weed, and Fat and Mary's involvement in the farm deepening, the seasons flew by like snowflakes. It wouldn't be long before the start of the Oley Valley Community Fair, the fair that celebrated Fall in the area since 1947.

Henry Shittler stopped by the house one bright morning late in the summer. Arsenic hadn't seen Henry in years, and he was eager to catch up on gossip even though he knew Henry was a *weisen-heimer*. But Henry's visit was discouraging in more ways than one, and Arsenic had no tolerance for discouragement these days.

When Henry said he'd heard about Arsenic's arterial surgery and wanted to know how recovery was going, the surgery seemed like old news, and so Arsenic thought maybe Henry wanted to talk about it because he was having a similar problem. And so, he sat with his old schoolmate at the kitchen table and talked over a cup of coffee, with Arsenic patiently describing the symptoms he'd experienced and the fear of Alzheimer's disease that preceded his consultation with Mountain Mary, and then his search for medical help, and finally the miraculous recovery when doctors "unclogged my pipes."

As it turned out, it was actually Mountain Mary that Henry was interested in. He'd heard rumors about Arsenic's friendship with her, and he said he wanted to communicate with the dead. He said, *"Some say Mountain Mary's a psychic medium?"*

Arsenic remembered that Henry had always been preoccupied with death, even in grade school. He was in no mood to go over this topic, and so he laughed loudly and said, "*Nah, I'd say she's a large, not a medium!*"

Henry didn't get the joke. He just went on as though Arsenic hadn't said a word, "*Ya heard bought Chake, I guess.*"

"*Chake Himmelreich?*"

"*Yah! He's dett!*"

"*Dett!?*" Arsenic responded with surprise. "*Hauw come? I ain't hert nothin bought it.*"

"*Some young kit loss control'a his machine dahn on route 422 an hit Chake's machine head-on! Chake's dett! So's da kit!*"

"*Vell, my Gott! Chake an me go back a lung vays! I can't belief it!*"

"*Vell's true! He vass sewenty fife yeahs olt. Hatt six grankits an a bunch a greatgran vons.*"

"*Gott im himmel,*" Arsenic exclaimed, but part of him was becoming aware that Henry was sucking him into a depressing discussion.

Henry continued, "*Rememper his son, name vass Kenny, got shot by his vife couple yeahs back, cause he vass foolin rount vith a nutter voman? His vife vass in bett sleepin vith Billy's shotgun stead'a vith Billy, an Billy comes home an tries ta schneak back in bett vithought her hearin. He vass puttin his clothes in da closet, vhen she pulls ought da shotgun an shoots im in da back vith his pants half dahn. And them both vith a haus full'a rotts näs kinder.*"

Henry's final phrase roughly translated into "snot-nosed kids," and Arsenic had just about reached his limit for negative talk, and so he tried to change the subject. "*Hauw's yoah farm dune? Yoah son schtill runnin it foah ya?*"

"*Nah. He chust found ought he got cansah. Lung cansah!*"

"*Oh cheese!*"

At this moment Randy came from upstairs and through the kitchen, said hello to Henry, and was headed for the barn, when

Arsenic blurted out, "*Oh. Randy. I foahgot I vass gonna help vith the horses! Sorry Henry, vee got verk ta do.*"

Randy looked surprised and started to say that Arsenic should just rest and continue visiting with Henry, but Arsenic cut him off, winked discreetly, and said, "*Nah! A promise is a promise. Ya can't do all dat verk by yoahself. Vee'd bettah get at it.*"

"Ah . . . o.k. . . . I guess."

"*Sorry Henry. I'm gonna haff ta go. Vee got verk ta do.*"

"*Yah vell,*" Henry said, and they all headed for the door. On the way to his car, Henry paused and said, "*I guess ya hert vott happened ta Chackie Schultz?*"

"*Yah, yah. I hert bought dat. Vee got'a get at it nauw. See ya. Thanks foah schtopin in.*"

After Henry had pulled out of the driveway, and Arsenic and Randy were almost to the barn, Randy said, "What happened to Jack Schultz?"

"*I ain't got no ideah, but it vass bad, I know dat! Henry talks too much, he's chust a bobble-maul. I'm gonna go see Fat.*" And with that, he turned up toward the trailer behind the barn.

"I thought you said you wanted to help me?"

"*Nah. Yoah dune fine. I'd chust get in da vay.*"

Randy had a perplexed look on his face as he watched his pop walk up to look for Fat and Mary, who were doing something at the trailer up behind the barn.

Fat had taken an interest in the horses, but he was afraid to ride horseback. Arsenic made it a personal challenge to get him to try.

There was a big old Morgan horse on the farm, a good horse for both draft and horseback riding. His name was *Koom'rod*, the *Deitsch* word for friend. Fat and *Koom'rod* were indeed becoming comrades. The horse was very big and gentle just like Fat. It was a match made in heaven, but Fat balked anytime Arsenic suggested he put a saddle on the Morgan and take a ride.

Randy had riden *Koom'rod* horseback from time to time over the years, but Arsenic had used him mainly to pull an Amish-style buggy at the family's horse shows. He had kept both Morgan and buggy for sentimental reasons, since they didn't have horse shows anymore, but he saw an opportunity to introduce Fat to horsepower via an indirect route. He dusted off that Amish-style buggy, laid away on the top floor of the barn.

Arsenic had bought the buggy from Yonnie Kibble's father. Yonnie was the Amishman who had purchased the semi-thoroughbred horse from Randy while Arsenic was up in the mountains "gettin bit with a snake."

The buggy was a bit run-down when first purchased, but Arsenic modernized the rig with a pair of black aluminum and hard rubber wheels and a dull black fiberglass top that closely resembled canvas. To the naked eye, the refurbished version looked very authentic. As a matter of fact, several of Arsenic's Amish friends were making similar improvements in their own buggies. Arsenic did no work at all on the chassis, since the original had been built of strong oak and poplar and painted with seven coats of black paint that looked new to this day.

Fat learned to drive the buggy with relative ease. He and Mary first started riding around the farm and then on back roads, sometimes with Jeremiah on Mary's lap. They often rode it up the road next to Maggie's to go work in Mary's garden. Arsenic, or Ricky, and sometimes Sabrina's kids, would go along from time to time. It was one of those long buggies, sort of like a van.

Arsenic's next step after getting Fat to drive the buggy was to tempt him to actually ride horseback. He took to putting a saddle on *Koom'rod* from time to time and riding the horse himself. It was only a matter of time before Fat got interested.

Arsenic helped Fat get on. First, he set a bushel basket upside down on the ground, thinking Fat could step on it for a boost up to the stirrup, but Fat was too heavy, and the basket collapsed.

Fat said, *"Ach I can do dis!"* And he was soon in the stirrup without assistance and in the saddle and then trotting around the horse ring.

Arsenic laughed eagerly and muttered, *"Im himmel gemacht, made in heaven."*

Now that *Koom'rod* was seeing action again, the horse seemed to find new life, just like Arsenic. Arsenic decided to take horse and buggy for display at the Oley Valley Community Fair. Fat and Mary were going to ride the buggy in a parade that would precede the fair. Regan bought Fat an Amish straw hat, and Mary made for herself a big gray bonnet that looked very Amish.

Arsenic's Amish friends would not have participated in such a conspicuous show, but many of the more liberal ones accepted the attention because they knew that the Amish were becoming more dependent on the tourist trade for cash these days, and the value of advertising had not escaped them. A lot of people would be attending the fair.

The Oley Valley Community Fair was held October 2, 3, and 4 since 1947. It was always a truly cooperative, communal endeavor managed by the democratically-run Fair Association. It was held on the Oley High School grounds, and so classes had to be dismissed on Wednesday to set up the fair. Exhibits were housed inside the school building and students helped set things up. Cars were parked on the Oley Fire Company grounds.

Each year the senior class ran a cake and cider stand at the fair. This was to raise money for their senior class trip. The cakes and also apples and equipment for squeezing were donated by residents. Maggie was committed to baking four cakes as donations toward the senior class effort. She was also busy selecting and planning her entries for the various canning and baking competitions at the fair.

This year the Fair Association constructed a ring for conventional equestrian horseshows and a corral for a cutting horse show.

The equestrian events included two of the three Olympic disciplines, show jumping and dressage, but the Association had to skip cross-country because they couldn't get a course set up. Ricky, Sabrina, and her kids, all were entered in dressage, and Sabrina was going to try some show jumping. Ricky, Michelle, and Michael were still learning the skills involved and didn't expect to win anything, but Sabrina was quite good at horsemanship and had high hopes. Her mother and father, the Plochmenschs, would be there rooting for her. Of course, Randy entered the cutting horse competition.

Everyone on the farm started preparing for the fair about two weeks ago. The family made their weekly visit to the Kutztown farmer's market, and there was a sign posted on the bulletin board near the entrance saying that the Oley Valley Area High School would be closed Wednesday of the following week so that the fair could be held. Right next to this notice was another poster listing and describing some of the events with lots of pictures, and this got the Schlank's enthusiasm flowing.

There were several farmer's markets in the area, but the Schlanks favored the Kutztown Market. All the markets were huge and consisted of a coalition of farmers, butchers, and produce stands, and several elaborate Delikatessens that often included candy, pretzels, cookies, and potato chips along with all the various meat and cheese preparations. Of course, it also included a great flea market with everything from junk to fine, expensive antiques. The markets all over Berks County were huge, often covering many acres. Some of them even had barber and beauty shops, as well as complete restaurants.

Denny Drexel, the strange little man who flew the big balloon onto the barn roof while Arsenic and Ricky were up in the mountains, had been hired to fly advertisements for the fair. He drifted over the suburbs of Reading with a big sign on the side of the balloon. Regan contacted the little W. C. Fields character and talked him into taking Ricky along on one of those flights. Insurance concerns usually made the little pilot shy away from such requests, but he owed Regan a favor for the patience he showed when the balloon-on-the-barn incident occurred. Thus, Denny agreed, and Ricky talked about the experience for days afterward.

While they were drifting above the known world, Denny told Ricky some of his many adventures, and Ricky made mental notes for future stories. At one particularly moving point in their floating journey, Denny waxed loudly and poetically, "Who would have thought. It could be so much fun. To do all of the things. That I have done!"

Ricky laughed and shouted, "You are a po-et that don't know-it!"

The Schlanks were preparing to haul all their paraphernalia over to the fairgrounds on the day before the fair started, and there was a great thunderstorm during the night. Actually, it occurred just before the sun was due to come up, about four-thirty in the morning. It was one of those that approaches silently and announces itself with a giant lightening bolt about the same time hail and rain start falling. While the family slept, a few huge drops started puffing up little dust clouds in the driveway like tiny meteor strikes, and then thirty seconds later "CRAAAAAAACK!" A giant lightening bolt struck the big tree next to Arsenic's farmhouse, the one he and Peach planted fifty years earlier.

The explosion about knocked everyone out of bed. Even Maggie, sleeping across the road, said later that she thought a gas tank or something had exploded.

It continued raining very hard as the family was getting out of bed. Arsenic met Randy in the kitchen.

"It rained pitchforks and hammerheads, ain't?"

It stopped by six o'clock, and Arsenic went outside to survey the damage while Randy prepared breakfast. He'd been peeking out the upstairs window and was prepared for the scene when he walked out in front of the house.

The big oak tree he and Peach had planted right after they inherited the farmhouse had a big stripe down one side and around the base. The bark was splintered away from the trunk all along the jagged stripe. There were long strips of bark laying all over the ground like pieces of rope. It looked like somebody had wrapped plastic explosive around the tree and detonated it. As Arsenic followed the stripe down and around the base, he saw that its destination was a big root that had grown itself above dirt over the years since planting. This was the grounding for the lightening strike.

There was a big rabbit next to that tree root. It was stretched out, laying flat on its stomach, stiff, dead. Its front legs reached forward, and the back ones stuck out behind like its last act was a gigantic jump. There was a jagged stripe of burned-off fur down its back where the electricity followed a path of least resistance. Its eyes were bugged out. Arsenic stared, shook his head, looked away, looked back, and shook his head again.

Ricky came out while his Pop Pop was standing there shaking his head in disbelief. Arsenic pointed at the base of the tree where the strike had girdled the majestic old oak as surely as if someone had sawed a circle around it.

Arsenic said, *"It's a gonner. Haff'ta cut it dahn nauw. Yoah Gammy an me planted dat bought fifty yeahs ago."*

He shook his head again in bewilderment.

Ricky was more fascinated by the dead rabbit. After having a closer look, he ran back into the house to tell his Pop. Soon Randy yelled that breakfast was ready. After Arsenic came in, they ate, mostly in silence.

After breakfast, Arsenic got in the pickup and drove past the horse arena and up to the family cemetery on the top of the hill behind the barn. He walked over to Peach's gravesite, and took an old feed store cap off his head, wiped his forehead on his sleeve, and then started talking.

"Dat tree vee planted is dett, Peach. I'm not shuah vott dat means.

He paused for awhile, shook his head for what seemed like the hundredth time, and said, *"I'm schtill alife, ya know. Ruby's baby is growin like a weed, an she an Regan are goot parents. Fat an Mary make a nice couple, an goot company, an Mary likes da baby. Randy's business is goin goot. Ricky's turnin inta a first-class writer, an he got ovah dat accident he hatt. Rosa and Chames got a goot schtart in colletch. Maggie's a goot frient. She ain't you, but a goot frient she is anyvays."*

Then, he sat quietly for awhile. Thinking. As he stood to return to the truck, he put his cap back on. Halfway to the truck door, he turned back to the grave again and said, *"Like I sett, I'm schtill alife, an I think I know yoah mind. I guess I'll go ta da fair, an haff fun til life ain't nomoah. Dat's vott ya vont, ain't? I'll schtop back tomarra an tell ya hauw it vent."*

Then, he climbed in, started the truck, and headed back down to the barn, where Randy was busy hooking up the horse trailer, and Fat and Mary were loading their costumes into Fat's station wagon.